Praise for

A 2021 Charlotte Huck Honor Book

"A fanciful adventure with a rich emotional core and a fairy tale flair.
An emphasis on Alma's mental health and circular thought patterns
proves an effective complement to the story's magical elements,
as her new endeavor and friends grant her the resilience to
navigate her needs. Reminiscent of Neil Gaiman's *Stardust*, this
is a clever, entertaining story with its own distinct identity."
—*Publishers Weekly*

"Redman's writing shines [in] the portrayal of Alma's mental health
and its effect on her sense of self and on those around her . . . Reassuring,
especially to kids struggling to articulate their own feelings
in the face of lingering stigma about mental health."
—*The Bulletin of the Center for Children's Books*

"A wildly imaginative tale full of wonder and hope that is grounded in our
everyday world and the very real problems that today's children face."
—Megan Frazer Blakemore, author of *The Story Web*

"A magical, wondrous book . . . The story is beautifully
written and gave me chills almost constantly—with that
magic-just-around-the-corner feeling."
—Gillian McDunn, author of *Caterpillar Summer*

"As bright and magical as a falling star, *Quintessence* is a
beautifully told story that collided with my heart and set it aglow."
—Heather Kassner, author of *The Bone Garden*

"While firmly grounded in real-world issues, *Quintessence* shimmers
with the perfect amount of magic. Redman's deft, sympathetic portrayal
of anxiety, a welcome and important addition to the middle-grade canon,
blends with scientific references to astronomy that are sure to engage
young readers. Well-rounded, relatable, and resilient characters
working together in a captivating setting make this the
perfect read for fans of STEM and the stars."
—Sarah R. Baughman, author of *The Light in the Lake*

Also by Jess Redman

The Miraculous
The Adventure Is Now

Quintessence

Jess Redman

SQUARE
FISH

Farrar Straus Giroux
New York

SQUARE
FISH

An imprint of Macmillan Publishing Group, LLC
120 Broadway, New York, NY 10271
mackids.com

Our books may be purchased in bulk for promotional, educational, or
business use. Please contact your local bookseller or the Macmillan Corporate
and Premium Sales Department at (800) 221-7945 ext. 5442 or by email at
MacmillanSpecialMarkets@macmillan.com.

The Library of Congress has cataloged the hardcover edition as follows:
Names: Redman, Jess, 1986– author.
Title: Quintessence / Jessica Redman.
Description: First edition. | New York : Farrar Straus Giroux, 2020. | Audience:
    Ages 8–12. | Summary: Middle-schooler Alma Lucas goes on a quest to return
    a fallen star to the sky, and along the way discovers friendship, magic, and
    the strength of her own soul.
Identifiers: LCCN 2019036430 | ISBN 9780374309763 (hardcover)
Subjects: CYAC: Quests (Expeditions)—Fiction. | Stars—Fiction. | Moving,
    Household—Fiction. | Family life—Fiction. | Friendship—Fiction.
Classification: LCC PZ7.1.R4274 Qui 2020 | DDC [Fic]—dc23
LC record available at https://lccn.loc.gov/2019036430

Originally published in the United States by Farrar Straus Giroux
First Square Fish edition, 2021
Book designed by Elizabeth H. Clark
Square Fish logo designed by Filomena Tuosto
Printed in the United States of America by LSC Communications, Harrisonburg,
Virginia.

ISBN 978-1-250-79184-9 (paperback)
10 9 8 7 6 5 4 3

For my mother,
who has a soul overflowing with love and wisdom and faith,
and who showed me how to grow the Light.

High above, high above, the sky is filled
with the never-ending brightness of the Stars.
Oh, how great and glorious and full of mystery they are!
But you, dear soul, did you know that you are made
of the same stuff as those Stars?
And did you know that you can be filled with the
same Light, filled with Quintessence?
Read on and you will learn these truths and far, far more.

—*Quintessence: An Elemental Primer for Star Restoration*
Written by the True Paracelsus, Child of the Skies, Watcher
of the Light, Illuminist of the Ages

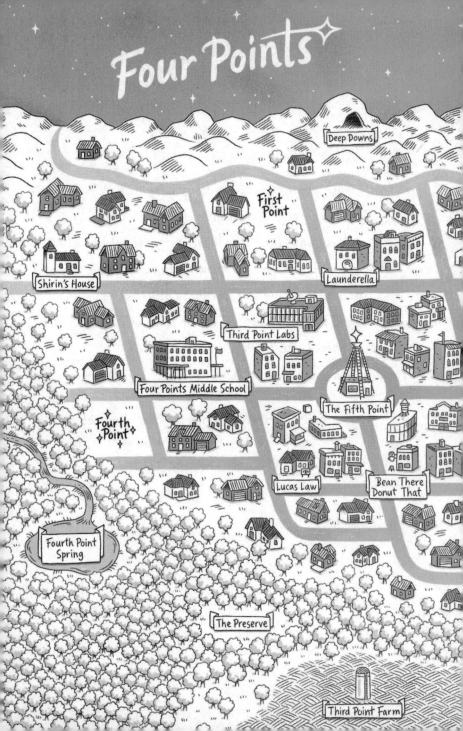

PART 1
The Flyer

....

CHAPTER 1

At the very center of the town of Four Points, there was a shop called the Fifth Point.

The Fifth Point was a shop, yes, but one that had never sold a single thing. It was small and square and brick and tucked between a coffeehouse and a launderette so that the air around it always smelled both bitter and sweet.

On each of the shop's four sides, there was a display window, with panes of glass so grimed and grubbed and smudged that nothing on display could possibly be seen. And next to each window, there was a door.

And above each door hung a wooden sign, with script that had once been glinty gold but was now tarnished and spotted. The signs all read:

The Fifth Point

And beneath:

Open by Appointment Only

How to make an appointment, the signs didn't say. What the shop sold and who owned it, the signs didn't say that either. And almost no one in Four Points knew, because almost no one in Four Points had ever been inside the Fifth Point.

But plenty of people had been above it.

Because rising out of the top of the Fifth Point was a twisting, tapering, midnight-black iron spire that blossomed—high above the other shops, high above the town of Four Points—into a star-shaped platform.

And on all four corners of the shop, welded to the roof, fixed and firm, there were ladders. Ladders with this message engraved on their eye-level rungs:

Come right up, dear souls.
See the lights above.
Grow the Light inside.

And inside the Fifth Point, someone was watching and waiting, watching and waiting, always watching and waiting for the right ones to come and see and grow.

CHAPTER 2

If the flyer had not been stuck to the school's front door, Alma Lucas would never have noticed it. She was in a hurry, after all.

Alma was in a hurry because it was the end of the school day. The bell had just rung, and the halls were filling with students, more and more with every passing second.

This was how almost every one of her episodes had happened—in these halls, full of students.

And more than anything else, Alma did not want to have another episode.

She was also distracted, even more so than usual. She was distracted because last night after dinner she'd had the Discussion with her parents. And she'd been turning the words over in her head all day long.

Over and over and over and over.

The Discussion had gone like this:

"So, Alma," her father said, lacing his fingers together the way he did when he was about to say something serious. "Let's check in. It's been three months since we moved. It's been more than two months since your last episode. How do you think you're acclimating to Four Points?"

Alma, staring at her plate of barely touched pasta, imagined herself in a vast and snow-filled tundra wearing a swimsuit. That was how she was acclimating. Like it was negative one million degrees and she was dressed for a pool party.

But she didn't want to tell her father that. She didn't want to tell him the truth. The truth, she knew, would only lead to more Discussions.

"Alma?" her father said. "Are you listening?"

"I am," Alma replied. "And I think that I'm acclimating really well. The weather's good. That's what I think."

She hadn't been smiling before, but she smiled then. It made her face feel strange, like she'd put on a very tight mask.

"I'm glad to hear that," her father said. "I'm sure you understand why your mother and I have been worried."

"I do," Alma said. "I certainly do. Who wouldn't be worried? But you shouldn't be."

Alma's father held up one finger. "We're worried about the notes from your teachers." Two fingers. "We're worried that you still don't want to leave the house." Three fingers. "We're worried that you aren't trying to make friends."

4

"I *am* trying," Alma replied. "I try all the time. All day. I am always, always trying to acclimate."

In the past, Alma's father had sometimes gotten a little too intense at this point in the Discussion, asking exactly *how* she was trying and exactly *what* she planned to do differently. So now Alma's mother took over.

"We know you are, Alma Llama," she said. "But three heads are better than one, am I right? So why don't we think together of new ways to try?"

Alma's mother smiled at her. Alma doubted that her mother ever felt like she was wearing a mask. Her mother was the kind of person who smiled a lot and who meant it every time.

"Maybe you could sit with a new group at lunch?" her mother suggested. "Say hello? Smile? Play a sport? Join a club? That's an easy one—why don't you join a club? Or even—even go for a walk outside?" Her chin rested on her fist, one finger tapping her lips, as if she had just come up with these ideas.

She had not just come up with these ideas. She said the same thing every time they had the Discussion.

And every time they had the Discussion, Alma reacted the way she had last night; she smiled and she nodded. She smiled and she nodded even as she felt the bright stuff inside her, the stuff that she imagined made her herself—her Alma-ness—grow dimmer and dimmer and dimmer.

Last night's Discussion ended the way it always did too. Alma's father, his forehead furrowed and his hands laced up tight again,

5

said, "I know that the move and James going off to college have been difficult, but it is imperative that you do something, that you make an effort. This is our home now. You must try, Alma."

Alma nodded and smiled and said, "I am trying. I really am. I really, really am."

Later, she had gone up to her new room that was the wrong color and curled up under her new bedspread that was too scratchy. She had lain awake for hours, listening to the thoughts that came over and over and over, like they did every night.

She had lain awake and felt dark inside, Alma-less inside.

Because the last episode hadn't been more than two months ago, like she'd told her parents. The last episode had been the day before.

And the episodes—they were never going to stop.

And she was never going to make new friends.

And this place was never going to feel like home.

And there was nothing, nothing, nothing to be done.

So that day, the day she saw the flyer, Alma was in a hurry and she was distracted. She had leaped up from her seat and raced out of her last class as soon as the bell rang, as she always did. She was running down the hall, as she always did. Her eyes were on the finish line—the handle of the front door.

Then her hand was on the door, and her eyes were just above.

And then there were stars.

CHAPTER 3

The stars were on a flyer—white and red and yellow and blue punctuating a black background. Gold letters crossed the paper sky.

You are made of elements and quintessence, the letters read. *Learn more at Astronomy Club in the Science Lab after school on Thursday.*

Elements and quintessence. Alma read the words again.

"Quintessence." She said it out loud, even though she knew she shouldn't talk to herself. Talking to herself had not made her any friends so far. Neither had weaving dried flowers and feathers into her long brown hair. Neither had having episodes in the middle of the hallway or dashing out of every class before anyone else had even gotten to their feet.

She didn't know what *quintessence* meant, but she liked the way it sounded. It made her think of that bright stuff she imagined inside herself, her Alma-ness.

She touched the little stars, one after another. They were, of course, paper. But they seemed warm under her fingers, bright to her eyes.

Thursday was tomorrow, and the flyer was new, she could tell. Untouched, uncrumpled.

It was as if it had been put there just now.

"Put here for me," Alma said to the stars.

Here was exactly what her mother had suggested, right in front of her.

Here was what her father meant by *acclimating*.

Here was something that could be done.

Alma pulled the flyer from the door, bit by careful bit. She folded it and tucked it into her schoolbag.

And for the first time in a long time, she felt her Alma-ness brighten instead of dim.

Alma felt herself spark.

There were stars shining at her back.

CHAPTER 4

Inside the Fifth Point, there were two types of light.

The first was whatever sunshine somehow managed, against the odds, to filter through the grime-coated windows of the shop. This light was amber tinged and irregular and awash in dust motes. This light made the shop look disused and run-down and dirty—and it was already very much all of these things.

The shop was full of dust. The shop was full of cobwebs. And the shop was full of stuff.

Piles of stuff, tons of stuff, mountains of old, thrown-away, broken, once-loved-now-lost stuff. Stacks of mildewed books with cracked spines. A heap of porcelain dolls with various fractures and amputations, their dresses a rainbow of time-muted color. A rusted wheelbarrow with no wheel. A silver tea set tarnished black. Model planes without wings. Kites without tails. Dozens of clocks, some silent, some ticking and tocking and ticking and tocking.

Hundreds and thousands of odds and ends that had been given a home in this shop where odd things ended up.

In the middle of the piles and the rotted shelves, in the center of the room, there was a spiraling iron staircase. It wrapped upward into a hole in the ceiling that looked like it had been made not by a carpenter but by someone who just happened to possess both a handsaw and a rudimentary knowledge of what a circle looked like.

It was from this hole that the second source of light came. This light was dim and blue and often flickered and sputtered and occasionally went out for minutes at a time.

It was shining right now, but barely, illuminating the somewhat circular hole, reaching down the spiral staircase and into the junkyard of a shop below.

And floating down with this light, there was a high, quavering voice.

"She'll be here soon," the voice whispered softly. "She'll be here soon."

CHAPTER 5

Outside the school, Alma's mother was waiting in the car line to pick her up.

She picked Alma up every day. Alma had told her many times that she didn't need to do this. She had told her mother that she would be just fine taking the bus home from Four Points Middle School.

Her mother had not listened and for this Alma was grateful.

"Alma Llama Ding Dong!" she said as Alma climbed into the car. "How was the day?"

On Alma's first day of sixth grade at Four Points Middle School, her mother had asked this same question. Alma had closed the door, put on her seat belt, and then collapsed into the shuddery, gasping sobs that she had kept inside for the past six and a half hours.

Her mother's usual smile had vanished.

"What happened, Alma?" she had asked. "Tell me what happened."

Alma hadn't known how to answer. Nothing had happened. Not really. No one had been particularly mean. No one had teased her or laughed at her or hurt her.

Yet all day, she had felt strange, different, off. She had felt it in her stomach, knotting and twisting. She had felt it in her throat, tightening and squeezing. She had felt it everywhere, like someone had poked a thousand holes in her, like she was leaking out a little bit at a time.

Back in Old Haven, she had never had a *best* friend, but she had always had *friends*. She had never been outgoing or popular, but that had never bothered her. Back in Old Haven, she just was the way she was. She was herself.

Here in Four Points, she didn't feel like herself.

On her second day, Alma was supposed to take the bus home. But that was the day she had her first episode.

So now her mother picked her up every afternoon and asked her a thousand cheerful questions, questions that Alma answered as cheerfully as possible, even though she never had good news to share. She never had anything to share.

But today she did. Today, she had the flyer. Today, she had stars in her bag.

She decided to keep that to herself though, for now.

Instead she said, "Oh, pretty good. I think I did some good acclimating today. I really do. I feel warm. Warmer."

Her mother beamed at her like this was the most wonderful thing she'd ever heard.

12

"Well, that sounds great," she said. "Really great. Listen, Dad and I are in the middle of something, so we're going to head right to the office. You can do your homework there, okeydoke?"

"Okeydoke," Alma said because she knew her mother wouldn't drop her off at home anyway. After a parent-teacher conference in February where it was revealed that Alma had not done any homework since returning from winter break, supervised homework time had become mandatory. She would be going to the office.

The office was the reason they had moved to Four Points in the first place. They had lived across the state in Old Haven for Alma's entire life, for her older brother's entire life. Her parents were both lawyers who had gone to law school—her mother first, then her father—throughout Alma's childhood. After graduating, they had worked together at a small firm.

Then a friend's father had decided to retire.

"It is imperative that we seize this opportunity," her father had said when they'd sat Alma down in November to tell her that they were buying the law practice in Four Points and leaving Old Haven forever.

"And Four Points is small, but there's lots to explore," her mother had said. "I think it will be a perfect new home."

Alma's brother, James, hadn't cared. James was only seventeen but he had skipped a year of school, and he was already in college. He'd never had many friends in Old Haven anyway. What did it matter to him where he spent winters and summers?

It had mattered to Alma, though. She hadn't wanted a new home. Old Haven had been her home. She might not have had a best friend, but she'd known everyone in that town. She'd known everything about that town. And Old Haven had known her.

Now that she'd left, nowhere and no one knew her, and she didn't know anywhere or anyone.

Not even herself.

CHAPTER 6

At the office of Lucas Law, Alma's father was at his desk, papers spread out before him.

"Hello, Alma," he said. "I absolutely want to hear about your day, at dinner. But Gwen, I really need another pair of eyes on these Third Point Farm files. Have a look?"

Alma's mother went over to his desk, and they started talking in their serious work voices. Alma stood by the table at the front window and unbuttoned her coat.

Alma's parents specialized in real estate law, and underneath the glass of the table there was a huge map of the town of Four Points. The map had come with the office, and it was very old and brown-edged. Alma imagined it would crinkle if she took it out and held it in her hands. She liked to look at the map. She liked to look at the map instead of doing her homework.

Through the glass, Alma would press one fingertip to Lucas Law in the downtown of Four Points. Then she would travel through the four neighborhoods that made up the town, tracing a path up to the green hills of First Point in the north, then over to the mountain ridges that lined Second Point in the east. South her finger would go, across the beginnings of the wooded Preserve and then into the farmlands that bordered her own neighborhood, Third Point. Finally, she would journey up to Fourth Point, where the Preserve broadened and spread to the far west edge of the map, the greenness broken only by the winding, weaving path of bright blue creeks.

Alma went everywhere on the map with her finger, but so far she had refused to visit any of those places in real life.

"But maybe today," Alma whispered, "I will."

Because today, she didn't want to do her homework—or pretend to. Today, she didn't want to do the same thing she did every day. Today, with the flyer in her backpack and the just-a-little-bit of Alma-ness sparking inside her—today, for the first time in a long time, Alma wanted to do something new.

"I think," she said, "that I'm going to take a walk."

Her parents both looked up.

"A little one," Alma said. "Around the town. It's just . . . such a nice day."

It wasn't. It was early March, and it was still freezing outside, windy and cloudy and miserable.

Alma's parents exchanged glances. Surprised glances, Alma thought. Unsure glances.

16

Which was understandable. In Old Haven, they hadn't been able to keep her inside. She had waded through streams and traipsed through fields and scaled trees, collecting rocks and feathers and flowers, lost in her own thoughts. But since the move, Alma had spent her time only at home, school, or office; home, school, or office, months without going to the library or the coffee shop or church or even the enormous backyard that her parents had been sure she would love.

"Well, I guess that would be okeydoke," her mother finally said. "We have been wanting you to get out there and see the sights."

"But stick close to the office," her father said. "And steer clear of that crazy tower."

"I won't go there," Alma promised. "I won't even look at it. I will be super safe."

She buttoned her coat back up. Her parents watched her—they watched her a lot ever since the episodes—then bent back over their papers, trying to make it look like they weren't watching her.

As soon as they did, Alma pulled the flyer out of her backpack and slipped it into her pocket.

CHAPTER 7

Very, very few people from Four Points had ever been inside the Fifth Point. The someone who was inside it, the owner of the quavering voice—and, in fact, the owner of the shop itself—was certainly not from the town. No, the ShopKeeper wasn't from Four Points or any of the neighboring villages or the city nearby. He wasn't from the state or even the country.

He was from far, far away.

Many years ago, the ShopKeeper had built the Fifth Point, as he had built many others like it. Up until that time, his earthly days had been spent traveling between these shops, training Keepers and accompanying them on quests. They were his dear friends, these Keepers, and the quests were his life's work.

But after completing the Fifth Point in Four Points, the ShopKeeper had decided his traveling days were over. Even back then, he had begun to feel old and faded. There were quests to be completed in

Four Points, of course—that was why he had chosen to set up a shop there in the first place—but not too many. Just enough.

At least it had been just enough until lately. Lately, the Shop-Keeper had begun to feel older than old. Lately, it was all he could do to climb to the top of the tower every evening to watch the Stars.

But old or not, faded or not, a new quest had begun.

"She'll be here soon," the ShopKeeper whispered again from his workbench.

Then, a little louder, "She'll be here soon."

Then, like a song, ringing through the shop from the top to the bottom, "She'll be here soon, she'll be here soon, she'll be here soon."

As tired as he was, the start of a new quest always gave the Shop-Keeper a spark. He had found the Elementals—one, two, three, four. The book had been picked up. The containers too, three first and then the final one. And this morning, he had opened the south door.

Everything was ready.

"Now we must wait. We must wait, we must wait. Now we must wait."

The words hung suspended in the lazy-floating dust motes, in the amber-blue rays of light. The porcelain dolls that had ears seemed to be listening. The clocks that still could tick-tock, tick-tocked on.

"Because she'll be here soon."

PART 2

The Quintescope

····················

CHAPTER 8

Alma wandered around Four Points. She wandered around all alone, in the startlingly cold air, with the stars folded in her pocket.

And she felt different.

Her thoughts, so gnarled and knurled for the past three months, seemed to be smoother. Her shoulders, so often drawn up by her ears, were at least down by her chin. What had changed, she really couldn't say. But she knew she felt bigger inside, lighter inside.

Alma was so distracted by these changes inside that she hardly noticed what was happening outside. She didn't notice until she was right in front of the Fifth Point.

The Fifth Point was the first thing that Alma had seen when her family arrived in Four Points three months ago. The iron spire had risen up into the sunset sky like a bean stalk, like a dark magic tower.

"That thing is a liability nightmare," Alma's father had said. "It looks like it's one gust of wind away from collapsing."

"No climbing, okeydoke, Alma Llama Ding Dong?" Alma's mother had said, using her full nickname for emphasis.

Alma had nodded, even though back then, back in December, that was exactly the kind of thing she liked to do. The Fifth Point was begging to be climbed. She had imagined herself at the top with Four Points spread out beneath her, like a queen surveying her kingdom, like a star twinkling down on a strange new world.

These days though, it was as if everything Alma used to enjoy was a picture that someone had covered with layers of black paint. She could hardly remember what was under there.

Even so, she found herself staring at the Fifth Point whenever her mother drove her to the office. She found herself wondering what was inside, what those grime-coated windows were hiding. She found herself wanting to knock on each of the doors—one, two, three, four. What if someone answered?

But today no one needed to.

Because one of the doors was open.

Just the slightest bit. Just enough that Alma could see a sliver of black between the door frame and the door itself.

And if it had been another day—if the air had not been so sharp and awakening, if she had not found the flyer—Alma might have left then. She might have been too afraid to go somewhere new.

But it wasn't another day. It was today.

Alma pushed the door open.

CHAPTER 9

Right away, Alma was disappointed. Horribly, terribly, gut-wrenchingly disappointed.

All those times she'd thought about the Fifth Point—so mysterious with its four doorways, shrouded from prying eyes by the thickly besmudged windows—all those times, she had always imagined that there would have to be something truly wonderful inside. A library of shining-spine books. A nursery of exotic plants. An apothecary with jars and vials and vats filled with unheard-of contents.

"But you're just junk," Alma said to the dust-blanketed heaps lit by the faint blue light of the shop. "Just a bunch of junk."

Piles and piles of dingy, moldering, thrift-store-rejected rubbish.

The disappointment, added to the many disappointments of the past three months, was so immense and so overwhelming that Alma felt tears in her eyes as she spun around to leave.

But then she paused.

On the shelf in front of her, blurred by her tears, something had caught the light.

Something was shining.

Alma moved aside a cracked lawn gnome. She moved aside a blob of melted wax that was once a candle, and a handleless teal pitcher. Behind them, there was a box.

It was a wooden case, covered in scuffs and scratches. The case had a copper latch—the shining thing—that was half-covered in a green patina.

"What are you, I wonder?" Alma asked, wiping her eyes with her jacket sleeve.

She knelt down and pulled out the case. Rusted wind chimes slid off, tinkling a minor-key tune.

The box was about two feet long and a foot wide, the size of a trumpet case. Alma opened the lid.

It wasn't a trumpet.

The object in the box was split into three tapered cylindrical pieces, large, medium, and small. The cylinders were wooden, as scuffed and scratched as the box they came in, with copper casings. They lay on a bed of red velvet.

"A telescope," Alma said.

At least, she thought it was.

She picked up the smallest cone. It had a glass lens on one end, and she peered into it, although she knew it wouldn't work without the other pieces.

But it did. Through the eyepiece, the entire shop seemed to shine with a golden light, and inside of Alma, that feeling of brightness grew too.

She sat there on the floor, peering through the telescope lens at the chipped blue of a doll's eye and the corroded black of an iron step, and she thought that this couldn't be a coincidence. How could it be a coincidence that she would find a flyer for an Astronomy Club and a telescope on the same day?

And this shop was obviously abandoned. No one had been here in a long, long time.

The telescope, like the flyer, felt like it was here for her.

"I'm going to take you with me," Alma said to the eyepiece as she placed it gently back in the case. "I'm going to take you home."

Alma closed the case and latched it shut.

And then a flash of blue light filled the shop.

And upstairs, the ceiling creaked, as if someone were walking above her.

The shop was not abandoned after all.

Alma leaped to her feet, leaving the case on the ground. She whirled toward the doorway, ready to flee, when a voice from overhead rang out, high-pitched and urgent, like the solitary chime of a clock at one:

"Wait!"

CHAPTER 10

Alma stood in the doorway of the shop, her hand on the doorknob behind her. For the past three months, she had avoided unpredictable places—like the busy school hallway, like anywhere new—because she was sure that being startled in an unpredictable place would lead to an episode. The flash of light, the sound of the footsteps, and the voice had all startled her.

But the episode hadn't come.

Instead, something else had happened: that light inside her—her Alma-ness—had flared along with the blue light, just as it had with the flyer and the telescope.

Alma waited because of that feeling.

She did, however, keep her hand on the doorknob.

Upstairs there was a flurry of activity. Alma heard cabinets creak open and drawers slam shut. She heard jars being unscrewed, feet shuffling here and there, a shrill humming. Then the blue light went out.

Someone was coming down the staircase.

The someone—the owner of the voice—was so tiny that at first Alma wondered if he was a child. Then the figure rounded a spiral in the steps, and she saw that he had an enormous white beard that covered most of his face and hung down almost to his stomach. Probably, she concluded, not a child.

The little man was wearing weathered brown leather gloves and a cream-colored smock-like garment that came to the tops of his weathered brown leather boots. On his head was what looked like a brass hard hat and covering his eyes were oversize bronze jeweler's glasses with the magnifying lenses all fanned out. The only parts of his skin that were visible were his nose and a bit of his temples. Both were smeared with blue paint. All of him, in fact— beard, hard hat, smock, and gloves—was smeared in paint.

"You're here!" the tiny, bearded, paint-covered man cried. "Oh, I'm so very glad you're here. I didn't mean to startle you."

Alma stayed pressed against the door.

"The door was open," she said uncertainly. "That's why I came in."

"Yes, yes, I know, I know!" the little man replied. His voice was rhythmic, almost singsongy, and tinkly, like wind chimes. "I opened it, dear soul! Do you like the shop? It's mine, you see. I am the Shop-Keeper."

The ShopKeeper had reached the bottom of the staircase now, and he was gazing expectantly across the room at Alma. At least

28

she thought he was. It was hard to tell since she couldn't see his eyes.

"It's . . . unusual," she said. "Are these—do you fix these things?"

"I try," the ShopKeeper replied. He started across the room, nimbly sidestepping a pile of rusted bicycle parts and a stack of half-disintegrated newspapers. "When I was younger, I traveled a great deal, and everywhere I went I collected." He wiggled his gloved fingers around him. "A holey hat on the side of the road here, a stuffing-spilled teddy bear in a garbage can there, an earring without a match, a shoe without a sole—homeless things, you see. Lost things. So I would take them along with me. And now that I don't travel anymore, I have more time to tinker with them, fix them up, paint them."

"Do you—do you sell them?" Alma asked. She glanced down at the telescope case, hoping that the answer was yes.

"Oh my stars, no!" the ShopKeeper cried. "I should, I should, but I'm quite sentimental. They have become part of my home, you see." Now he was on the other side of the shelf in front of her, where the telescope case had been. The shelf was almost as tall as he was, and he had to stand on tiptoes to peek over at her. "Where, may I ask, is your home, my dear girl?"

Alma's disappointment about the telescope-she-could-not-have was interrupted by a jolt of surprise at this unexpected question.

"I—I live here," she replied. "In Four Points. But I'm new. I mean, I'm not from here. I'm from Old Haven." She paused before finishing, "That was my home."

The ShopKeeper was nodding, his brass hat chinking gently

down onto his jeweler's glasses and then rising back up, his beard wagging along sympathetically. "Then you understand," he sighed. He reached a hand through a gap between the shelves and pointed down at the telescope case. "I see you were admiring my quintescope. I made it myself."

Again, Alma found herself surprised by his words, this time because *quintescope* sounded so much like the word from the flyer—*quintessence*. "Quintescope," she repeated. "Is that like a telescope?"

The ShopKeeper fluttered his gloved fingers this way and that. "Sort of," he said. "Kind of. A bit. But a telescope, my dear soul, shows you what your eyes could see if they were better, sharper. A quintescope, well, a quintescope shows you what cannot be seen with the naked eye—the invisible things, the true things, the Light within!" His voice had grown higher, more melodic as he spoke, so that the last words were not just singsongy but an actual, belted-out melody. The last note was held for quite some time before the ShopKeeper ended with a loud trilling cough. "Excuse me!" he said, his voice back to normal. "Tickle in my throat."

Listening to the ShopKeeper, Alma felt again that the quintescope was for her. This was what she had been hoping to find here in this mysterious place—something special, something magical. She had to try again. Steeling herself with a deep breath and gripping the doorknob even tighter, she asked, "Wouldn't you ever sell just this one thing? Give it a—a new home?"

But the ShopKeeper shook his head sharply, the hat smashing

into one side of the jeweler's glasses and then the other with a loud *crack! crack!* "No, no, indeed! I would never sell it," he cried, smashing Alma's hopes as well. Until he added, "But! I do lend it out to very particular someones. And I think you may be the next particular someone I've been waiting for. Let me see now!"

The ShopKeeper came dancing around the edge of the shelf. He flipped down the magnifying lenses on his glasses and craned his neck toward Alma.

Alma pressed herself more firmly against the door. Her heart began to pound. She started to twist the doorknob, and she might have run away then and there if the ShopKeeper hadn't given a little leap and let out a high-pitched, ringing laugh.

"Yes, indeed! Mostly fire, as I predicted!" he sang. "Only a spark, it's true. But it's growing brighter, it's growing brighter."

This was the most astonishing thing the ShopKeeper had said so far, because it sounded to Alma like he was talking about her Alma-ness. But how could he be? She wanted to ask what he meant. She wanted to ask if he knew what quintessence was. She wanted to ask who on earth *he* was. But she felt too flustered to gather her thoughts. All she could manage was, "I can bring some money. For the quintescope, I mean."

"Heavens, no," the little man said, pulling the magnifying lenses back up. "No money. I only ask that you use it. Use it tonight, my dear girl—what was your name?"

"Alma," Alma replied. "Alma Lucas. I promise I'll take good care of it. And I'll bring it back!"

The ShopKeeper bent down and hoisted up the quintescope case. "Not until the end, Alma Lucas," he said, pressing it into her hands. "You come to the top at the end. Until then, I'll be in and out, I'll be around, but really most of the quest has to be done with the other three elementals."

Alma clutched the quintescope case to her. "What quest?" she asked. "The other three who?"

The ShopKeeper was reaching around her now and pulling the door open. "You'll know, dear soul, you'll know," he assured her with a radiant smile. "Just remember: Find the Elements. Grow the Light. Save the Starling. And now goodbye!"

"What elements? Save who?" Alma asked.

The ShopKeeper took her arm and pivoted her toward the door. His glove was so warm that she felt the heat through her jacket.

"I'll see you by and by, Alma of the Growing Light!" He gave her back a gentle push, moving her through the doorway and out into the sunset streets.

"But—"

"By and by!"

And the south door of the Fifth Point slammed shut in Alma's face.

CHAPTER 11

Before she returned to the office, Alma shoved the quintescope under the backseat of her parents' car. She hadn't told them about the flyer, and she didn't want to tell them about the quintescope either. It would be too easy, she knew, for the flyer and the quintescope to become part of another strategy to help her acclimate.

She still wanted these things to be hers for now. Hers and hers alone.

But that night at dinner, Alma's father said, "Alma, we want to talk to you about something."

No, Alma didn't want to tell her parents about the flyer and the quintescope. But she also very much did not want to have the Discussion again.

"I have an announcement," she said before her father could continue. "I'm going to be joining a club. Like you said I had to. Astronomy."

Her father's eyes blinked wide open with surprise. Her mother clapped her hands together.

"Alma Llama, that's fantastic news!" she said.

"It certainly is," her father said. "Although no one ever said you *had* to do anything, just that it would help."

"That's what I meant," Alma said. They were only suggestions, of course, even if they didn't always seem that way. "To help me acclimate."

"You've always liked astrology, am I right?" her mother said.

"Astronomy," Alma corrected her. "Astrology is horoscopes and things like that."

"Oh that's right," her mother said with a laugh. "Leo, Aquarius, moons in the second house. That could be fun, of course. But astronomy—stargazing and supernovas and galaxies—well, you've always loved nature and exploring. It's perfect for you."

"I think it really is," her father said. "And that's exactly what you've been needing. Something for you. Just for you."

Alma smiled. "That's what I was thinking too," she said.

Her father smiled back at her, and it was the proudest look Alma had gotten from him in a long, long time.

She had done something right at last. There would be no Discussion tonight.

"They even gave me a telescope to use," she said, feeling guilty about the lie but wanting now to show them. "Well, it's a special kind, actually, called a *quintescope*. And it's really old and really dirty, but it works."

After dinner, Alma cleaned the quintescope. Her parents helped, her father bringing orange oil to polish the wood of the case and the cones, her mother contributing a salt-and-lemon-juice mixture and a bristly sponge to scrub the green patina from the copper clasp and from the quintescope's casing.

When she climbed into bed that night, Alma put the case next to her pillow. Just a flyer and a quintescope had made her Alma-ness so much bigger, so much brighter.

She felt more like herself than she had in a long time.

CHAPTER 12

Alma couldn't sleep.

This wasn't unusual. She hadn't slept well since she moved to Four Points.

At first, she had blamed the new house, which was actually a very old, creaky-squeaky house. Then she had blamed her new bed, which her parents had bought her, along with a new desk and a new bookshelf, to try to trick her into being excited about the move. The bed was bigger than her old one and made of white wood and really very lovely. But it wasn't her old bed.

And even though her collection of Old Haven rocks was on the shelf of her new bookcase and her collection of Old Haven feathers was pinned to a board above her new desk and her collection of Old Haven dried flowers was pressed between the pages of her books as always, this still wasn't her old room. This wasn't her home. And she was sure that this was what was keeping her awake every night.

It didn't help, of course, that all night every night, Alma's mind spun through thought after thought, like speed-reading a thousand fear-filled books.

You live in Four Points, her mind said. *You don't live in Old Haven anymore.*

You don't have any friends, her mind said. *Your parents are disappointed in you. And James is gone.*

You are going to have another episode, her mind said. *You're never going to stop having episodes.*

And there's nothing you can do about any of it. There's nothing to be done.

Usually, Alma lay and listened to these thoughts, listened as she drifted fitfully in and out of sleep, listened over and over and over.

But tonight, Alma was not in the mood to listen.

"Be quiet," she said to her thoughts, and she got out of bed. She had promised the ShopKeeper that she would use the quintescope, and she was going to do it. Right now.

When they first moved into the house, both of Alma's parents had talked to her about never, ever going onto the flat roof outside her new bedroom window, because when they had first moved, climbing onto the roof was exactly the kind of thing Alma would have liked to do.

But in the last three months, she had not so much as unlatched her window.

Now she did. She lifted the frame upward as slowly as she could, as smoothly as she could. There was a grating shriek about halfway up, but when she paused and listened, everything was quiet.

She pushed the quintescope case out onto the roof. Then she followed it, quickly, before she could think twice, before she could stop herself.

Out on the roof, the wind caught her by surprise. It also woke her up, the way it had earlier as she walked to the Fifth Point alone. She opened the case and set about putting the quintescope together.

First, there was a tripod, with three shiny legs that did not want to stay upright. Then there were the bigger cones of the quintescope that extended, and the eyepiece that fit on, but how she did not know. She spun knobs, twisted joints, pulled, and pressed.

But she couldn't do it.

She felt the just-a-little-bit of Alma-ness inside her dim.

She couldn't do it.

Even in the cold air, Alma's face felt hot, flushed. The thoughts started back up again. Why had she thought the quintescope was for her? James was the smart one, not her. She couldn't join an Astronomy Club full of strangers anyway. She would almost certainly have an episode. And then what? Had she really imagined that things would change because she found a flyer?

She couldn't put the quintescope together. She couldn't even do that much. She couldn't do anything.

Now the wind wasn't waking her up. Now the wind seemed to

blow straight through her. Now the wind was frozen fingers that reached up the sleeves of her nightgown and into her collar and held on tight, squeezing her down, shrinking her small as the world grew large and howled around her, howled through the blackness that surrounded her on the roof.

But above her, there were stars.

And inside, on her nightstand, on the flyer, there were stars.

You are made of elements and quintessence.

Everything that had happened today—

"It has to mean something," Alma whispered.

She sat back on her heels and picked up the eyepiece from the roof. She looked through it, up at the sky. Gold light shone back at her, distant but near, strange but familiar.

Then she turned the eyepiece around and held it in front of herself. If the stars were looking down, they would see her. They would see her tall and strong and brave.

"And bright too," she said, thinking of what the ShopKeeper had said when he looked at her through his jeweler's glasses. "And growing brighter. I am still Alma."

She started putting the quintescope together again.

It took time. It took twisting and turning and fumbling and the tripod collapsing on itself at least a dozen more times.

But finally the quintescope was assembled.

She had done it, she had done it.

It was time to see the stars.

CHAPTER 13

If anyone had been walking through the town of Four Points so late at night, they would have seen a faint blue light spitting and sputtering high above the ground. They would have seen a light at the top of the Fifth Point tower.

The ShopKeeper was up there, and he had his own quintescope, nearly identical to the one he had lent out that afternoon.

Lowering one gleaming blue eye to the glass, he aimed the scope at the heavens. Through the lens, Stars that were invisible to the naked eye could be seen, clear and shining and made stunningly huge by the extraordinary power of the scope. Quintessence was visible as well, spheres of brilliant, burning gold within each Star.

The ShopKeeper located the red supergiant first. She was easy to find, as enormous and scarlet as her name suggested, more brilliant than a hundred thousand suns, and filled with the golden Light that could only be seen through the quintescope.

"What a sight, what a sight!" the ShopKeeper breathed. "Such marvelous Quintessence!"

As the ShopKeeper knew well, a Star so large did not live very long, several million years or less. This Star was surrounded by her sisters and brothers, but although they had begun forming around the same time as her, they were still very young. They were mostly red dwarf Stars, smaller and cooler and able to live for ten trillion years or more—practically forever.

It was to one of these, a young copper Star, that the ShopKeeper now turned his attention.

"There you are," the ShopKeeper sang out. "Oh, I fear it will be hard for you, little Starling! It is always hard when one so young falls. But the Elementals are here. They will help you. And you will help them!"

The Starling shone on, and the ShopKeeper moved the eyepiece back to the red supergiant. She was more luminous than ever.

Because Stars always shine brightest right before their end. And two hours ago, the red supergiant's core had collapsed.

"Three," the ShopKeeper whispered.

Once that happened, it was only a matter of time.

"Two."

The great red Star gave an immense shudder and then—

"One."

—she exploded.

The sky was suddenly lit by a blinding light as Elements and dust and gas and Quintessence were hurled outward in tendrils of swirling, reaching radiance.

"Glorious!" the ShopKeeper cried. "Glorious!"

He knew that this Star's end was truly a beginning. New Stars would be born in the nebula being created. Elements that could be created no other way were now in the Universe. And the Star's Quintessence—it would continue, and it would be used again too, perhaps even on the tiny planet he now called home.

The ShopKeeper gave the explosion site one last, longing look. Then he moved the quintescope down, down below the light and the debris, down where the Universe was still dark and undisturbed.

He moved the quintescope down until he found what he was looking for: the young copper Star, falling, falling, falling.

"Here comes the Starling."

CHAPTER 14

The stars took Alma's breath away.

Through the quintescope, she could see far more of them than without. Thousands more, millions more, stars hiding in places that had seemed black and blank.

They weren't just silvery white either. Through the quintescope, they appeared in startling detail. They were icy blue and molten yellow and blazing red, each with a gleaming golden sphere at the center. The sky was a box of jewels. The sky was a fireworks display that extended and expanded endlessly, forever.

As old as it was, the quintescope moved at Alma's slightest touch, guiding her around the universe. She moon-gazed for a while, following the paths of the craters and pits, then journeyed from star to star to star.

She paused on a small, golden-centered copper star. It was sur-rounded by other stars and it wasn't particularly noteworthy except that it seemed extra shimmery. Alma imagined, as she watched it, that each twinkle was a message.

"What are you saying, star?" she wondered. "Can you see me down here?"

Then, in an instant, in less than an instant, the star was gone, lost in a wave of rapidly expanding, color-saturated light.

Alma jerked her head back, and the quintescope swiveled away. She lunged for it, and pressed her eye against the ring of the eyepiece, hard enough that she felt its circle imprinting on her skin. Her fingers fumbled with the focus knob and twisted too fast, too far, light smearing across the blackness. She slowed down, turning back, pivoting the quintescope.

Where the star had been was now an ocean of light, vast and chaotic and as full of dust as the light in the Fifth Point had been. Alma knew there was a name for the wild, terrible, beautiful thing she was witnessing, but she couldn't remember what it was.

Then she saw it—right below the light and dust, streaking downward, copper and swift and gold-centered—the star that Alma had seen before.

The star was falling.

And as she stared, following the path of the light, Alma saw that it was no longer just a star. There was something else where the gold sphere had been—a brighter, burning something that made her gasp.

Because it looked like a person.

It looked like a golden person was falling from the sky.

Down, down, down came the star until it was so big and so close that Alma pulled away from the quintescope, and there it was, in front of her eyes—a cape of fire and a glowing ball and inside of it, no longer golden but fiery copper, an unmistakably human shape.

And not just human.

A child—a girl, perhaps.

"A girl in a star," Alma whispered to herself. "A—a Starling!"

Alma couldn't remember the exact words, but she knew the ShopKeeper had mentioned Starlings right at the end, right when he'd said so many things she didn't quite understand. The Starling—if that was what she was—was beneath the clouds now, close to Earth. Alma could make out long hair streaming above her head and dark places where two eyes and a mouth would be. Her thin arms and legs were spread out from her small, compact body.

The world seemed to be silent. Alma felt as if everything had stopped, absolutely everything, except for this falling, shining, luminous thing.

Then the Starling reached the tops of the trees that grew behind Alma's new house, and there was a crashing of leaves and branches.

And then there was a flash like a great bolt of lightning and a *boom* that shook the house.

And then—nothing.

Alma was left kneeling on the roof in a dark, silent night.

She gulped in the air she hadn't been breathing. Her hands were shaking. Her whole body was shaking.

"What should I do?" she said, and her voice was shaking too.

The first answer that came to Alma was this: *Save the Starling.* That, she remembered now, was what the ShopKeeper had said. *Save the Starling.* She should climb down from the roof. She should cross the backyard she had never set foot in and walk to the edge of the woods where the sound and the light had come from. She should go and save the Starling.

But this answer was overwhelming. This answer made Alma's heart pound and her throat tighten. Neighbors would have seen the light, would have heard the noise. Her parents must have too. What if they came outside to investigate? She should not be on this roof in the middle of the night. She should not have opened the door to the Fifth Point. She should not have waited, should not have listened to that strange ShopKeeper's confusing ramblings about homes and Starlings and elements.

What should she do?

"Nothing," she answered herself. "There's nothing to be done."

Alma didn't look through the quintescope again. She disassembled it with trembling fingers, shoved the pieces into the soft red cushion, and latched the case shut tight.

Then she crept back through the window, closed it as quietly as she could, and climbed into bed. She lay there, wide awake, and she tried not to think about the golden child who had fallen out of the sky.

She tried not to think about anything at all.

PART 3

The Astronomy Club

....

☽

CHAPTER 15

When Alma woke from her half sleep the next morning, the events of the night before seemed hazy and confusing. The most reasonable explanation, she decided—the *safest* explanation—was that it had been a dream.

"It was a dream," she said as she brushed her teeth.

"It was a dream," she said as she combed her hair.

"It was a dream," she said as she went down the stairs.

Even so, she couldn't help but check the woods behind her house. Well, at least she tried to. She hadn't gotten far when she heard her father calling from the back door.

"Alma, are you out here?" He was standing on the steps, his hand shading his eyes against the morning sun. "It's imperative that we get moving!"

Alma turned reluctantly from the sunlit trees and brush. Her father hated to be late.

Inside, her mother was pouring coffee for herself and for Alma's father.

"Alma Llama! Today's the day," she said, smiling a big, encouraging smile. "Astrology Club!"

"Astronomy," Alma said as she took her seat at the table.

"I really do have a mental block about that, don't I!" her mother said with a laugh.

Alma tried to smile, but her mind got in the way of her mouth. Yesterday, she had gotten carried away. Yesterday, with the flyer and the quintescope and the ShopKeeper calling her *Alma of the Growing Light*, she had felt braver, bigger, brighter.

Now, though, on the day of the meeting, after maybe dreaming about a falling Starling she was supposed to save—now, she was afraid. She wished she hadn't told the truth. She wished she hadn't told her parents anything.

"Have some breakfast," her father said, pushing a plate of toast toward her. "Remember what the doctor said about regular meals. And you certainly need energy today. This is a big step you're taking. A very big, important step in the right direction."

"It sure is," her mother agreed. "We are so proud of you."

Her father nodded. Twice.

"Oh. Well," Alma said. "Thank you. Thank you."

She took a piece of toast while her parents watched.

She would, of course, have to go to the meeting.

"I hope that lightning storm didn't keep you awake," her father said. "Sleep is very important too."

49

"I only heard one crash," her mother said, "but it was so loud it woke me up!" She took a sip of her coffee.

"March storms, I guess," her father said. He sipped his coffee too.

Alma listened to this with her toast gripped in her hand. She waited, breath held, for her parents to say more, but they didn't. They had seen the flash. They had heard the boom. But they thought it had been lightning and thunder.

"I did hear it," Alma said, her voice almost a whisper. "But I thought it was a dream."

She took a bite of her toast.

CHAPTER 16

The quintescope didn't fit in Alma's locker, so she had to carry it around all day.

Every time she looked at it, her stomach turned into a knotted, gnarled rope, and her throat felt like it was being squeezed by invisible hands, and her mind started whirring through the latest book of fears.

She was going to make a fool of herself at Astronomy Club. She didn't know anything about astronomy, except that she liked looking at the stars. She'd barely even been able to put the quintescope together. She was going to have an episode in front of the other kids. They were going to laugh at her.

If those thoughts weren't bad enough, there was also the little matter of the Starling who had come hurtling out of the sky and crash-landed behind her house last night.

"It was a dream," she muttered. "A dream, a dream."

By the end of the day, Alma was a knot-stomached, squeeze-throated, racing-thoughted mess. She thought she should just go home.

But she didn't.

She had the flyer. She had the quintescope. And she still had that light—that little bit of Alma-ness—inside her.

She was going to Astronomy Club.

At the end of the last period, she stood in the hallway right next to the door of her History class instead of running out the front door like she usually did. She stood there and watched as the hallways filled and filled and filled, and then emptied.

Then she picked up the quintescope.

"Elements and quintessence," she said to herself as she walked toward the Science Lab.

The lab was a big, sunny room with shining metal surfaces and glass tubes behind glass doors and neat rows of white aprons and goggles. Mrs. Brisa taught all the Science classes there, so Alma knew exactly where it was.

When she reached the lab, she peeked through the open doorway.

Seated on high stools were a boy dressed entirely in gray with a poof of curly black hair and a girl with two long braids and a butterfly-patterned dress. Their backs were to her. A pristine black telescope case was open on the counter in front of them, revealing a shiny white optical tube, new and modern.

The boy was staring down at his lap and talking in a loud,

monotone voice. The girl was twirling a braid around with one hand and drumming the table with her other hand, both motions in rhythm, *spin-tap*, *spin-tap*, *spin-tap*.

Alma stood and watched. They looked friendly enough, she told herself. They looked fine. There was nothing to be afraid of.

But her legs wouldn't move.

She was here, she told herself. She could sit by the door, leave if she needed to. It was time to go in.

Her legs still wouldn't move.

"Elements and quintessence," Alma repeated quietly.

But not quietly enough.

The Astronomy Club kids turned to stare at her.

CHAPTER 17

Alma's first impulse was to run.

She might have if the boy hadn't closed the book that she could now see was resting on his knees and said, "Greetings. I am Hugo. Enter, newcomer."

Hugo was wearing a gray dress shirt, gray pleated pants, and the strangest glasses Alma had ever seen. The frames were made of shiny silver and instead of two lenses, there was a single long one, stretching across both eyes like a visor. They made him look, Alma thought, like a robot. He sounded like one too. She wondered if that was on purpose.

Robot or not, now that someone was speaking to her, Alma didn't feel like she could leave. She took a deep breath.

"Hello, um, Hugo," she said. "I'm Alma. I'm here for—I mean, this—this is the club, right?"

Hugo started to shake his head, the wispy ends of his curls waving with each movement, but the girl leaped up from her stool and shouted, "Right! Right!"

She didn't, however, leap far enough.

The girl's foot caught in the stool's rung. She pitched forward, her arms windmilling so fast they turned into blurs. Alma let out a warning cry as the stool came crashing to the ground, but the girl didn't fall with it. She spun to the right, then to the left. Her dress fanned out around her, butterfly wings seeming to flutter as she staggered across the room until finally coming to a stumbling stop in front of Alma.

"I'm Shirin!" she said, breathless. "Thank goodness you got here before Hugo bored me to death. Are you the club starter?"

Alma gaped at her. "Am I the what?"

"Club starter," Shirin said. "Like the president, founder, supreme leader."

"Me? No, not me." Alma shook her head hard. "I just found the flyer yesterday."

"Flyer! Flyer! See, Hugo?" Shirin spun back to the boy. Her braids spun with her, nearly smacking Alma in the face. "See? I told you there was a flyer!" She whipped back around to Alma. "Mine was in my locker. *Inside* my Science book. On the *exact* page as my homework for that night. Isn't that so bizarre? That's pretty bizarre, isn't it?"

"It is," Alma agreed. She thought about the flyer she had found, how new it had looked, how perfect. "Mine wasn't—it wasn't in my books or anything. Not like yours. But it did seem—it seemed like it was for me? Somehow."

Shirin was nodding along with her. "Yes! Yes! Like someone chose us to be in this club. And oh! I like your feather."

Alma touched the blue jay feather stuck behind her ear. She'd done this since she was little, added bits of her nature collections to her outfits. And since the move, it seemed all the more important, like she was carrying Old Haven around with her, even though she'd heard kids laughing behind her back more than once about these fashion choices.

But Shirin wasn't making fun of her. Alma felt the pressure in her throat releasing. She felt her stomach untangling. She had been so worried that she wouldn't fit in, and here was someone complimenting her and telling her that she was exactly where she was supposed to be.

Hugo, however, was shaking his head. "Apologies, but I have no knowledge of any club," he said, "or any flyers."

"So you say," Shirin said. "But then why are you here?"

"I am always here," Hugo replied.

"Always?" Shirin walked backward and boosted herself back onto the stool next to him. "I doubt that. Do you even go to school here? Are you in sixth grade too? I've never seen you in any classes."

"Yes, I am a sixth-grade student," Hugo replied. "But, I'm in advanced classes."

"So am I," Shirin said.

"I'm in very advanced classes."

"I didn't know we had those," Shirin said.

"Officially," Hugo said, pushing his visor-glasses up on his nose, "we don't."

At this, Alma's throat began to tighten again. The feeling of belongingness faded. Shirin was smart. Hugo was smarter. And she, Alma, was failing every single class.

She shouldn't have come.

But she had the quintescope and she had made it this far and now, after what Shirin had said about the flyers and about being chosen, now—

She didn't want to leave.

"Maybe whoever put up the flyers just knew you would be here, Hugo," she said, her voice trembling slightly. "Maybe they knew it was something you'd like and they thought you should join. What about that? That's possible, isn't it?"

Hugo tipped his head to one side, then the other, considering this. "I did speak with Mrs. Brisa about giving a series of lectures to the student body on astrophysics, my latest interest." He gestured to the shiny telescope open on the table. "But she seemed to think that wouldn't be well received. Perhaps this 'club' is her alternative; I can give my lectures here."

"Lectures?" Shirin pulled her chin back and scrunched her face up. "I don't know about that."

"I wouldn't mind," Alma said. "I just got this quinte—I mean,

57

telescope and I saw the flyer and I—I like the stars, but I don't know much about astrology yet."

She realized her mistake immediately.

"Astrology." Hugo's visor made his face difficult to read, but his tone was unmistakably disdainful. "Astrology is a ludicrous pseudoscience that claims to predict the future using the movements of planets and stars. Apologies, but I have no interest in an astrology club."

"I meant astronomy," Alma said quickly. "Astronomy Club! That's what I'm here for. That's what the flyer was for." She struggled to think of what to say next, how to erase her mistake. "I've been stargazing, and I even—well, I maybe even saw a star explode and another one fall last night."

It was out of her mouth before she had time to really think things through. But as soon as she said it, Alma realized that although she'd been telling herself that the Starling had been a dream and although her parents had thought the Starling was lightning, the truth was—she didn't really believe either of those things.

The Starling was real, whether Alma wanted her to be or not.

Then she noticed that both Hugo and Shirin were staring at her again.

Shirin had a braid in each hand and her mouth was hanging open. Hugo seemed catatonic, his visored gaze fixed on her. No one spoke.

Then Shirin screamed, "Oh my goodness! What?"

And Hugo shook his head and muttered, "Zounds."

58

CHAPTER 18

It was not exactly the reaction Alma had expected.

Of course, the explosion and the falling star had been over-whelming, but the most unbelievable part had been the child inside the star. She hadn't even mentioned that, and Hugo and Shirin already seemed shocked.

Hugo was leaning forward, gray elbows on gray knees. "When you say you saw a 'star explode,' are you referring to a supernova?" he asked. "That is, the death of a massive star during which its core collapses and its outer layers are blown off?"

Here was the word that had eluded Alma last night. "'Super-nova,'" she repeated. "Yes, that's what I saw! I saw it through my quinte—through my telescope."

"At what time did you see this?"

"Around midnight," Alma replied, her excitement increasing at Hugo's interest. "Why? Did you—did you see something?"

Hugo leaned back and gestured to the open telescope cases. "As I said, astrophysics is my latest hobby. And as it happens, I was also stargazing last night. My telescope is not very powerful, but I did see some . . . unusual astronomic activity, including a possible meteor and—"

"Okay, this is too bizarre!" interrupted Shirin, who was now pushing off the table so that her seat rotated around and around. "My sister was talking on her phone incredibly loudly until so late last night. And even after she hung up, I couldn't sleep so I was just lying there looking out my window, and I didn't see any explosion, but I *did* see a fiery thing falling out of the sky! At first, I thought it was some really crazy lightning, but maybe it was a meteor, like Hugo said?"

"A meteor—is a meteor a star?" Alma asked. Inside her, the spark flared.

"Meteoroids are bits of space stuff—pieces of comets or asteroids or even other planets," Hugo replied. "When they enter Earth's atmosphere, most meteoroids immediately burn up, producing the fiery glow that we call a *meteor*—or, unscientifically, a *falling star*. Fascinating fact: approximately 20,000 tons of cosmic dust falls to Earth each year. So seeing a so-called *falling star* is not an uncommon occurrence."

Alma shook her head as disappointment welled up, dousing the light. That wasn't what she'd seen. She wasn't explaining it right. "It was—it was a star, a real star," she stammered. "Glowing, sort of reddish-gold. It wasn't moving at first. And then—and then there was this wave of light, and it was like the star came flying out of the sky. I watched it fall all the way down and land somewhere behind my house!"

Neither Shirin nor Hugo responded right away. Alma studied the ground, embarrassment building with every ticking second. They had seen *something*, but they had a reasonable explanation for it—an explanation that didn't include a golden star-child. She wondered if she should leave before she looked even crazier.

Then Shirin said, "You know, I've seen meteor showers, and they're gorgeous—aren't they gorgeous?—but that thing last night *was* different."

Hugo was pushing his glasses up and then down, up then down. "There is such a thing," he said, "as a runaway star. It can sometimes happen during a star system collision, or when a star gets too close to a black hole—or after a supernova, as you describe. The star is essentially catapulted through space at an extremely high rate of speed."

Alma jerked her head up, mouth open. "That must be what we saw! It was a runaway star!"

"What if?" Shirin cried back. "That would be amazing!"

"However," Hugo continued, shaking his head, "the fastest recorded runaway star is US 708, which is moving at around 2.7 million miles per hour. That star is incredibly far away from us, but even if the sun—the closest star to Earth—were traveling that fast, it would still take it almost thirty-five hours to get to Earth. You

61

wouldn't be able to watch it fall in a few minutes, as you're describing. *And*, of course, if a star actually fell into the Earth, we would be incinerated. Apologies, but what you're describing is impossible."

Alma heard Hugo's explanation, but in her mind, she was seeing the supernova detonate and the Starling being flung toward Earth again, and she was sure that this was what she had seen. Maybe it was impossible, but it sounded like Shirin might actually believe her—and Hugo was at least offering hypotheses.

"Well, I want to know more anyway," Shirin said. She drumrolled on the table, then pointed to the quintescope case. "Is that what you saw the falling star with, Alma? Can we see?"

"Yes, I have"—Alma pulled the case upward—"I have a—"

"Hey, weirdos!" The voice came from behind Alma, near the door of the classroom.

Alma's heart stopped. Her breath caught in her throat.

And the handle slipped from her grasp.

The crash was extraordinarily loud, the velvet lining apparently doing little to cushion the fall. The cones cracked against each other. There was a sound like glass scraping across metal. Shirin shrieked. Hugo winced.

"Telescope," Alma whispered. "I have a telescope."

"You *had* a telescope," the voice from behind her said.

CHAPTER 19

Alma hadn't dropped the quintescope just because she was startled.

She had dropped the quintescope because of the voice.

She knew that voice.

She knew that voice from her second day of school.

From the day of her first episode.

On that day, she had left History class with everyone else, one of the herd heading into the halls. It had been a long day. She had been taking her time getting her books while lockers slammed and voices called and laughter echoed around her. She had felt more tired than she ever had, but tense too, brittle and thin, like she might shatter if someone touched her, spoke to her.

It had happened as she turned away from her locker. Someone had shoved her. Someone had yelled, "Watch out, weirdo!"

And then—she really had shattered.

At least it had felt like it.

Now here he was, the owner of the voice.

She wanted to run all over again.

The boy was tall, taller than Hugo, who was standing up now, and much taller than Shirin, who had also jumped to her feet. He had dark blond hair and a scowl, and he looked as unfriendly as his voice sounded.

"Let's get this over with," he said.

"Get what over with?" Shirin asked. She scrunched up her face and pulled her head back. "Ugh. Please tell me you didn't get a flyer too."

"What are you talking about?" the boy said. "I'm here for tutoring."

Shirin let out a long sigh. "Oh, thank goodness," she said, sinking back onto her stool.

Hugo did not relax. He stayed standing, awkward and stiff, as he faced the new boy. "This isn't tutoring, Dustin," he said, his voice flatter and even more robotic than ever.

"Figures you'd be here," Dustin said. He pushed past Hugo and plopped onto one of the stools. "This is the worst."

"This isn't tutoring," Hugo repeated. "It's Astronomy Club."

"I got a letter!" Dustin said impatiently. "It said that I had to come here today after school to get tutoring if I wanted to pass Science. Why else would I be here?"

Alma had been afraid that the boy might say something else to her, but he wasn't looking at her. He seemed to be trying not to.

She reached down with trembling fingers and gripped the handle of the quintescope case. She held on as tight as she could as she backed slowly toward the door again.

"Listen, I'm pretty sure you're in the wrong place," Shirin said.

"I'm not in the wrong place," Dustin insisted. He fished a piece of paper out of his pocket and threw it on the table. "See?"

Shirin didn't look at the paper. Instead, she turned her back on Dustin. "Can we see the telescope, Alma?"

Hugo glanced over at Dustin quickly, then, following Shirin's example, he half turned his back on him too. "Yes," he said. "It appears quite antiquated. Perhaps this falling star was simply an optical distortion."

Alma stopped moving toward the door, but she didn't want to take the quintescope out. She couldn't, not with Dustin there. To take it out in front of him—broken, scuffed, all wrong—seemed impossibly painful. It would be like taking out the broken, scuffed, all-wrong pieces of herself.

And more than that—her heart was beating so fast and her breathing was so rapid and short and everything inside her was being turned upside down. She was seconds away from an episode. She knew it.

She had to leave. She had to leave now.

"I actually have to go," she managed to choke out. "I just wanted to—"

"Smash my billion-year-old telescope into a thousand pieces," Dustin finished, his words high and quavering in what Alma imagined was an imitation of her own voice. He still didn't look at her, but he gave a snort of laughter.

Alma was so rattled that when she turned to leave—turned to flee—the quintescope case slammed into the wall.

Dustin laughed again.

The laughter rang in Alma's ears as she hurried down the hall. Louder than her own breathing. Louder than her own heartbeat. That laughter was the loudest thing Alma could hear.

Until someone yelled, "Hey! Hey! Alma!"

Alma turned to see Shirin speeding down the hall toward her. Hugo was behind, his pace slow and measured, his hair following a beat behind his body.

"Sorry about that!" Shirin said, coming to a skidding stop in front of her. "Ugh. Seriously, what is with that kid?"

"Sorry about what?" Alma held the quintescope case in both hands. She tried to smile. "I'm fine. I'm not upset. I just have to go home. I'm fine."

Shirin studied her, tugging on one braid, then the other. "So you say," she said.

"Apologies," Hugo said. "I've known Dustin for a long time and he is often socially inappropriate."

Shirin rolled her eyes. "Understatement. But listen—he's in the wrong room. He's not part of the club."

"Correct," Hugo agreed. "He is not."

Alma felt like she was holding back a tidal wave as she listened to them. Everything inside her was so chaotic, so intense, that it was hard to understand what they were saying. "Part of the club? Is there still going to be a club? Even after—even after what happened?"

"Of course there is!" Shirin cried. "Why not, right? I need—I need something. Something to do, I mean. And we got the flyers, didn't we?"

"I did not," Hugo said.

"Okay, okay, we know, Hugo," Shirin said. "You have 'no knowledge of any flyers.' But you said yourself, you're always in the lab. Mrs. Brisa obviously wants you to join. And we all saw that runaway-falling-star-meteorite thing! What are the chances of that?"

"Highly improbable," Hugo admitted. "And Mrs. Brisa does often tell me I need more human interaction. The first topic of my lecture series will be stellar nucleo—"

"We can go stargazing on the top of the Fifth Point!" Shirin cried. "I don't think you can go inside the shop, but people are always up on that platform, and I'm pretty sure I have a telescope somewhere in my room. Maybe we'll see something else amazing!" She grinned at Alma. "What do you say? Do you want to be in the Astronomy Club?"

It had been so much—too much—all day. All day Alma had been moving closer and closer to an episode, then inching away at the last minute. All day she had teetered on the edge of disaster. It was a miracle she was not in pieces right now. She couldn't do this again. She couldn't. She had to tell them no.

But she didn't.

"Yes," Alma said. "Yes, I want to be in the club."

Inside her, the spark grew.

PART 4
The Starling

....

CHAPTER 20

That night, as usual, Alma couldn't sleep.

But it wasn't for the usual reasons. It wasn't because she was listening to thought after thought, spinning through fear after fear.

Tonight wasn't a monologue.

It was an argument.

Not a very good one, but an argument nonetheless.

You sounded so stupid, her mind said. *And you're going to keep sounding stupid because you don't know anything about astronomy.*

Maybe, Alma said back. *But maybe not.*

You almost had an episode in front of everyone, her mind said. *And you definitely will have one if you go to another meeting.*

Maybe, Alma said back. *But maybe not.*

Even if you really did see a Starling, her mind said, *there's nothing you can do about it.*

Maybe, Alma said. *Maybe.*

But maybe not.

Because no matter what her mind said, something had happened to Alma yesterday. No matter what her mind said, she didn't feel as empty, as dark, as Alma-less as she had felt only a day before.

Yesterday she had sparked. And today, today that spark had grown.

So finally, after lying under her covers and arguing and arguing and arguing with herself for far too long, finally, Alma said, "I told you last night. Be quiet."

She got out of bed.

She didn't know what she should do. And she was still afraid of what she might find out there behind the house.

But she tucked the quintescope eyepiece into one nightgown pocket and a flashlight into the other. She opened her window, and she stepped out onto the roof.

She had to do something.

CHAPTER 21

It was another cold and windy night, and Alma had forgotten a coat again. Her nightgown whipped around her as she lowered herself down from the roof. When she was hanging by her fingertips from the gutter, she let go. She was surprised and pleased when she landed on her feet.

She took the eyepiece from her pocket and gripped it tightly in one hand. She had been relieved to find that the quintescope was still intact when she opened the case that afternoon, although there were a few new scuffs here and there. In her other hand, she held the flashlight. She swept its beam across the mud and the dead grass as she crept through parts of the huge yard she had never set foot in, toward the cover of the woods behind it. The flashlight's beam was small and weak, however, and instead of making her feel less afraid, the tiny bit of light only made her even more aware of how dark and hidden the world around her was.

"I shouldn't be doing this," she said, because now that she was out in the coldness, out in the blackness, with thunder rumbling threateningly somewhere nearby, she knew that this was a mistake. "I should go back."

But she didn't.

And then there was a rustling somewhere ahead and a small noise like wind chimes.

"Who's there?" Alma whispered. She pointed the flashlight forward, illuminating a small circle at the far edge of the yard.

She didn't really expect to hear anything.

But the strange noise came again, a sort of high-pitched pulsing that made Alma shiver.

"Who's there?" she said again.

And then the circle of Alma's light disappeared in a wave of red and gold.

CHAPTER 22

The light was so bright.

Alma closed her eyes and threw her arms over her face. Even so, she could see red on the insides of her eyelids and she could feel heat, blazing, burning heat, pressing on her cheeks.

She scurried backward. Her feet crunched over dead leaves, but she couldn't hear the sound over the pulsing, drawn out and bell-like.

Only when she felt like she was out of danger of being incinerated did Alma stop and slowly, warily, peek out from behind her arms.

Her first thought was that it was a good thing her parents' room didn't face the backyard. Her second thought was that it was a good thing there were plenty of trees between them and the next neighbors. Because the backyard—and the whole world, it seemed—was lit up like day. A copper-tinged day.

Not more than fifty feet away was the source of this illumination. There, at the bottom of a wide, shallow dip in the earth, was the thing that Alma had watched fall from the sky.

There was the Starling.

Alma could hardly look at the Starling, she was so blindingly brilliant. Alma had to glance quickly, then cover her eyes; glance, then cover. The Starling was much shorter than Alma. She was slender and topped with an oversize round head. Her back was to the house, and her body seemed to be in constant motion, hands clasping and unclasping, head bobbing, waves of light radiating outward. Long wild tresses streamed from her head, held aloft as if by the wind, gleaming red and gold. Her skin shone a brilliant copper.

Hoping to get a closer look while keeping her distance, Alma pressed the quintescope eyepiece to her eye. Peering through the lens, she could see that same golden sphere that had been in each of the stars in the sky, the same golden glow that had been in the Starling as she had fallen the night before.

Light-filled and otherworldly, the Starling was the most beautiful thing Alma had ever seen.

And somehow, she was not one bit afraid.

Instead, she felt the way she had when she found the flyer, the way she had when she found the quintescope, the way she had in the Fifth Point—only more so. She felt like the brightness from the Starling was flowing to her and like her Alma-ness—small and weak though it was—was flowing back, connecting them to each other.

And she felt a terrible ache of sadness for the Starling too. She seemed so out of place, so small and lost here on the edge of the woods. She was alone, and she was so far away from home.

Alma knew exactly what that felt like.

She knew then that she had to save the Starling, like the Shop-Keeper had said, no matter what.

"Hello," she whispered.

The small, bright figure whipped around. Her huge black eyes stared unblinkingly at Alma.

"Hello," Alma said again.

The Starling's eyes grew even more enormous. The pulsing sound pitched higher, faster. The heat grew even more intense. Alma took a step backward.

Then the Starling ran.

And Alma ran after her.

At the end of Alma's backyard, the Preserve began. It wasn't wide here, only a mile or so across, but it was thick and untouched, a dense tangle of trees and underbrush. It was into this wildness that the Starling fled, moving fluidly, gracefully, flitting around trunks, feet seeming barely to touch the earth.

Alma, on the other hand, stumbled and tripped her way over roots she could not see and through bushes that seemed to spring out at her. She was keeping up though, keeping up until she fell once, then twice.

The light started to get farther away.

"Wait!" Alma cried. "Wait for me!"

The Starling didn't wait. Alma realized as she staggered forward again that she had ruined things. She should never have chased the Starling. She was probably terrified; Alma knew *she* would be. But now she couldn't give up. She ran on through the woods, which had begun to smell smoky, smoldering from the Starling's heat.

"Wait!" she cried again. "I want to help you!"

The Starling was too fast. Soon all Alma could see was a faint glow that wove in and out of her vision somewhere far ahead among the trees, like a sparkler writing in the air, then fading into nothingness.

Then Alma was through the woods.

On the other side of the Preserve was the abandoned Third Point Farm. Alma knew it was abandoned because her parents were working with the erstwhile farmer. The fields spread out before her, black in the light of the full moon, then blacker as dark clouds crossed the sky. In the distance, a lone silo stood guard over an empty kingdom.

In desperation, Alma pressed the eyepiece to her eye. Crossing the field, there was a shining trail, as if the Starling had left behind some of that golden light that was inside her, as if it was leaking out.

But the trail stopped, suddenly, abruptly in the center of the field.

There was no sign of the Starling.

She was gone.

Alma was left standing alone, surrounded by darkness and silence and the smell of ashes. She was left alone, wondering yet again what she should do.

CHAPTER 23

"Alma!" Her father was calling up the stairs. "Alma! Are you ready for school?"

Alma woke with a start. Her eyes felt gritty, and her mouth was dry. Pulling back her covers, she saw that her nightgown was shredded, brambles clinging to the mud-coated fabric. She was still wearing her shoes. She ran her fingers through her hair and came away with two leaves and a stick. She smelled like smoke.

Her father was on the stairs now. "Alma! It's imperative that you come downstairs! We're going to be late!"

If her father came in here, if he saw her covered in foliage and smelling like a campfire, what would he say? What would he think?

Nothing good, that was for sure. There would be a lot of Discussions if her father found her like this.

Alma leaped out of bed and pulled the covers over the

dirt-caked sheets. She grabbed her school clothes from the day before and flew out of her room and into the bathroom across the hall, slamming the door as her father reached the landing. She clicked the lock and turned on the shower.

"Alma?" her father called through the door. "Are you almost ready?"

"Oh! Yes!" Alma replied. "Almost."

There was silence on the other side of the door. Then, "Alma, is the shower on? You don't have time for a shower."

"Don't worry!" Alma cried. "I'll just be a minute!"

Another silence, and then her father sighed a long, exasperated sigh. "Okay, Alma," he said. "Okay. You're going to be extremely late, but I suppose that's your choice."

Alma stepped into the shower, nightgown, shoes, and all. The water ran sludgy and thick, a waterfall of mud.

When she got out, she hung her sort-of clean nightgown over the showerhead and pulled the curtain shut. She dressed as quickly as she could, then ran downstairs, past her parents, and out the back door. She could hear her father calling after her, his voice frantic, but she rushed on, pushing her way through the bushes, the still-bare twigs scratching at her in protest.

Until she reached the far edge of the yard, the border of the Preserve.

Where she found the pit in the earth. The pit where the Starling had been last night.

The pit was wider than her bedroom—two or even three times as wide—and it looked almost as deep as she was tall. There was no grass there, and the earth was smooth and undisturbed.

"A crater," Alma said.

"Alma!" Her father was yelling from the back door. "Alma! We really have to leave! Right now!"

Alma took a tentative step into the crater. The dirt here was redder than the earth around it and more loosely packed. It shifted under her feet. In the center, the ground was black, charred by something very, very hot. Across from the crater, Alma saw that some tree trunks were singed as well.

After last night, she'd felt sure the Starling was real.

Now she had evidence.

CHAPTER 24

Alma had evidence, but she didn't really know what to do with it.

What should I do? What should I do? All day the question played over and over in her mind.

The most obvious first step was to go back to the Fifth Point and talk to the ShopKeeper. He was the one who had given her the quintescope. He was the one who had told her to save the Starling. But why? How had he known about the Starling in the first place? What was the gold light that the quintescope showed? And how, exactly, was she supposed to save a fallen star?

She would go to the Fifth Point that afternoon, she decided. She would go and ask the ShopKeeper everything.

The next thing she had to do, Alma thought, was check to see if the Starling had returned to the crater. Alma hoped that she had, because she couldn't save the Starling if she didn't know where she was. But what if she hadn't? How would Alma find her? And how had she disappeared so suddenly, so completely?

At lunch, she saw Shirin sitting at a table full of girls. They were talking loudly and giggling and every single one of them looked so happy and easy and light.

Shirin sat at the end of the table. She was twirling a braid with one hand, twirling it fast, and holding a slice of pizza with the other. She was smiling at the other girls. She was laughing when they laughed. She looked like she belonged with them. Alma wondered why Shirin had come to the Astronomy Club alone when she had an entire table of friends.

She wanted to talk to Shirin. Shirin had seen something, and she didn't think it was a meteor. Maybe Alma could tell her about the Starling. Maybe they could work together. Maybe they would become friends.

But the longer Alma watched her, the more convinced she became that she could never, ever tell Shirin about the Starling. Shirin was too popular and too pretty and too perfect. And the truth sounded too crazy.

There were other places to look for information, of course. There was the library, but Alma had never been to the Four Points Library. She had gone to the Fifth Point and into the woods, but she didn't think she was ready to go to a new, unpredictable public place.

She thought about calling James. He used to help her with her schoolwork all the time. But she hadn't spoken to him since winter break, and she had never called him on the phone. Or she could ask the Science teacher, Mrs. Brisa. Mrs. Brisa knew so much—everything, it seemed—and she was always so excited when students asked questions. But what, exactly, could she ask James or Mrs. Brisa?

No, she had to start at the Fifth Point. It was the ShopKeeper who had the answers she needed. No one else could help her.

CHAPTER 25

That afternoon, Alma left her last class ten minutes early. She followed the rules and took the hall pass with her, but she didn't plan to come back. She couldn't sit at her desk for another minute. Hurrying down the hall, her thoughts were whirring so fast and she was listening to herself so intently that she wouldn't have stopped at all, wouldn't even have noticed that anyone else was there, if that someone hadn't said, "Greetings, Alma."

Hugo was standing by a hallway bulletin board. He was wearing another totally gray outfit and his robot glasses. In one hand, he held a stack of papers. In the other, a tape dispenser.

"Oh. Hi," Alma said. "Hi, Hugo. What are you doing?"

Instead of answering, Hugo stuck one of the pieces of paper onto the bulletin board.

It was a flyer.

A very plain flyer, Alma noticed. White paper with words written in cramped black-marker letters: *Astronomy Club Lecture. Next Tuesday. After School. Science Lab.* There were no stars, no shimmering gold words.

"Mrs. Brisa had no knowledge of the flyers you and Shirin received," Hugo said, "but she was very pleased to hear about our club." He gestured toward the flyer with the tape dispenser. "She suggested that I offer my lectures in addition to our regular meetings rather than replacing them. Will you be attending? If you are truly serious about the study of astronomy, I would highly recommend it."

Alma did want to go. But she didn't know who might be there.

"There will be no tutoring at the lecture," Hugo said, as if he could read her mind.

"Oh," Alma said. "Oh. Well, then yes. I'd love to come. What's it about again?"

"I will be discussing stellar nucleosynthesis," Hugo replied. "The material will be purely introductory."

"That sounds very . . . nice," Alma said, even though she had no idea what stellar nucleosynthesis was and highly doubted there was anything introductory about it. "It's about—it's about stars then? I mean, astronomy."

"Of course," Hugo said. "This planet, as you know, and everything in it, including human beings, is made of elements. And those elements are created in stars through stellar nucleosynthesis. So really, everything is astronomy."

"The elements," Alma said. The ShopKeeper had mentioned them too. *Find the elements*—wasn't that what he had said? She didn't know anything about the elements.

But Hugo did, and Alma suddenly realized that if anyone besides the ShopKeeper could help her, it was him. True, he had already said there couldn't be a fallen star, but she had evidence now. She had the crater and the charred trees. She had seen the Starling up close.

What if she could get him to help her? She had to try.

"Can I—can I ask you something?" she asked.

"There is nothing preventing you," Hugo said. He pulled a piece of tape from the dispenser and rolled it into a circle.

"I—I need your help," Alma said.

"You need my help," he repeated, sticking the tape circle to a flyer.

"Yes," she said. She straightened up, took a breath, then said, "Can you come to my house tonight?"

"Come to your house tonight." Hugo didn't move toward the wall with the flyer, just held it.

"Yes. But late. Like . . . maybe midnight?"

"Midnight."

"Yes." He was repeating her, but he had also gone extremely tense and his voice was very robot-y now. Alma tried to see his eyes, but the light bouncing off his visor made it impossible. "Will you come?"

"I am profoundly confused," Hugo said.

Alma felt her resolve begin to seep away. He was going to laugh at her.

"It's about the—the star," she said. "The one that fell into my backyard."

"Apologies, but if you recall our discussion yesterday—"

"There's a crater," Alma said. "From where it fell. And the trees are blackened and everything. Burned."

Hugo pressed the flyer onto the bulletin board. "This may be socially inappropriate to say, but that is ludicrous."

"It's true! I saw the star fall. There was a—a bright light and—" She had told him all this before. She needed to say something new, something that would make him want to help her. "The star," she said, "there was something inside it."

Hugo was silent. He was silent for so long that Alma wondered if that was his way of getting her to leave.

"What kind of something?" he finally asked.

"Just a—it was a thing," Alma replied. She couldn't tell him the truth, not here in the school hallway, where everything was so fluorescent-lit, with students hovering inside classrooms, like bees in a hive, waiting to swarm out any moment, stingers sharp and ready. "I'm hoping we can see it again tonight," she said, knowing that would not be enough, knowing she had lost him.

But then Hugo asked, "Did you say something about quintessence the other day, right before you walked into the lab?"

Alma flushed, remembering how she had been caught talking to herself. "It's just a word I've been hearing a lot lately," she said. "I'm not even sure what it means."

"I'm not entirely sure either," Hugo said. Then he reached into his shirt pocket and pulled out a pen and a tiny spiral notebook. He held both items out to her. "Please inscribe your address on the first blank page," he said.

Alma didn't know what she'd said to make Hugo agree, but she took the pen and notebook. She wrote her address inside in careful blue letters. "It's on the edge of the Preserve," she said. "In the Third Point neighborhood. Do you know it?"

"I am familiar with the Preserve," Hugo said. He took the pen and put it back into his pocket. "We should discuss, however—"

The bell rang. Alma's heart began to race. She felt her throat grow tighter, so tight that her words came out choked and fast. "Midnight," she said. "Back of the house, at the very end of the yard, on the edge of the woods. I'll be waiting there."

Then she ran for the school's front door.

She hoped Hugo would show up.

CHAPTER 26

Every Friday, Alma's mother asked her the same question: "Anything fun planned for this weekend, Alma Llama?"

Every Friday, of course, Alma said, "Not a thing."

But today, after she climbed into her seat and buckled her seat belt, she had a new answer. "Not really," she said. "But on Tuesday afternoon, there's another Astronomy Club meeting. It's a lecture. On star . . . nuclear . . . physics? Or something like that."

"Wow!" her mother cried. "Heavy stuff! And you're going to—" She snuck a sideways glance at Alma. "You're going to go?"

Alma nodded. "Yes," she said. "I think I like astronomy. A lot."

Her mother beamed. "That's wonderful. That's really wonderful, Alma Llama Ding Dong."

Alma smiled back. Until her mother took a left turn instead of a right turn—toward the house instead of toward the office.

"Where are we going?" Alma asked.

"Home!" Alma's mother said. "Dad and I thought we would work from there this afternoon for a little change."

Any other day, Alma would have welcomed a chance to escape the boredom of the office and supervised homework time. But since she had spent the entire day planning her visit to the Fifth Point, this was the worst possible news.

She tried to think of a good reason she'd want to go to town, but there wasn't one. All she could do was crane her neck around her seat and watch through the back window as the tower of the Fifth Point grew smaller and smaller as they drove farther and farther away.

After dinner that night, Alma took out the quintescope. She cleaned the cones and the glass, even though they didn't need to be cleaned again. She put the pieces together and then took them apart. Put them together, took them apart. Over and over until she could do it easily.

She thought as she worked, thought about the red-gold light that had washed over her and the gold-gold light that had spilled from the Starling. She thought about where the Starling might be now and whether she would come back tonight. She hoped so. More than anything, she hoped so.

Her parents were heading to their room for the night when Alma finally put the cylinders gently back into their velvet-lined beds.

"Time for sleep, Alma Llama," her mother said.

"Sleep is very important," her father said. "You remember the doctor said that."

"I remember," Alma said. She shut the lid of the quintescope's case and latched it. "I'm ready."

CHAPTER 27

*Inside the Fifth Point, the ShopKeeper was hunched over his work-
table. He had pushed aside the cogs and wheels of the clock he'd
been tinkering with and spread out his quest papers—charts, book-
lets, maps that would span the entire room when unfolded, calen-
dars that began before this stardust-speck of a planet even came into
existence.*

*Most of the papers had been made by the ShopKeeper himself,
the work of many, many, many lifetimes. But some had been made
by those who had fallen before, and a few had even been written by
Elementals—that is, humans.*

*Here was what the ShopKeeper knew: He knew a Starling had
fallen. He knew the third Elemental had the quintescope. He knew
that the book and the containers had been picked up by the other
three.*

Here was what the ShopKeeper did not know: If the third

Elemental had found the Starling. If the four Elementals had found one another. If they were beginning the task of growing the Light.

He hoped that all those things had happened, but if they had, he would have expected the third Elemental to come back this afternoon seeking more information, seeking answers.

No one had come.

What if he had read the Elementals wrong? Oh, it was tricky to find exactly the right four! Each one had a part to play, and those parts were so intricately interconnected. The third was the most concerning. She was young and her Light had obviously been dimmed by some recent change.

But that shouldn't matter. No one started a quest full of Quintessence.

"She must be the one," he whispered. "She must be the one for the Starling."

Even more disconcerting, last night he had set up his quintescope and scanned the town of Four Points, searching for the Starling. He had found the trails of Quintessence, golden paths that circled and crisscrossed over hills and down streams and through woods. They were everywhere, those Quintessence trails.

But the Starling herself was nowhere to be found.

Fallen Stars were unpredictable, of course. Some immediately charged into populated areas, terrifying Elementals and occasionally burning down whole towns. Some climbed to great heights and leaped again and again, exhausting themselves in a desperate effort to get home.

And some hid.

The Starling, the ShopKeeper was sure, was hiding now.

Usually, he could find those who hid, using his quintescope. The Light of Quintessence could be seen through most Elements, but, alas, the scopes were not perfect. Metals, in particular, often proved impenetrable. His own shop had iron in its doors and in its ladders and in the spire above, and so even if the shop's inside was filled with Quintessence, that iron would prevent anyone from seeing the Light from the outside—even with a quintescope. And the ShopKeeper remembered a Starling who had once hidden in a steel storm-water tunnel for nearly two weeks until it was almost too late.

Almost, but not quite. He had found that Starling in the end, and his Elementals had sent the Starling home.

The ShopKeeper would find this Starling too.

He would go tonight. He would search for her on foot.

But he didn't have much time left.

The blue light flickered, off and on, off and on. The ShopKeeper studied his papers.

CHAPTER 28

"Little star? Starling? Are you there?"

Alma was in the woods behind her house. She'd been so tired from the night before that she'd drifted off to sleep while waiting for time to pass. When she'd jerked awake to a room lit by moon-beams, her clock had read 12:03.

Now she was running through the brush, the quintescope case banging against her leg, and calling as loud as she dared, but there was no bell sound. There was no red-gold light.

There was no Starling.

Disappointed, Alma went to the very edge of the yard, behind the bushes and leafless trees, to wait for Hugo. The crater was there, and she climbed to the bottom and sat cross-legged, clutch-ing the quintescope case in both hands. She waited for what felt like a long time. She waited until she was sure that Hugo was not going to come, sure that he thought she was stupid or crazy or both.

Then she heard a whisper.

"Alma?"

Alma jumped up and scrambled out of the crater. She pushed through the bushes—and there was Hugo, robot-glasses flashing in the just-less-than-full moonlight, wispy hair tips blowing wildly in the wind, yellow gloves on his hands.

"You came," Alma said. "I didn't think you'd come."

"I wasn't sure if I would be able to," Hugo replied. "But my mother had an unexpected night shift and my stepfather always retires very early, as do my younger siblings. Also, your house is in very close proximity to my own. I'm on the south edge of Second Point." He pushed his visor-glasses up on his nose. "And there are . . . additional factors as well."

"I have something to show you," Alma said. "Something you're not going to believe."

Sitting there in the crater, Alma had been thinking about the best way to tell Hugo about the Starling, since she couldn't show her to him. She couldn't just say it; Hugo would probably back away slowly, gloved hands held up.

The crater, she had decided, would impress him.

She was right. When Hugo saw the smooth, red-earthed pit, his squinty eyes popped open behind his visor-glasses and he murmured, "Zonks. I can certainly see why you would assume that this is a meteorite-impact crater."

"Isn't it?" Alma asked. "I mean, don't you think it is? That's what it looks like to me."

Hugo crouched down. He craned his neck until he was almost upside down, first one way, then the other way. "I can't be certain," he said after a few minutes. "It's extremely small. The smallest crater I'm aware of was approximately three hundred feet across. This is not even thirty feet across." He scooped up some of the dirt from the edge of the pit, held it up to his visored eyes, then let it fall back to the ground. "Although there does appear to have been a fire here. Perhaps if there was—was there anything else? A larger piece of rock, perhaps?"

"There was the Starling," Alma blurted, forgetting her plan.

She glanced quickly at Hugo, and she could tell by the way he wasn't looking at her that she should have stuck to the crater.

But now that she'd started talking, Alma didn't think she could stop. All day she'd worried about the Starling. All day she'd tried to figure out what she should do. Then she hadn't been able to go to the Fifth Point, and the Starling wasn't here.

She needed help. She needed Hugo's help.

She had to tell him the truth.

"I told you a star fell from the sky and into my backyard," she said. "But the star wasn't just a star—not just a ball of gas—it was a person. A girl, I think. A—a Starling maybe. And this was where she landed two night ago, and then last night—last night I saw her and she started to run. I chased her through the woods, but then she disappeared. I was hoping she'd be here again tonight. I think—I think she needs me. And I thought if anyone would know what to do, it would be you because you know all about stars and nuclear stuff and elements. And I know you probably think I'm crazy, but it really happened, and I really, really, really need to figure out what to do next."

Alma said these words very fast. She only breathed twice. And when she was done, Hugo was still studying the crater—and not her—very intently.

Alma waited, but he didn't say anything.

"Hugo?" she finally said.

"You've provided me with a lot of information," Hugo said, "and I think it would be wise for us to sit down somewhere out of the wind for a few moments. It feels as if a storm is approaching."

"You're not going to leave?" Alma asked, relieved.

"Not yet," Hugo said.

"You don't think I'm crazy?"

"No," he said. "Not crazy." He reached into the pocket of his coat. "I have this."

He took out a book, and he opened it to a page near the middle, a page taken up by an illustration.

An illustration of the Starling.

CHAPTER 29

They went to sit on the back steps of Alma's house. Alma felt breathless and strange, but it wasn't, for once, a bad feeling.

"I found the book outside of the Fifth Point," Hugo told her.

"*Outside* of it?" Alma asked.

Hugo nodded. "Propped up against one of the doors. I thought—" He pulled one of his yellow gloves off, then the other. "In ordinary circumstances, I would never commit a crime. But it was—I was curious. I'm going to return it."

Alma hadn't known Hugo for very long, but it was obvious that taking the book had been a big deal for him. She wondered if he had felt about the book the way she had felt about the quintescope— like it was there for him.

"I got the telescope from the shop too," she said. "Well, the Shop-Keeper actually called it a *quintescope*."

"There's a ShopKeeper?" Hugo asked. "I wasn't aware that the Fifth Point was occupied."

"I wasn't either," Alma replied. "But one of the doors was open, and he was in there. He's very—well, strange. He told me to save the Starling, and I think that must be the star-girl I saw. I think maybe—maybe that's why he gave me the quintescope? So I would see her fall. So I would help her."

"I remain highly skeptical," Hugo said, tucking his gloves into his pockets, "but the book would agree with you."

He set the book on the steps between them. It wasn't much of a book really, more like a pamphlet, with a cracked, red-brown, leathery cover. It was clearly very old, and engraved in gold across its front was the title: *Quintessence: An Elemental Primer for Star Restoration.*

Alma gasped as she read the words. "*Star Restoration!* So this is about—"

"It's about sending a star back to space," Hugo said, "in the most unscientific way possible."

Alma opened the book. The pages within reminded her of the map in her parents' office—brown, faded, crinkly—with handwritten words in such fancy script that some of the letters were hard to decipher. On the first page, she read:

High above, high above, the sky is filled
with the never-ending brightness of the Stars.
Oh, how great and glorious and full of mystery they are!

But you, dear soul, did you know that you are made of the
same stuff as the Stars?
And did you know that you can be filled with that same Light,
filled with Quintessence?
Read on and you will learn these truths and far, far more.

"It's just like the flyer," Alma breathed. "'You are made of elements and quintessence.'"

Hugo turned the page but didn't answer.

On the next page, there was an illustration of a four-pointed star.
In each point, there was a symbol—an upside-down triangle with a
line through it at the top, a right-side-up triangle with a line through
it on the right, a right-side-up triangle at the bottom, and an upside-
down triangle on the left. And in the center of the star there was
a circle with lines extending from it, like light rays. Alma read on:

It is common knowledge that there are four elements:
Earth, Wind, Fire, and Water.
But I tell you a new thing:
There is a Fifth Element, unseen by the natural eye.
This Element is the Great Light of the Stars.
It dwells within each Elemental, a spark that must be grown,
and it can be created when the four Elements
in their truest forms are connected.
This Fifth Element is called Quintessence.

Alma felt these words at her core, in the center of herself, where her Alma-ness had been sparking and sputtering for the past two days. More than ever, quintessence sounded like Alma-ness.

The next illustration was of a four-pointed star falling from the sky. Waiting on the ground for the star were four human shapes. At the center of each was a circle containing one of the symbols from the page before, which Alma realized must represent the four elements. She read:

This Universe is marvelous, this Universe is magnificent,
And this Universe is in a state of perpetual change.
At times, imbalances and shifting forces and sudden endings
will shake loose a Star from its place in the firmament.
That Star, my dear soul, will fall.
And in that terrible fall, the Star's Quintessence will be depleted.
But take heart!
The fallen are drawn to worlds
where true Elements can be gathered.
With the assistance of Elementals,
these Elements can be connected,
Quintessence can be created,
And the Star can be restored to its home in the Universe.

"So the elementals are us?" Alma asked, studying the four human shapes. "People, I mean? And the fallen stars need—need our help?"

"As best I can gather," Hugo replied.

Alma turned the page, eager to learn more, and there was the Starling illustration. The image showed a slight body, a large head, and enormous black-hole eyes. The figure had its thin arms and legs outstretched, and it was surrounded by the lines that radiated out. In the center of its torso, there was a circle with its own ray lines. Beneath the picture were these words:

For a very young Star—a Starling, that is—a fall often results
in catastrophic Quintessence loss.
Thus, the Elementals must act swiftly and boldly.
A fallen Starling is a Starling in mortal peril.

Alma felt her heart not just sink but plummet into her stomach.
"'Mortal peril,'" she whispered. "But what do we do?"
Hugo reached over again and flipped through the pages. Alma watched as entries on Earth, Wind, Fire, and Water passed. And then, on the very last page, next to an illustration of a brilliant star now shining high above the four human shapes, were these words:

Now you know these secrets, dear souls.
Now you know how we are all connected to one another,
how we all need one another.
And be you an Elemental of Water or Wind, of Earth or Fire,
your quest is before you.
Find the Elements.
Grow the Light.
Save the Stars.

CHAPTER 30

It felt to Alma as if the pieces of the puzzle that had been scattered across her mind two days ago had very suddenly come together.

"This is what the ShopKeeper said!" she cried, lifting the page close to Hugo's visored gaze. "'Find the Elements. Grow the Light. Save the Stars'—well, he said 'Starling.' I guess that's a young star. He told me what to do, and here it is again. We have to find the elements!"

Hugo shook his head. "Apologies, but this entire book is ludicrous."

Alma stared at him, perplexed. "What do you mean?" she asked. "How can it be ludicrous? This book is very old. Ancient, even."

"Science is cumulative," Hugo replied. "That means the older the information is, the less correct it is, for the most part."

"But what about the elements it talks about—earth, wind, water, fire? Isn't that what you're doing your lecture on? How the elements were created in the stars?"

"It is very important," Hugo said, "that you come on Tuesday. I am astounded by the gaps in the education system." He tapped the cover of the book. "This is alchemy—pseudoscience from medieval times. Earth, wind, water, fire—those are not the elements I'm referring to. And neither is quintessence."

"Quintessence is the fifth element," Alma said, flipping back to the page with the elemental symbols in the star. "See? It's the 'Great Light' that fills the stars—the spark in us—and we can make it by combining the other four elements."

Hugo pushed his visor-glasses up on his nose. Then he pulled them down. Then he pushed them back up. He seemed confused, Alma thought. Conflicted.

But she wasn't. Not anymore.

Because here was what could be done. Here was what had to be done.

They needed to get started as soon as possible.

"It might be ludicrous," she said, "but I think it's true. And you— you know so much, Hugo. I could really use your help finding the elements."

Hugo scooped up a rock from the ground. "Eureka," he said, holding it out. "Here is some earth. You're one-fourth of the way done."

Alma didn't take the rock. "I don't think that can be it," she said. "I think it has to be . . . special-er."

"Special-er," Hugo repeated.

"Truer," Alma said. "The most true. That's what the book says."

"That doesn't make sound scientific sense," Hugo replied. "True earth? I have no hypothesis about what that would consist of or how to find it."

Alma turned back to the Starling and traced the illustration, the lines emanating from the little form, the circle at her center. "We both saw something, Hugo," she said. "And you have this book, and I have the quintescope. That's too many coincidences. I think—I think we're the elementals who are supposed to save this Starling."

Hugo was silent. He was silent for a long, long time. By now Alma had figured out that she just had to wait while he thought, while he processed and figured out what he wanted to say. So she waited.

"You really think this?" Hugo finally asked. "You really think that a star, defying the laws of physics, fell out of the sky? And turned into a child? And now requires pseudoscientific assistance to return to outer space?"

"Yes," Alma said. "That's what I think. Absolutely."

He was silent again. Then he said, "I do agree that the number of coincidences surrounding this incident is highly unusual. I'm not saying any of it is true! But since scientific knowledge is about an open-minded spirit of inquiry, I suppose I can explore the hypotheses set forth in this book."

Alma couldn't contain her smile. Hugo might not be fully convinced, but he believed enough to help her. That was all she needed.

They were going to find the elements. They were going to create quintessence, that Great Light. And they were going to save the Starling.

"You won't regret it, Hugo," Alma said. "Neither of us will. I can feel it."

CHAPTER 31

Before Hugo left that night, they decided to meet the next after-noon at the Fifth Point.

"The ShopKeeper will know what we have to do," Alma had assured Hugo.

"Perhaps," Hugo had said. "But I will do some research on my own as well." He had sounded delighted by the prospect.

Since the next day was Saturday, Alma had been able to sleep in late, and sleep she had. It was nearly eleven by the time she came downstairs. Her parents were in the living room, doing the "light weekend work" that they always brought home from the office.

"So I think," Alma told them, "I'm going to go into town."

The other day, when she had announced that she was going for a walk, her parents had been surprised and concerned. Now they looked surprised and pleased.

"You are really Miss Social all of a sudden!" her mother said.

"Yes, indeed," her father agreed. "What's going on in town?"

"I need to meet someone at—at the library," Alma lied, guilt making her stammer. "A partner. For a project. An Astronomy Club project."

"Alma Llama Ding Dong!" Her mother jumped out of her seat. Her coffee sloshed over the sides of the mug she was holding, but she didn't seem to notice. "That's fantastic, am I right?"

"It should be fun," Alma said with a small smile. "I mean, in an educational kind of way."

After lunch, she headed out. She hadn't been on her bicycle since moving to Four Points, but she used to ride all over Old Haven. Today, she pedaled as hard as she could. The wind—still cold and fierce—was in her hair, and although there were rumblings of thunder in the distance, the sunshine was splendid and warming. She zipped up a hill, and then the center of the town was beneath her, the Fifth Point rising out of it like a magic wand, like an arrow pointing to the heavens.

For the first time ever, Alma felt excited to find out what Four Points had in store for her.

CHAPTER 32

Hugo was waiting by the south door of the Fifth Point. He lifted one yellow-gloved hand as Alma pulled up to a stop.

"Greetings, Alma," he said.

"Hi, Hugo," Alma replied. She locked her bike to a lamppost, then joined him at the door.

"Remember the ShopKeeper is a little strange," she warned him. "But I'm sure he'll know what to do."

Then she knocked on the south door.

No one answered, so she knocked again. And again. And again.

Five minutes later, Alma's fists were red and stinging, and all four doors remained shut and locked.

"He is not here," Hugo informed her.

Alma felt like crying as she pressed her nose to a display window. She shielded her eyes, but she couldn't see anything inside the shop, not even the blue light. She was slightly consoled by the thought that the ShopKeeper had said that he would be in and out. Maybe he was "out" today.

"We'll come back," she said after giving one final knock on each door. "We'll just have to keep coming back until he's here."

"Does that mean you're finished?" Hugo asked. "If so, I propose we purchase some supplies."

This had not been part of the plan. "Supplies?" Alma said. "Like what?"

"I haven't had much time to research," Hugo admitted. "But I thought I might find some promising materials at the General Store. Let us proceed."

She didn't want to go inside anywhere. Her stomach had already begun to churn and her throat had already begun to constrict at the thought.

They approached the store, which was a great, red warehouse-like building. At its entrance were big, heavy barn doors that were propped wide open. Open doors, Alma told herself, were a good thing; she would be able to get out quickly if she started to have an episode. Through the doors, she could see that the store was brightly lit with a high ceiling and wide aisles. And there didn't appear to be many people inside. Two more good things.

Maybe she would do it. Maybe she would go into the store. She still had that spark inside her, that little-bit-of-Alma-ness. And she was here for a reason. She was here because she wanted to help the Starling.

But at the entrance to the store, Alma stopped.

"I'm going to wait right here," she called to Hugo, who was selecting a shopping basket. "So I can keep an eye on the Fifth Point. In case the ShopKeeper comes back."

Hugo glanced over at her, frowning slightly, then shrugged. "That's your choice, I suppose," he said. "It will be easier for me alone. But you are the one who wanted to find the elements."

"I do," Alma said, her voice choked and high. "I do but—"

A delighted shriek of, "Daddy, it's Hugo!" cut her off.

In the middle of the store, there was a counter with a cash register. Behind it was a man with buzzed dark hair, deep brown skin, and a child hanging from each of his arms. The kids were young, maybe three years old, and they were both laughing hysterically. The man tried to free one hand to wave, but then settled for a shrug and a smile when the giggling kids refused to release him.

"That's my stepfather, Marcus," Hugo said. His voice was even more robotic than usual, and while he lifted his still-gloved hand, he didn't wave it. "He owns this store. And those are my twin siblings, Lexi and Isaac. Whenever my mother works a night shift on the weekends, they come here so she can sleep." He sighed. "Usually, I stay home too. It's so quiet and peaceful."

"I'm sorry you're missing that," Alma said. "I'm at home a lot. Or at my parents' office. I don't—I haven't been going out very much."

Hugo picked up his chosen basket. "I will return," he said.

From the door, Alma watched as Hugo moved methodically through the store. He went down every aisle and he took a very long time on each one. When he finally started back toward her,

112

Alma stepped just inside the store's barn doors to meet him. She was surprised to see that after all his searching, there were only two things in his basket: water-purification tablets and a rock-polishing kit.

"The problem with the tablets," Hugo said, holding up the packet, "is that they add iodine or chlorine to the water. Chlorine water isn't *pure*. Iodine water isn't *pure*. And the polishing kit will make stones prettier, I suppose. But not—not—"

"Earthier," Alma finished. "Not true earth."

"As I've said, I don't know what *true* earth really means," he replied, "but it seems unlikely that it means *smooth* and *shiny*."

Alma tried to think of a way to save the trip, an idea, any idea that would help Hugo. "What about a windmill? For wind, I mean."

Hugo blinked his eyes, squinty and warm brown behind his visor-glasses. "That's a possibility," he said. "But typically windmills are used to convert wind into energy. The wind itself is a means to an end. Fascinating fact: windmills were invented by Hero of Alexandria, an inventor and mathematician during the first century. He used the energy to power an organ. He also invented the steam engine. And vending machines."

"Really?" In spite of her disappointment that they were no closer to finding the elements, Alma laughed.

Hugo didn't reply, and for a moment, Alma worried that he hadn't been trying to be funny. Then he smiled back at her.

"Really," he said.

"Okay, so no windmills," Alma said. "What about a funnel? Like a huge cone that would catch the wind and then direct it into a—a bottle or something?"

Hugo pushed up his glasses. "I understand what you're saying," he said. "There are some wind turbines that use funnels. But once the air is bottled, it would be cut off from the things that make it move— the forces that make wind. It would be regular air in a bottle. And fire—I have no idea what to use for fire. Maybe a flint stone? A lightning rod?" He shook his head in frustration. "No. Nothing is right."

In the end, Hugo talked himself out of every purchase. Alma slouched against the outside wall of the store as she waited for him to put his basket back. The ShopKeeper hadn't been at the Fifth Point, and now they were leaving the General Store empty-handed.

But when Hugo said, "We have to think harder. And I have to do more research," she felt a little better.

They weren't giving up.

They were just getting started.

CHAPTER 33

Alma and Hugo were unchaining their bicycles by the Fifth Point when they heard a buzz of voices, many voices, coming their way.

Somewhere in that buzz was a voice Alma recognized.

She looked behind her to see a group of girls coming down the street. They wore vibrant colors and the sun bounced off their sequined and shiny accessories. Their teeth flashed as they smiled and laughed. And with them, right in the middle like she fit perfectly, was Shirin.

Alma jerked her eyes back to her bicycle lock. She had liked Shirin from the moment she met her, but she didn't want her to know what she and Hugo were up to. It was weird. It was bizarre, even. And Alma was pretty sure that the last thing she—a girl who talked to herself and wore feathers in her hair and fled from every classroom every single day—needed was one more thing that made her weird.

A boy who wore visor-glasses and gave lectures on astrophysics and said things like "Zonks" didn't need another thing to make him weird either. But Hugo didn't seem to be aware of this.

"Greetings, Shirin," he said.

"Oh. Hi, Hugo! Hi, Alma!"

The girls, every single one, giggled.

Alma glanced up. Shirin was smiling, but she seemed like she'd rather not be. She seemed, Alma thought, like she would rather not be there at all.

"Hi," Alma mumbled.

"What are you two up to?" Shirin asked.

"Noth—" Alma started to say, but Hugo was already answering.

"We're gathering supplies in order to create true forms of the four elements of alchemy," he said. "We want to test some hypotheses based on a pseudoscientific book that I found."

Alma felt like someone had snuffed out every possible light in her as the girls with Shirin started to giggle again.

"Whatever that means," one of them said.

"Yeah," another said. "Pseudo-what?"

But Shirin's rather-not-be-there smile had slid completely from her face and the expression left behind was startled and wide-eyed. "You're collecting elements?" she said. "Elements like wind, water, earth? Those kinds of elements?"

"Yes," Hugo confirmed. "Classical elements rather than chemical elements."

The other girls were drifting away now, moving in twos and

threes farther down the street, toward the coffee shop, Bean There Donut That. None of them, Alma noticed, waited for Shirin, who was now inching closer to her and Hugo.

"So, like, do you know how to get true elements?" she asked, her voice nearly a whisper. "Or how to store them? How are you going to keep wind in a jar? Have you asked anyone for help—like Mrs. Brisa or Mr. Newton in the school library or your parents or anything? What's the plan?"

Alma had no idea why Shirin seemed so interested, but she desperately did not want Hugo to be the one to answer these questions. It was bad enough that Shirin knew about the elements—she did *not* want her to know about the Starling.

"We're not sure yet," she said quickly. "We're still gathering ideas."

"Creating true forms of the elements is proving somewhat confounding," Hugo explained. "And, as you point out, storage presents another issue."

Shirin nodded emphatically. "Yes. Yes! A big issue. You'll probably need some super-specialized equipment." She paused for a moment and glanced around her. She seemed to have just noticed, right then, that none of her friends were with her anymore. "Oh," she said. She straightened up and her voice went back to its usual volume. "Well, I have some ideas for you. And some things you might need."

"We don't—" Alma began.

"We meet at midnight," Hugo said. "Under the stars. It's very top secret."

117

Shirin grinned. "I like that!" she said. "Where?"

"Alma's backyard," Hugo said.

"I'm in Fourth Point," Shirin told Alma. "Where are you? Here, I'll write it on my hand."

Shirin pulled open the tiny, bejeweled bag she was carrying and dug around for a minute before producing a flower-topped pen. Alma stammered out her address, and Shirin scrawled it across her palm in fuchsia ink.

"Meet you there tonight," she said, slinging the bag back over her shoulder. "Trust me, you're going to want what I have."

"Okay," Alma said. "Sure. Tonight. What do you have though?"

But Shirin was already gone, on her way to find the group of happy and sunny and beautiful girls who had left her behind.

PART 5

Water

· · · · · · · · · · · · · · · · · ·

▽

CHAPTER 34

When Alma arrived at her backyard at midnight that night, quinte-scope in hand, Hugo and Shirin were already there. Shirin was sitting cross-legged in the middle of the crater, her sequined school back-pack beside her, a flashlight in hand, and *Quintessence: An Elemental Primer for Star Restoration* open on her lap. Hugo was lying next to her. His gloves were off and he was holding tiny pieces of charred rock up to his visor-covered eyes, studying one after another.

"Can you believe this?" Shirin called to Alma, holding up the book. "Have you read this? I mean, wow."

"I've read some of it," Alma said. She climbed into the crater, where it was a little less windy, and sat next to them.

"And this thing," Shirin continued. She flung out her arms, taking in the whole of the pit. "I guess this is where you saw the meteor or whatever fall?"

Before Alma could answer, Hugo said, "Alma thinks it was a star." He took the book from Shirin and flipped it open to the illustration of the black-eyed Starling. "Like this one. She thinks we're the elementals and we need to collect true water, wind, earth, and fire in order to create quintessence and send the star back home."

Shirin studied the picture for a long moment before looking back up at Alma. Alma could feel her throat constricting as she met Shirin's raised-eyebrow gaze.

"That's what the book says to do," she said quickly. "And I thought I saw a Starling. I mean—I did see her." She swallowed hard and waited for Shirin to laugh at her and leave.

Instead Shirin shrieked, "Oh my goodness! It all makes sense now!"

"Shh!" Alma shushed her, glancing back at her house. "What do you mean?"

"Yes, what makes sense?" Hugo asked.

"I'll show you," Shirin said, only slightly softer.

She unzipped her backpack. From inside, she drew out three small containers.

All three were transparent, like glass. The first was tall and angular, like a stretched-out pyramid, with a bluish tint, a corked top, and an inlay of an upside-down triangle made of a white metal that shone with a rainbow of colors depending on the angle of the moonlight. The second was short and square, brownish in color, and featured a rusted metal inlay of an upright triangle with a line through it. The final container was decorated with opaque swirls and a silver inlay of an upright triangle with a line through it. Inside that container—which was curved but tapered at the top—there was a tiny white windmill.

"Zonks," Hugo murmured. "What are these made of?" He picked up the first container and held it up to the moon. The light shining through it cast a bluish glow on his face. "I've never seen material like this. It's like glass. But metal. Is it some kind of acrylic? No, too light for that."

"These are the symbols from the book!" Alma cried. She picked up the third container, the one with the windmill in it. The blades turned with the movement.

"I drew them and showed my mother," Shirin said, "because she knows a lot of, like, science stuff. That's how I knew they were the element symbols. There were only three, though. The fire container is missing."

"You think these were designed to store elements?" Alma asked.

"Maybe," Hugo answered. He was now tapping experimentally on the sides of the second container. "But designed by whom? How did you procure these, Shirin?"

"I . . . found them," Shirin replied.

"Where?" Hugo pressed. "I would like to contact the manufacturer."

Shirin was quiet for a moment before blurting out, "The Fifth

Point! They were outside of it. Like outside one of the doors when I was heading home last Saturday. They weren't there when I walked past the first time—I know because I always look in the windows. And then—they were. It felt like—I know it's bizarre, but it felt like I was supposed to take them. I was going to take them back, but then I found that flyer in my Science book, and you two have this." She shook the book.

"Alma also has the telescope," Hugo said.

"Quintescope," Alma said. "It's from the Fifth Point too. I never got to show you at Astronomy Club. Do you want to see it?"

She handed the case to Shirin, who flipped the copper clasp and opened the lid.

"Wow," Shirin said, leaning over to touch each cone. "This is so gorgeous! I wish I could've seen the Starling with this like you did. Although I bet it was really sad. I mean, can you imagine? Being up with your star friends, shining and everything, and then all of a sudden—bam! You fall out of the sky!"

Hearing this, Alma wished she had asked Shirin for help from the beginning. Shirin—who had seen the Starling from her window, who had shown up in her backyard, who had brought element containers—belonged here, with them.

"She was here in the woods the other night too," Alma said. "She was in the crater, but I—I scared her. By accident. Now I don't know where she is."

Shirin shut the case decisively and jumped to her feet. "Then

123

we'll go find her *and* the elements," she said. "After reading this, I know exactly where to start!"

Hugo had been listening without comment to this exchange. Alma wished she had been able to convince him so easily. "Where exactly are you proposing we go?" he asked.

"Yes, where?" Alma said.

Shirin grabbed the angular blue container from Hugo and held it up to the starlight. The colors in the inlay shone, iridescent and glittering. "To true water!" she cried.

CHAPTER 35

Before they left, Alma read the page on water. Next to an illustration
of the upside-down triangle, the water symbol, were these words:

Water, Water, the genesis of life.
Water that bubbles and flows and refreshes.
And the deeper you go, the truer it becomes.
At the source is where the wonder awaits.
And those Elementals of Water,
do they not possess these same qualities?
Though they be vainglorious and inconstant at times,
are they not adventurous and active,
overflowing with vim and vigor?
Do they not restore the weary and inspire the downtrodden?
Do they not contain hidden depths, waiting to be found?

It seemed fitting, Alma had thought reading those words, that Shirin would be the one leading them to this element. Fast-paced and quick-tongued, Shirin was certainly full of vim and vigor. And now here they were following her toward the Fourth Point neighborhood in the middle of the night.

Alma had never been out so late, never pedaled down streets that were entirely devoid of people and cars, with only the sound of the wind around her. It was unnerving, but it also made her feel awake and energized, almost like she was borrowing some of Shirin's sense of adventure.

"I live right there," Shirin said in a voice that Alma felt was much too loud given the lateness of the hour and the definitely not parentally approved nature of their expedition. She was pointing at a lovely blue Victorian with a wraparound porch and a round tower, which was something Alma had always wanted. "Where we're going is a little farther west though. My sister and I used to go there a lot before she started high school and got too cool. Ugh."

"I've never been over here," Alma replied. "But I've never really been anywhere in Four Points."

At the end of one of the streets, the houses stopped. Ahead of them were only trees. It was the Preserve, the same one that wrapped past Alma's house in Third Point, but here in the west, that thin strip of woods became a true forest. Alma didn't know how far the Preserve extended; on her parents' map, it went to the very edge of the crinkly brown paper.

"We have to leave our bikes," Shirin said. She jumped off hers, letting it crash to the ground.

"We're going into the woods?" Hugo asked, coming to a hesitant stop. "Is that wise at this hour?"

"There's a trail," Shirin said impatiently. "Like I said, I used to come here all the time."

Hugo frowned at her. He stayed on his bike.

Alma felt a shiver of anticipation at the thought of traipsing through the woods after midnight, but she found that she wasn't scared. After moving to Four Points, she had cooped herself up indoors, afraid of what might happen if she ventured out. But before, in Old Haven, she had always felt more like herself when she was outside. She wondered what the Four Points forest would be like.

"Come on, Hugo," she said, hopping off her bike and taking the quintescope, set up without its tripod, out of her basket. "We have to find the elements, remember? And we can look for the Starling as we go. She could be in these woods."

Hugo sighed deeply, but he climbed off his bike.

"This is truly ludicrous," he muttered.

At first, the trail was wide and easy, and the three walked side by side. But the farther they went, the narrower and more overgrown it became. Soon they were hiking in single file.

Every now and then, Alma paused to peer through the quintescope, scanning the trees for signs of light. It was hard to walk and do this though, especially since Shirin kept tripping over roots and sprawling to the ground right in front of her.

"Ugh, I'm so clumsy," she said, dusting herself off after her third fall. "It's because I move so fast. My sister always makes fun of me for it. Well, everyone does, actually. But I can't help it. Anyway, this is exciting! We're helping a *star*! As soon as I read about water, I saw this place in my mind. You'll see why."

They moved farther and farther into the woods. Shirin kept up a steady stream of conversation, but Alma was only half listening to her. And she was not listening at all to that voice that had taken up every bit of space in her mind for the past three months.

Instead, she was listening to the woods around her—the few hanging-on dead leaves rustling, the wind through the branches, the hoot of a watchful owl, a far-off roll of thunder.

And another sound, a sound that was growing louder with every footstep. A sort of hushing, a sort of swooshing, a sort of rhythmic lullaby. The path took them past a tall river birch, its peeling white bark like a mummy's wrappings in the darkness.

And on the other side of the tree, there it was. The source of the lullaby.

"It's the Fourth Point Creek!" Shirin cried, throwing up her arms. "Isn't it gorgeous?"

It was. The trees cleared around the stream bank, letting the moonlight and starlight in. The brightness danced on the water as it flowed past, like fireflies or fairies or specks of shining stardust. Alma was seized with a sudden desire to wade into that water, to feel it on her toes. The stream that ran past her backyard in Old Haven had been one of her favorite places. She used to gather rocks for her collection there in the summer and slip-slide down its shining ice path in the winter.

She could see why Shirin had led them to this place.

Here was water. True water. She was sure of it.

"I'm going to put some in the jar," Shirin said.

She took the container from her backpack, then knelt by the creek, uncorked it, and placed it underwater. Then she pulled it out.

"It's empty," she said, confused. She lifted the container up, and Alma saw that there was nothing inside—not a drop.

"Allow me to assist you," Hugo said, moving carefully over the rocks to stand by Shirin. "This may not be socially appropriate to say, but you don't strike me as being particularly meticulous or mechanically inclined."

Shirin wrinkled her nose at Hugo, but she handed over the bottle.

After a few seconds of holding it under, Hugo brought the container back up—still empty.

"Something must be obstructing the opening," Hugo said, peering into the little hole at the top.

"Oh really, Mr. Mechanically Inclined?" Shirin said.

While Hugo and Shirin tried over and over to fill the bottle, Alma watched the stream. She thought of what the book said and how the water seemed to flow right around the bottle top, like it was refusing to fill it up.

"Maybe," she said after another failed attempt, "this water isn't true enough or pure enough or something."

"This water is extremely pure!" Shirin replied. "It's a spring-fed creek."

"What does that mean?" Alma asked.

"It means that the source of the creek is not another body of water such as a lake or a river," Hugo said, putting the jar under the water again. "The water comes instead from the aquifer—from underground."

"Oh," Alma said, the solution suddenly clear to her. "Then let's go there."

"Where?" Shirin asked.

"To the spring," Alma replied. "To the start of the creek. Remember what the book said? 'At the source is where the wonder awaits.'"

"You want to go farther into the woods?" Hugo asked uncertainly. He took the jar out of the water again. Empty.

"We have to," Alma said. "Don't we? For the Starling?"

"Yes! Yes!" Shirin leaped off her perch on a stream rock, then lost her footing. She started stumbling into the many-limbed embrace of a leafless weeping willow before Alma caught her arm and steadied her.

"For the Starling," agreed a now-breathless Shirin. She grinned at Alma, and Alma felt herself smiling back.

CHAPTER 36

They followed the shimmering stardust. Shirin, flashlight in hand, led the way, tromping through the underbrush and over the stones in a way that might have worried Alma if there had been any houses nearby. Shirin was not made for stealth missions.

Before long, everyone was tired. Hugo dragged behind them and even Shirin stopped talking—mostly. The farther they went, the more Alma worried. How long would they keep going? It was getting later and later—or rather, earlier and earlier. They needed to turn back soon. What if the spring was miles and miles away? Or worse, what if they found the stream's source and water wouldn't go into the bottle there either?

She tried to feel the cool air filling her lungs. She tried to watch the moon peekabooing through the tree branches. She tried to listen to the deep murmurings of the thunder in the distance, a sound she had always loved. But with every step she took, the woods seemed to grow fainter and fainter, and her thoughts grew louder and louder.

Then she paused for a moment to look through her quintescope, and for the first time that night, she saw it: trails of gold.

"The Starling was here!" she cried.

Without the quintescope, there was nothing to be seen except, Alma now noticed, a few slightly singed tree trunks. But when Shirin and Hugo took turns looking through the eyepiece, Shirin oohed and aahed and Hugo muttered, "Zonks."

"When I accidentally scared the Starling," Alma told them, "she left bits of this stuff all over the woods behind my house."

"How come you can only see it through the quintescope?" Shirin wondered.

"If I may propose a very unscientific hypothesis," Hugo said, "I believe the gold substance is quintessence, which the book says is 'unseen by the natural eye.' This quintescope makes it visible."

It was what Alma had thought when she'd first seen the trail across the farmland. The Starling was losing her quintessence. "That must be it," she said. "The ShopKeeper—he said the quintescope showed 'true things.' Maybe it will show true water too!"

"Perhaps," Hugo said.

"There's quintessence everywhere in here," Shirin said, nearly taking off Hugo's head as she swung the quintescope around. "Maybe she was looking for something."

Alma had seen that too—trails every which way, in circles, overlapping—but she'd interpreted it differently. The random, scattered paths had reminded her of something else.

Sometimes, when she felt like she was about to have an episode, Alma would run—from classrooms, from the cafeteria, from her locker. She would run until she found somewhere that felt safe and private, usually a bathroom stall or an unoccupied classroom. Maybe, Alma thought, the Starling had fled in that same way, blinded by panic, frantically searching for somewhere safe.

Her thoughts were interrupted when Shirin let out a sharp cry, thrust the quintescope into Hugo's hands, and starting racing toward the stream at top speed.

"We made it!" she screeched. "We're here!"

Alma and Hugo hurried after her, and a moment later, they saw what she meant.

Ahead of them, the stream opened up. It wasn't a flowing line anymore, but a pool. A pool of water that caught the moonlight magnificently and reflected it back like a spotlight. Steam rose from the surface, and Alma could see bubbles coming up.

There was no doubt that this was the source.

"I'm going to get some of the water," Shirin said, pulling out the container.

Before she could plunge in, Hugo grabbed her arm. "Cease and desist!" he shouted, louder than Alma had ever heard him. "I have no scientific explanation for what's happening here, but if we are

133

going to investigate further, I would like to begin by pointing out that this appears to be a thermal spring. See the steam? Thermal springs are heated in the Earth's crust."

"But that's perfect," Alma said. "If it's coming from deep in the Earth, it's sure to be true!"

"Perfect," Hugo said, "except that water at the source could be very hot, even boiling. This presents a very serious obstacle to our quest."

Alma studied the water for a moment, then pulled off one shoe. "I think I have an idea," she said.

"If you are thinking of putting your feet in this water, I would not suggest it!" Hugo cried.

"Hugo!" Shirin said. "Oh my goodness. Calm down."

"Don't worry," Alma reassured him. "I'm not going in."

She removed her sock, then pulled it onto the end of the longest stick she could find. Leaning as far over the water as she could, she dipped the sock in, then brought it back to her and gave it a tentative poke with one fingertip.

"It feels warm," she said. "But not hot."

"I would propose additional testing," Hugo said, but Shirin was already pulling off her coat, then her shoes and socks. She splashed out into the water.

"It's okay, Hugo! See?" She lifted one foot. "Not boiled. Not even poached. Come on, you two. It's amazing! And look!"

She held up the little oblong water container, full and corked.

"I guess it wasn't blocked," she said. "Use the quintescope, Hugo! Maybe you'll be able to tell if it's true water!"

Reluctantly, Hugo pressed the quintescope eyepiece to his glasses and aimed it at the bottle. After gazing silently for a long moment, he passed the scope to Alma.

"Eureka," he murmured, shaking his head in disbelief.

When Alma looked through the quintescope, it was like someone had flipped a switch. Light was streaming from the water that was bubbling out of the ground, iridescent and brilliant.

Inside the bottle, the water was like a rainbow in motion, gleaming and sparkling in the starlight. Even Shirin, holding the bottle, seemed to shine.

And inside herself, Alma felt like she was shining too.

"We have our first element," she said. "Water."

CHAPTER 37

For a while, they took turns staring at the iridescent white water in the jar through the quintescope. Then they waded into the stream and took turns staring at the iridescent white water flowing from the source.

But ten minutes later, they weren't staring or wading. They were floating. The three of them were in the water, clothes and all.

Alma wasn't sure if it was Shirin's influence or the reckless feeling of being out in the middle of the night or something about that place, something about the source of the creek. But as she floated in the water, steam rising up around her, stars blazing above her, Alma thought that this was exactly where she was supposed to be.

"What a night," said Shirin. She was bathed in moonlight. She looked, Alma thought, like a mermaid. Or like another fallen star. Alma was sure that wasn't how she herself looked, but that was how she felt. "I'm so glad I found those jars and asked my mom about the symbols. She's a scientist, actually. She works for Third Point Labs. Did you know that?"

"*Your* mother?" Hugo asked. He turned his steam-fogged visor gaze toward Shirin. "Really? I would not have expected your family tree to contain scientists."

"Well, it does," Shirin said, splashing water Hugo's way. "Lots, in fact. My mom works with, like, bacteria and stuff, but she knows tons about astronomy because that was what her mother studied. My mom always wanted me and my sister to learn about it too, but Farah is always too busy to do anything with anyone. And I guess I was never really interested before. I've tried lots of other hobbies though—tap dance, ballet, piano, trumpet, basketball, ceramics, archery, fencing, opera, watercolor—"

"So why are you interested now?" Hugo asked, interrupting Shirin's seemingly never-ending list.

"Yes, why?" Alma asked. She had been wondering about this since the day of their first meeting. Why would Shirin—popular and outgoing—join a club with a nobody like her?

Shirin was uncharacteristically silent. Then she said, quietly, "I guess I thought it would be something new. Something where I could just be, like, me."

"But you said you had all those hobbies," Alma said. "And you have a million friends."

"That's true." Shirin swished her hands in the water, moonlit wakes rippling out with every motion. "But I always get bored with my hobbies. And my friends—I like them, but—"

"You find them vapid and mindless?" Hugo suggested.

Shirin's head bobbed back and forth. "It's not like that," she said. "Plenty of them are smart and funny and amazing. But they—they spend a lot of time worrying about who's popular and who's pretty, and I don't want to think about that stuff all the time. Maybe some of them feel the same way I do, I don't know. It's hard to tell." She sighed, her eyes on the sky. "Anyway, my sister said things get better in high school. She said everyone isn't so obsessed with fitting in and being perfect and everything. Even though she thinks she is. Ugh."

Alma thought this might be true. James hadn't had a lot of friends in high school, but he'd seemed less moody than he'd been in middle school. He had smiled more, talked to her more, helped her with her homework more. And when he'd come home from college for winter break in December, he'd seemed almost like a different person. But still . . .

"High school is a long way away," she said as she stretched her arms above her head, letting the water rush into the empty spaces left behind.

"Too long," Shirin agreed.

"The life expectancy for American women is 81.6 years," Hugo said. "Assuming you live that long the remainder of middle school is just two percent of your life."

138

Shirin laughed and splashed Hugo again. "Thanks, Hugo. Alma and I are super relieved," she said. "But I don't really want to spend even two percent of my life trying to be someone else. I guess that's why when I found the flyer and bottles and we'd all seen the Starling, it felt like—like this adventure was meant for me. The real me."

Alma remembered what she'd thought when she'd read the water section, and even though she felt silly, she said, "You know, when you got the water, you were kind of shining too. It's almost like—like this is your element? Like you're an elemental of water, like the book says."

"Are you saying I'm—what was it? Vain and inconsistent?"

"No!" Alma cried. "No, not that part. But you're—you make things exciting. And you're fun. You brought us here. You brought us to the water. And I'm pretty sure this counts as an adventure."

"Uh, yeah, I'd say so," Shirin agreed with a grin. "What do you think, Hugo?"

Hugo was staring up at the sky. His visor-glasses reflected the shining disk of the moon. His feet kicked slowly, keeping him afloat.

"The last few days," he said, "have mostly been profoundly confusing for me. But I cannot deny that this is the biggest adventure I have ever had."

CHAPTER 38

The journey home was decidedly less enjoyable. Even wrapped in their dry coats with knit caps jammed over dripping hair, and socks and shoes pulled over damp feet, the night air was biting and sharp. Once out of the woods, they biked in shivery silence.

Alma didn't know what Shirin and Hugo were thinking about, but her mind was on the golden trails that had filled the woods and the iridescent light that had illuminated the water. She was thinking about how she and her new friends were on their way to creating quintessence.

"We're coming, Starling," she whispered into the wind. "We're coming."

Shirin left them first, heading toward her house in Fourth Point with a too-loud "Bye!" and a grin that gleamed in the moonlight.

Hugo went almost the whole way with Alma, the two of them

pedaling side by side. When they reached her street, he waved a gloved hand and kept on toward Second Point.

Alma rode the last few minutes alone.

And even alone, inside her mind, her thoughts stayed wondrous and sparkling.

At home, she closed the window she had just climbed through and changed into her nightgown. She hung her damp clothing up in her closet and then shut the closet door. It was so late, but she pressed the quintescope to her eye one last time.

Through the eyepiece, Alma stared at the jar of water that Shirin had let her keep, watching the glowing colors swirl and gleam.

Then she put the scope away, set the jar on her nightstand, and crawled into bed.

She fell asleep within seconds.

It was a deep, wave-rocked, light-filled sleep.

CHAPTER 39

The ShopKeeper lay flat on his back at the top of the tower as the morning sun rose. Often, his platform was occupied by tourists or stargazers, but if no one was around, this was where he preferred to be. He would rest and watch the Stars above and absorb the bits of Quintessence that drifted down with their light. He hoped the Starling was coming out of hiding at least every now and then, to do the same. That Quintessence had been what kept him alive before he had learned to grow his own.

He reflected, as he lay there, on the sorrow and joy of the night.

The joy, of course, had come when the three Elementals had found true Water. Through his quintescope, he had watched as the Water Elemental bottled it. The true Water had shone so brightly in the container. And the true Water inside the Water Elemental had shone. And the other two Elementals, they had shone too, in their own ways.

Light, of course, begets Light.

In past quests, the ShopKeeper had always had to search far and wide for precisely the right Elementals, one for each Element. He had been shocked when he had found these four right here in this very town, although he had been uncertain about the third and, of course, the first had not actually joined the quest as yet.

There was still so much that could go wrong, so much that could fail. "There is no easy way to the stars from the Earth," as the Shop-Keeper's old friend Seneca used to say. There was no easy way to create Quintessence.

But an Element had been found, and that was cause for joy.

"Water, Water, Water," the ShopKeeper sang to the blushing sunrise sky and the gradually fading starlight. "True, true Water."

The sorrow had come after that magnificent finding, once the ShopKeeper had left his tower and begun his search for the Starling in the earliest hours of the day, before dawn. He had trekked through the hills and caves of the North, over the mountain peaks of the East, across the farmlands of the South, and around the creeks and woods of the West. Everywhere there was Quintessence—clinging to a dead leaf, smeared across a stony outcropping—but the Starling herself was hidden away again.

"Starling!" he had sung out everywhere he roamed. "Starling!" He had tried his best to make his voice sound the way a Star from her home would sound, but it was impossible to get it just right with his earthly lungs in this thick, earthly atmosphere.

He would try again. The Elementals would continue gathering their Elements, and he would search for the Starling. Tomorrow night and the next night and the night after that.

He would try for as long as he was able.

PART 6

Wind

....

CHAPTER 40

Alma usually sat alone at lunch. It was something that had happened gradually.

On her first day of school, she had given herself a long pep talk. "Time to acclimate," she had told herself. Then she had picked a table that was a little out of the way, a quieter table with kids who didn't look too perfect, kids who didn't look like the sun followed them around. Kids who might be her friends.

None of them had talked to her.

True, as her father would point out later, she had not talked to any of them either.

It had hurt, nonetheless.

The next day, she had sat at the same table, with the same results.

By the third day, after her first episode, she was afraid of what would happen if she tried to sit with a crowd. So she had found a seat at an unoccupied end of a table in the far corner of the cafeteria. She had sat there, alone, unnoticed, unspoken to, for the last three months.

But on Monday, Hugo plunked his lunch box next to her and sat down.

"I have been considering our options for wind," he said without preamble. "I don't know of any feasible possibility other than the funnel you suggested, and since the jar that Shirin provided has a windmill inside of it"—he shrugged, a jerky up and down of his shoulders—"I suppose it's just one more hypothesis to test."

Since Alma had been thinking about the Starling and the elements too, it didn't take her too long to recover from her surprise. Setting down her bag of pretzels, she asked, "What's wind made of anyway?"

Hugo shook his head, his curls fluttering back and forth. "This is what I've been trying to tell you," he said. "Wind is simply the movement of atmospheric gases—air moving around because of differences in pressure and the rotation of the Earth."

"What would make air *true* though?" Alma wondered.

"If it was unpolluted, possibly?" Hugo pulled out a turkey sandwich and a bag of carrot sticks. "Or less polluted, at least. My best hypothesis is that wind on top of a mountain would be the *truest* or purest. Generally speaking, air speed increases with height, so it's windier the higher up you go. There are pollutants, of course, but likely fewer than in the air in closer proximity to towns and highways. And we do have mountains, you know, to the east of Four Points, although they're quite small. Perhaps we can meet tomorrow after the lecture to conduct further research."

"That sounds perfect," Alma said, popping a pretzel into her mouth to celebrate their successful brainstorming.

She was smiling to herself when she felt eyes on her. Someone was looking at her.

Across the cafeteria, there was Shirin. She was at her usual table, a table that Alma would never have considered sitting down at in a million billion light-years. When she saw Alma looking at her, Shirin grinned and gave a tiny, quick wave.

Alma waved back. Then she watched as Shirin turned to her group of friends, laughing at something another girl had said, her big smile for them now.

In Old Haven, Alma had thought she knew everyone and everything. But here in Four Points, there were thermal springs hidden in the woods and popular girls joining Astronomy Clubs and her own Alma-ness growing day by day. Now that she was getting to know Four Points, she wondered how much of Old Haven she had missed.

"The deeper you go, the truer it becomes." It was amazing how much there was to learn about everyone and everywhere.

CHAPTER 41

That afternoon, Alma's mother picked her up, and they headed—finally!—to the office.

"How was the day, Alma Llama?" Alma's mother asked as usual.

"Not bad," Alma replied. "Not too bad. My Astronomy Club friend and I had lunch together. And don't forget, the lecture is tomorrow, and then the club is working on a project, so can I maybe come home at dinnertime?"

Alma hadn't said so much on a car ride home since before the move, and she had never had multiple social engagements in one day.

For a moment, her mother seemed stunned. She kept glancing over at Alma: quick, probing looks.

"Astronomy Club, huh?" she finally said. "This club is really—well, you seem so different than you did only a week ago!"

"I'm the same," Alma said. "It's just nice to have something fun to do."

But she wasn't the same, and she wasn't surprised that her mother was noticing. Alma felt like she was just waking up after a long, long sleep. She felt like she was stretching out stiff muscles, shaking the fog out of her head.

She felt restless too. At the office, she didn't want to do her homework. She didn't want to sit quietly and work on her English essay while her parents typed and highlighted and occasionally murmured to each other from their desks. There was so much she needed to be doing, so much she needed to be figuring out. She needed to talk to the ShopKeeper again.

"I think I'm going to go for a walk," she said. She hadn't even sat down yet. Her backpack was still on.

Alma's father looked up from his papers, brow furrowed. "Alma, I think it's great—I mean, really great—that you're suddenly so active," he said. "But what about your homework? It's imperative that you do not fall behind again."

"I don't have much," Alma said. "And I've been sitting in class all day. I want to move around."

"Well, okay. Maybe just a quick stroll?" Alma's mother suggested. Then she frowned. "Oh, except it's raining now! This weather!"

Alma turned to the door and saw that it was true. It was a light, misting rain, the kind of rain that could have been snow but wasn't. From the south came a crack of thunder.

"How about if I make you some hot chocolate to drink while

you do your homework?" her mother said. "I think we have some packets in the back. Want more coffee, Peter?"

Alma sighed as she sank into her usual chair at her usual table. As soon as she sat down, she realized how tired she was. She wasn't sure how much sleep she'd gotten last night, but it wasn't enough. She knew she wouldn't be able to concentrate on her homework.

Instead, her fingers traced the old map again.

She started downtown as usual, but this time at the Fifth Point instead of Lucas Law. The Fifth Point, she noticed, was at the exact center of the map. The four neighborhoods and their surrounding areas curled out from that center, like the petals of a flower— green-hilled First Point to the north; rocky Second Point to the east; farmland-bordered Third Point to the south; and then the stream-filled woods of Fourth Point to the west.

After she made her loop, Alma moved her fingers back to the outskirts of Second Point and then farther east, where the mountains began. She traced the ridges and wondered if true wind was there, waiting for them even now.

CHAPTER 42

That night, Alma slipped out her window. She had tried to use the quintescope earlier in the backyard, but it hadn't worked very well in the sunlight. She had only been able to make out a slight shimmer on the trees and in the bottom of the crater.

So now she was out on her roof, hoping that the night would reveal what she was searching for: the Starling and the next element.

First, she looked for the Starling. She had been right about the sunlight blocking the quintessence; the golden fragments were now shining again, and from above, it was even clearer how far the Starling had journeyed. There were trails of light everywhere Alma looked.

The gold was thickest in the backyard and along the path through the woods that the Starling had taken when Alma had chased her. With the quintescope, Alma could see the farmland with the silo, but the trail still dead-ended in the middle of the field.

"Where could you be, Starling?" Alma wondered.

She turned now to the east. Without the quintescope, the mountains in the distance blended into the night sky. But with the quintescope, the sky was so full of stars that it was easy to tell where the uninterrupted darkness of the mountains began. Alma found the top of the first peak and followed the line of the ridge.

It was at the summit of the tallest mountain that Alma saw it.

There was a faint, silvery glow. It was not a stationary thing but a writhing, twisting glimmer, not in the empty darkness of the mountain but above it. In the sky.

"Wind," Alma said. "That has to be the wind."

As she crept back into her room, Alma felt a pang of guilt as she thought about what her parents would say if they saw her now. She had snuck out in the middle of the night three times, and she was planning to do it again. She was lying to them.

But she had been doing that for months, ever since she told them that the episodes had stopped. Before that, Alma had tried to follow their suggestions. She had tried to smile and tried to pay attention and tried to do all the somethings. But none of those somethings had worked, and she had felt, more and more, as if nothing could be done, as if she couldn't do anything. So she had lied and lied and lied.

Now she was doing something, a new something, a something she had chosen to do. And it was working. Gathering the elements was working. Saving the Starling was working. She was making friends. Four Points was turning into a place that she knew.

She could feel her Alma-ness—her quintessence, if that was what it was—growing and growing.

She couldn't stop now, and if she told her parents, they would certainly stop her. None of their suggestions had included sending stars back to space.

She still felt guilty though.

She would tell her parents the truth, she finally decided, but not until she saved the Starling. After she saved the Starling, she would tell them everything.

CHAPTER 43

Shirin sat with her friends at lunch the next day, and Hugo wasn't there at all. Alma had been waiting impatiently to tell them about the light on the mountain, so this was especially disappointing. And even though Hugo had only eaten lunch with her one day, sitting by herself felt lonelier than ever. At least, Alma thought, taking her old, out-of-the-way seat, she would see them at the lecture.

That afternoon, she did what she had done on the day of the first club meeting. She waited next to the door of the classroom until the last student had left, then waited ten minutes more for the halls to clear. Then she headed down the empty hallways to the Science Lab, which would hopefully now also be empty except for the two people she wanted to see.

In the lab, Shirin was spinning distractedly around on one of the high table's swivel stools. Hugo was straightening one of many stacks of paper, each covered in colored tabs and highlighter marks, which Alma guessed was how he had spent his lunch period. Mrs. Brisa was there too, wearing one of her earth-toned dresses with an earth-toned scarf around her neck and gray pebble earrings that looked distinctly handmade.

"Hello, Alma," she said warmly. "I was so pleased to hear that you started this club."

Alma was surprised that Mrs. Brisa recognized her outside of class, and even more surprised that she knew anything about her.

"I didn't start it," she replied nervously.

Mrs. Brisa smiled, as if Alma was being modest. "It was a team effort then? Well, I love it. The sciences are full of beauty and mystery and joy, but people seem to miss that a lot."

"Well," Alma said, "the stars aren't easy to miss."

"They are if you're not looking up," Mrs. Brisa replied.

"Apologies," Hugo called from the head of the table, "but it is four o'clock, which means it is time for the lecture to begin." Hugo's voice, Alma noted as she sat by Shirin, sounded as unrobotic as she'd ever heard it. "You may each take a stack of notes. They are three-hole punched for your convenience. Future lectures will build on this material."

Shirin spun toward Alma. "Alma," she whispered. "Oh my goodness. What have we gotten ourselves into?"

Alma smiled back and pulled a set of notes to herself as Hugo put a slide of the periodic table of elements up on the overhead projector.

"My lecture has been somewhat altered in light of recent developments," Hugo began. "When we talk about elements in science, we are usually referring to those listed on the periodic table. Everything on Earth is made of these chemical elements. Everything in the universe is made of these elements. And that includes the so-called classical elements, which I will focus on today."

He put a new slide up. This one showed the ocean, vast and blue under a vast and blue sky.

"The first classical element is water, which, of course, is made of the chemical elements hydrogen and oxygen," he said. "In the ocean, there is also sodium and chloride—that is, salt—as well as additional ions."

"What about the water from the Fourth Point Spring?" Shirin called. "What's that made of?"

Ignoring Shirin, Hugo flipped to a new slide, this one of a field of windmills. "The second classical element is wind, which is simply air in motion. Earth's atmosphere—that is, air—primarily consists of nitrogen and oxygen. There is also carbon dioxide, water vapor, and other elements like argon and neon."

Alma didn't shout out like Shirin, but she thought of the light she'd seen on the mountain last night. What kind of wind would they find up there?

Hugo's next slide was a cross-section of the Earth's layers. "Earth is the third classical element," he said. "Over ninety-eight percent of the Earth's crust is made up of eight chemical elements: oxygen, silicone, aluminum, iron, calcium, sodium, potassium, and magnesium. Additional elements include titanium, hydrogen, copper, silver, bismuth—"

"Do I seriously have to listen to this weirdo?"

Alma felt her whole self go tense. It was that voice again. She looked over her shoulder and sure enough, there he was.

Dustin.

CHAPTER 44

Mrs. Brisa had stood up the moment Dustin spoke. Now she gestured toward the stool next to her. "Dustin, if you're here for the lecture, please sit down," she said in a voice that was somehow stern yet kind.

"I'm not here for anything," Dustin muttered, but he threw himself onto a stool. It wasn't the one next to Mrs. Brisa though. It was one that was, thankfully, at the far table, away from everyone else.

At the front of the room, Hugo was standing awkwardly in front of the projector, his silhouette covering up most of the picture. He pushed his glasses up, then back down again, then up, his shadow-self mimicking him.

"Keep going, Hugo," Mrs. Brisa said encouragingly.

"Yeah, Hugo," Shirin said. "What about fire? What's fire made of?"

Hugo stood for a few seconds more, then shuffled out of the projector's light. He fumbled with the slides before a forest engulfed in flames beneath a lightning-lit sky appeared.

"Fire is a chemical reaction," he said, his voice now emotionless and robotic. He was not, Alma could tell, enjoying himself anymore. "It requires oxygen, fuel, and heat."

"But what are the, like, flames made of?" Shirin persisted. "And is lightning fire?"

"Usually, flames are made of carbon dioxide, oxygen, and nitrogen, as well as water vapor. Lightning is not fire, but they do share some properties, and lightning can, of course, create fire."

He shrugged and took the slide off the projector. "So—so those are the four classical elements—water, wind, earth, and fire—and the chemical elements each is composed of."

Off to the side of the room, Dustin yawned loudly. Hugo began to gather his stacks of papers, the projector still blank, but Alma saw from her notes that there was more he wanted to say. Shirin had asked questions to keep him talking; now, Alma decided, it was her turn.

Spinning her stool so that she couldn't see Dustin, she asked, "But where do the chemical elements come from?"

Shirin jumped right in. "What's their source, Hugo?"

Hugo was silent, his eyes fixed on the ground, but Alma knew they just had to wait. When he was ready, Hugo set down his papers and met Alma's gaze. She smiled at him.

"If you really want to know," he said. "I can tell you. The answer to that is—"

He put a new slide up, and this one made Alma's breath catch in her throat, but in a good way, in a glorious way. There was the Milky Way, the galaxy she lived in, all black and violet and silver, all swirls and clouds and bright points of light. It was beautiful, so beautiful.

"'Made of the same stuff as the stars,'" she whispered to herself.

"Stars," Hugo said, starting to relax back into his lecture mode, "are primarily composed of just two elements—hydrogen and helium. These are, of course, the lightest of the elements by weight. Yet we know that all chemical elements come from stars. We know that *everything* comes from the stars. So the question is how?"

Hugo paused dramatically, and Alma scooched forward on her stool.

"The answer," Hugo said, his voice now back to full animation, "is nuclear fusion. Or, more precisely, stellar nucleosynthesis."

"Booooooring," Dustin muttered from his table.

"Dustin," Mrs. Brisa warned.

Shirin glared at him. "It's not boring!"

"No, it's not," Alma agreed, a little quieter. "Keep going, Hugo."

"Uh, okay," Hugo said, and this time Alma thought he was not quite as shaken. "Within a star there is basically a constant nuclear explosion. As the star gets hotter, more and more elements are created—heavier and heavier elements. Even the elements that make up human beings—oxygen, carbon, hydrogen, nitrogen, calcium, and phosphorus—are created within stars. But all of these elements are mostly contained within the star itself."

"So how do they get into the universe?" Alma asked. "How did they get into—into us?"

With a small smile on his face, Hugo put up a new slide, a slide of something that Alma had seen before. It showed light, a blazing, burning flash of light captured at the point of detonation, a light that seemed too bright to look at, even in a picture. The light radiated outward, blossoming into swirls of color and heat that reached into the black void of outer space.

"Supernovas," Hugo said, his voice laced with awe. "When a star collapses and then explodes, there is so much energy that almost every element is created."

"Supernovas," Alma repeated, remembering the power of that wild and terrible explosion, remembering all the dust and brightness streaming across the universe. "That's how elements get from the stars to us?"

Hugo nodded. "Supernovas are one of the most powerful forces in the universe," he said. "They destroy." He held his hand over the projector's light, blacking out the image. "And then"—he pulled his hand away and the light returned—"they create."

CHAPTER 45

After the presentation, Mrs. Brisa started to clap. Alma and Shirin clapped too. Shirin even whistled.

Dustin did not clap.

"Is this over now?" he demanded. "Can I leave?"

Mrs. Brisa stopped clapping and turned to him, eyebrows raised. "Whoever told you that you had to come, Dustin?"

"You did," Dustin grumbled. "You said I had to come for tutoring."

"I never said that," Mrs. Brisa said, shaking her head. "You don't need tutoring. You need to do your homework. And you need to come to class."

"You sent me that letter," Dustin insisted.

Shirin jumped up from her stool now. She almost tumbled over but Hugo caught her arm. "Even if Mrs. Brisa did tell you to come for tutoring last week," she said, "this is a lecture. You know that. There's no reason for you to be here!"

"Unless you want to be," Mrs. Brisa corrected gently. "Mr. Evans—your teacher from last year—told me that you love science. He told me that you and Hugo used to be quite the duo."

Alma saw Shirin's eyes bug and her mouth drop open in shock. It was exactly how she felt. Dustin and Hugo—a duo?

Before she could think about it further, Dustin started to yell.

"I *don't* want to be here!" he shouted, right at Mrs. Brisa. "I thought I had to come! Why would I want to come here on purpose? Like I haven't listened to that show-off enough in my life!"

"Dustin," Mrs. Brisa began. "Let's take a breath."

"You are so rude! Ugh!" Shirin was advancing toward Dustin. "No one made you come here. You just don't have any friends. Or maybe you just like making people feel bad. Maybe you're just mean!"

There was a long silence, a thunderhead silence, a silence waiting to crackle into lightning and fire.

But instead, Dustin grabbed his backpack. "Whatever," he muttered. "You're the mean one."

Then he ran from the room.

Mrs. Brisa watched him go. She didn't look nearly as flustered as Alma thought she should be after being screamed at. "Hugo, that was an excellent presentation," she said, turning to the front of the room. "I do want to remind you three that you cannot exclude anyone from a school club. However, if someone is being a bully or making themselves a nuisance, we can go through proper channels to have them removed." She raised her eyebrows at Shirin. "Proper channels, not yelling, right?"

Shirin nodded, but she didn't look apologetic.

Alma didn't want to talk about Dustin anymore, and she didn't want to stay in the Science Lab in case he came back.

"I have some things to show you two," she said, glancing between Hugo and Shirin. "Maybe we can go now?"

"Yes," Hugo said, gathering the remaining stacks of notes. "Thank you for coming, Mrs. Brisa. But if you'll excuse us, we have some elemental hypotheses that are in need of serious attention."

CHAPTER 46

When Alma told Hugo and Shirin about the light on the top of the mountain, Shirin shrieked with excitement, which was not surprising. What was surprising was when Hugo smiled and said, "Zonks. I thought so!"

"Does this mean you believe now?" Alma asked. They were sitting on a bench outside of school, *Quintessence* open on Hugo's lap.

Hugo shrugged at this, his curls bobbing noncommittally. "I haven't drawn my conclusions yet," he said. "That would be very unscientific. But I am eager to continue testing the book's hypotheses."

"That's a change from thinking it's 'ludicrous,' though," Shirin said. "Was it the shiny water that convinced you? Was it? Was it?" She wiggled her eyebrows and grinned so big that Alma laughed.

"I propose that we stop talking," Hugo said, ignoring them both and flipping through the pamphlet, "and study the section on wind." Pushing his visor-glasses up, he began to read aloud:

> *Let us turn high, high up to the wind.*
> *Who can hold the wind? Who can calm its restless pursuit?*
> *The Earth spins, the pressure shifts,*
> *and the air moves ever onward.*
> *And those Elementals of Wind,*
> *single-minded and excessively focused*
> *though they can seem,*
> *are they not engaged in their own pursuit—*
> *the pursuit of wisdom?*
> *Do they not blow hither and thither,*
> *asking "Why, Why, Why?"*
> *Do they not challenge us to do the same?*

"Fascinating fact!" Shirin cried when Hugo finished. "That sounds exactly like Hugo!"

Alma had been thinking that too. Hugo had been the one prodding them to plan, the one asking questions every step of the way. If Shirin's element had been water, then Hugo's was definitely wind. As she nodded her agreement, Alma tried not to feel jealous that both of them seemed to have an element. There were four elements, she reassured herself; hers would be next.

"I will take that as a compliment," Hugo replied, "although I don't believe there is such a thing as 'excessively focused.'"

"It also says 'high up,'" Alma pointed out. "The light was on the tallest mountain peak. But how are we going to get to the top of the mountain? And then how are we going to get the wind into the container? I still can only think of the funnel."

"Funnel?" Shirin asked.

Alma explained her idea of creating a funnel that would direct the wind into the windmill bottle while Shirin listened intently.

"You're so creative, Alma!" she said when Alma was done. "You always have the best ideas, like the spring and, well, this whole quest really."

Alma didn't know what to say. She didn't think she had the best anything. Hugo was the one who knew everything, a never-ending supply of information spilling out of him and filling him up, as easy as filling his lungs with air. Shirin was the one who did everything, rushing from place to place, bubbling with life and laughter and fun. What did Alma know? What did Alma do?

It was still nice to hear, though. It made Alma feel warmer inside, brighter inside.

"It's certainly the best idea we've come up with," Hugo said. "I do have supplies for such a venture at my house, but we may need to pay a visit to the library for further instructions. I want to research wind funnels and turbines, as well as other elemental possibilities and, of course, alchemy. Given its pseudoscientific nature, that subject is one I have only cursory knowledge of."

Alma felt her stomach knot. "You want us to go to the library?" she asked.

"I find it to be the most efficient way of collecting information," Hugo said. "Also, my mother received an automated message this morning about several books that the library claims are overdue but that I no longer have in my possession. I would like to resolve that issue before my ability to check out further materials is compromised."

"Let's go!" Shirin cried, leaping to her feet and pulling her sequined backpack on. "Then we can stop by the Fifth Point and see if Alma's mysterious ShopKeeper is finally there."

Of course, neither of them was one bit afraid. Who would be afraid to go to a library?

Only Alma.

But if she was going to bottle the wind, it was a fear she would have to face.

CHAPTER 47

The library was in the downtown of Four Points, one block farther east than the General Store. Four Points Middle School was on the west side of the downtown. As they walked, Alma watched as the dark tower of the Fifth Point grew larger and larger. Inside, her dark thoughts grew larger and larger too.

She almost told Hugo and Shirin that she had changed her mind. She almost told them that she had made a mistake, that she did not, in fact, want to go. She didn't want to go anywhere at all ever.

Instead she thought about the Starling.

"Hugo," she asked, fighting to keep the tremor from her voice. "How far away is the nearest star?"

"You mean the sun?" Hugo asked.

"Oh, right," Alma said. The sun was still shining down on them now. It was a safe bet that it had not fallen from the sky and into her backyard. "No, not that one. The next one."

"The next closest star," Hugo said, "is Proxima Centauri. It's about twenty-five trillion miles from Earth."

Twenty-five trillion miles. Alma couldn't even fathom a distance that far. The Starling had fallen *at least* twenty-five trillion miles through space. She had fallen and fallen and fallen. What would it be like to fall so far? Alma didn't know. But she knew that the Starling had to be afraid. She had to be lonely. No one could be farther from home than the Starling was.

And the book said the Starling had lost quintessence in the fall. From what Alma had seen through the quintescope, she was losing more and more every day. The Starling was in mortal peril, while she, Alma, was feeling brighter than ever.

She had gone to new places now, and she hadn't had episodes. She was with her friends. She was on a quest. So surely she could go to the library. She had to. It was up to her to save the Starling.

Shakily, tentatively, Alma followed her friends through the library doors.

Behind the library's front desk, there was a librarian. Well, Alma assumed she was a librarian because of where she was sitting. She didn't exactly look very librarian-y.

She was wearing a dress that started high on her neck with sleeves that trailed to the ends of her fingers, which were covered in white gloves. The dress appeared to be made of scarves, dozens

171

of scarves sewn together in a hodgepodge sort of pattern. She had huge, round sunglasses that obscured most of her face, and she wore her hair in twists tipped in rainbow colors—scarlet, gold, teal, fuchsia. Her name tag read SUSIE.

Even before they approached her desk, Susie leaped to her feet.

"Welcome!" she cried in a very unsuitable-for-the-library voice. "How can I help you today, my dear souls?"

Alma's nervousness was coursing through her, energizing her in a high-wire, live-wire, barbed-wire way. "We need—we need books," she blurted to the rainbow-garbed librarian.

Susie beamed at her, showing shiny teeth. "You're in the right place, aren't you? What kind of books do you need?"

Alma looked to Hugo to respond, but Hugo seemed momentarily overwhelmed by the librarian. Alma didn't blame him. Susie didn't seem very acclimated to Four Points. She seemed as out of place as a tropical parrot in a gray concrete city.

"Books about building wind funnels," Shirin said. In her own colorfully striped dress and sequined backpack, her voice loud and clear, Shirin didn't even seem to notice how odd the librarian was. "And wind turbines, if you have anything like that."

The librarian nodded emphatically, her twists nodding along. "Wind funnels and turbines!" she practically sang. "How marvelous! Marvelous! What else?"

"Geology." Hugo spoke up now, a little uncertainly. "And mining, alchemy, and natural spontaneous combustion."

"Also a local bus schedule, please," Shirin added.

"That's quite a varied list," Susie said, still grinning at them. "Is this for a school project, my dears?"

"Yes," Alma replied. "Sort of. It's for a—a club."

"Just the three of you are in it?" Susie asked. "No one else?" Then, before they could answer, she shook her head and laughed, a bell-like sound that rang around the room. "Never mind, never mind! There's a schedule posted at the bus stop outside of the library. As for the other topics, let's see what we see!"

The librarian came out from behind the desk. She was, Alma noticed, extremely short, and as she led the way to the stacks, her feet were hidden by her dress, so that she seemed to glide.

Hugo and Shirin hurried to follow. Alma took a deep breath and then went after them.

They searched through the sections together, gathering up book after book until each of them had a tower. Alma tried to focus on the task. She tried to listen as Susie chattered on and on about this book and that book, about engineering and wind direction, about cave systems and lightning, about the alchemist Paracelsus, who had written about the elements during the early Renaissance—and about the phone call that Hugo had received about his fines, which Susie admitted must have been an error on her part.

Alma tried to pay attention to Susie, and she tried not to pay attention to her mind.

Which was telling her over and over and over to run.

"I think," Susie said after placing a final book on the already

173

head-high pile in Hugo's arms, "that should be enough to get you started." She nodded happily at Hugo, then at Shirin. Then she looked at Alma and her smile slipped from her face. "Oh my stars! You look a bit flickery. What's the matter, dear soul?"

"Nothing," Alma said. "I'm fine. I'm absolutely fine. I'm not flickery at all."

But that wasn't entirely true. Because in spite of the librarian's concern and in spite of the books in her hands, books that would no doubt lead them to wind and possibly the other elements, and in spite of the light that had been growing in her and the new friends by her side, Alma's stomach had begun to knot. Alma's throat had begun to tighten. Alma's breath was coming faster and the edges of the world had begun to blur.

The library suddenly seemed so cramped, so small. There were people here, on the other side of the bookshelves, at the computers, surrounding her, everywhere. She was going to shatter and everyone was going to see it. She wasn't only going to flicker, she was going to go out, she was going to go dark. She should never have come here.

It was happening again.

Alma dropped her books, and she ran from the library.

She ran all the way home.

CHAPTER 48

Here was what it felt like to have an episode:

It felt like someone was squeezing and squeezing her throat and pressing and pressing on her chest. Her stomach cramped and twisted and turned to stone, a heavy, hard stone. Her hands shook. Her whole body shook.

Worst of all were the thoughts. It was as if those thousands of fear-filled books all flew off the shelves of her mind and opened at once, as if every single word was being screamed at her, flung at her, piercing and deadly. Those words made Alma feel like she was caving in, collapsing into the empty, Alma-less space that her insides had become.

When she'd had the episode at school, her first ever, she had sunk to the ground. She hadn't known what was happening to her. She had only known that it was terrible, that it was unbearable, and that she wanted it to end.

The doctor that her parents had taken her to see had told Alma that what she'd experienced was a panic attack. She'd explained, in medical terms, what had happened to Alma's body. "Simply put," she had said, "your brain sensed danger. In response, it released adrenaline—fuel for you to use to fight or run. But there was no danger. So you were left with lots of fuel and lots of fear and nothing to do with it."

"But why?" Alma had asked. "Why does my brain think I'm in danger?"

"Anyone can experience anxiety, and most first panic attacks feel like they come out of the blue," the doctor had said. "There are, however, external factors that can contribute. Stress, hormonal changes, and genetics too. Some people have very reactive nervous systems. Their brains respond quickly to even the possibility of danger."

The doctor had told Alma to get enough sleep. She had told her to eat well and never skip meals. She had told her to take walks. She had told her to keep living her life normally.

"When you start to avoid situations or places because you're afraid of having another attack," the doctor had said, "that's when the real trouble begins. Your brain starts to think that everything you're avoiding is dangerous, which leads to more panic attacks. You don't want to give your brain more things to be afraid of."

Alma had heard the doctor. She had heard her again at her follow-up visits, where she had lied and said that the episodes had stopped. She hadn't known at the time exactly why she was lying,

176

but her parents' relief at hearing that she was better had been palpable. And once she'd told that lie, she had kept going. The truth had felt overwhelming. The truth had felt like failure.

Then she had done exactly what the doctor had told her not to do. She started running from her classes. She refused to go anywhere except school and her parents' office. The number of places where she felt safe shrank and shrank and shrank. And the light inside her shrank and shrank and shrank too.

When Alma got home, no one was there yet.

She took the quintescope into the backyard. She didn't set it up though. Instead she sat inside the crater, her arms wrapped around her legs, her cheek resting on her knees. She watched the woods for some light, for some sign that the Starling was out there.

She had thought they were connected somehow. She had thought that the flyer and the quintescope had been for her. She had thought that she could do something.

And she'd thought—she'd been sure—that the episodes had ended. What was the use of making friends, what was the use of being involved in a mysterious, magical quest, what was the use of growing brighter, if this terrible emptiness could open up at any moment, dark and vast and consuming? What was the use of any of it?

You'll lose your friends, her mind said, *if they find out how strange you are.*

You're going to keep having episodes forever, her mind said. *No matter how bright you feel.*

You'll never be able to save the Starling, her mind said. *No matter how hard you try.*

You can't do anything, her mind said.

The sunlight faded and the shadows spread, but the woods stayed dark and empty.

And inside Alma, it was the same.

CHAPTER 49

In the musty, dusty, amber-blue light-filled Fifth Point, a new clock was now ticking and tocking. A wagon had been painted a cheerful cherry red. The floors had been swept and mopped until they shone. The ShopKeeper had neglected his home for too long, and he wanted to put things to rights. Before the end.

He sat now, exhausted from his work, on a cushionless armchair, the springs poking through here and there. Distractedly, he stitched a new arm onto a rag doll who had been through a great deal, while he mulled over what he had seen in the library that day.

"It is hard," he confided to the doll, "to grow your Light, you know."

After the third Elemental had run from the stacks, the other two had gone to the Fifth Point. He had seen them from the library window, knocking and knocking and knocking. Of course, he had not been there to answer.

That was the way it had to be though. He could consult his papers, find the Elementals, put a hundred pieces into motion and then coax them along with the help of disguises and impressions and well-timed wisdom. But the four had to find the Elements together. It was the surest way to refine the Elements inside them.

To the rag doll, arm half on and half off, he sang, "But me oh my, what a struggle it always is!" These quests, they involved so many risks, so many failures, so many heartaches and questions and challenges. And these Elementals, they were so young, like Starlings themselves.

Yet each one of them held such glorious possibility, and he could see how connected they were becoming. He could see how they were beginning to plumb their own depths, brightening day by day—if the final one would ever show up!

The ShopKeeper set the rag doll, limbs secured, back with her friends. Then he sifted through a pile of old scrap cloth until he found a tattered blue jumpsuit. Sinking back into the battered armchair, he began to sew again.

At least he was sure now that he had the right four. Even as the third Elemental had flickered and fled that day, he had known that she was not a mistake. She was the right one. He remembered what she had told him, here in his shop, about her home. He understood, oh yes, he understood.

The ShopKeeper knew about longing for home, like the third Elemental, Alma Lucas. Like the Starling.

After all, he himself was a fallen Star.

CHAPTER 50

Alma went to bed early that night, but she woke up feeling some-how even more tired, even heavier. She moved through her classes like a sleepwalker, dazed and dull and barely aware of what was happening around her.

At lunch, she sat across from Hugo, who eyed her from behind his visor-glasses and seemed to be about to speak several times but never actually got any words out.

Then someone crashed down next to her and she had to grab the table to keep from tumbling forward as arms embraced her.

"Alma!" Shirin cried. "Oh my goodness! Where did you go yes-terday? I was going to go to your house, but I didn't know if you'd like that, and I didn't have your phone number—so obviously I need that right now. You scared us to death! You seemed—well, you were like—"

"Frantic," Hugo said. "You were frantic."

"I'm fine," Alma said, even though she didn't feel fine. She did feel a little better though hearing her friends express their concern and with Shirin's arm around her shoulders. "I'm really okay. I just felt sick. But I'm better now."

Shirin studied her skeptically. Hugo took a bite of turkey sandwich and watched her too.

"So you say," Shirin said. "Hugo and I decided to meet up at his house this afternoon to build the funnel. Can you come?"

Alma remembered what her mind had told her yesterday. She wasn't going to be able to save the Starling. She was going to fail, the way she had failed at everything since the move.

But if she stopped trying, then Shirin would return to her perfect group. Hugo would go back to working on his own genius projects. She would go back to being alone. She would not only have failed but given up. She would have given up on the Starling.

She couldn't do that.

"I can come," she said. "But if we go to that mountain, we'll have to go at night. When I look through the quintescope during the day, the quintessence isn't very bright. I don't think we'll be able to see the true wind unless it's dark out."

Shirin covered her eyes with her braids. "I was afraid you'd say that," she said. "It's going to be like really, really tricky to go that far in the middle of the night."

"We can do it though," Hugo said. "My stepfather once forced me to hike with him on that mountain—it's called the Second Point

Peak—and I think we'll have sufficient time to get there and back before daylight. In fact, I'm sure of it."

Shirin went back to her usual table after that. Alma called her mother from the front office before lunch ended and got her surprisingly hesitant permission to come home late again.

They met by the door of the Science Lab that afternoon. Alma was ten minutes late, as usual, but Hugo and Shirin either didn't notice or decided not to comment. They set off for Hugo's house at the bottom of Second Point, the mountains peeking over the horizon in the far eastern distance.

Hugo's house was old, like Alma's, but it was obvious that someone handier than Alma's parents lived there. There were no potholes in the driveway, the paint was a fresh, cheerful-looking yellow, and the yard was free of dead leaves and winter detritus. It wasn't as secluded as Alma's house either. If a star fell in Hugo's backyard, his neighbors would certainly know about it.

"Marcus is always asking me to help him out here," Hugo said. "He's very invested in the upkeep of material possessions—house, cars, various electronic gadgets."

"I would think you'd like the electronic-gadgets part," Alma said. She could picture Hugo taking things apart—toasters and televisions, cameras and radios. "That's very scientific."

But Hugo frowned. "Not the way Marcus does it," he said.

Alma remembered how tense Hugo had seemed greeting his stepfather in the General Store, but she didn't really understand why.

"What, you don't like your stepdad?" asked Shirin, right to the point. "Because he wants to climb mountains and do yard work with you?"

"I didn't say I didn't like him," Hugo replied, his voice flattening. "He's fine. However, I have a father already. He lives a few hours away, but I see him quite frequently and he is superior in every way. I don't need Marcus."

He strode, quick and stiff, toward his house's front door.

Hugo's mother was in the kitchen. Alma felt, when she saw her, that she would have recognized her as Hugo's mother anywhere she met her, not only here in her own house. She was tall and thin like her son. Her skin was the same deep gold color, and she had the same slightly squinty eyes, although hers were behind tortoise-shell, square-framed glasses—two lenses, not one.

She smiled while Hugo introduced her—the kind of huge, thrilled smile that Alma thought her own mother would probably have if she came home from school with two friends.

"Isn't this a surprise?" she said. "A wonderful surprise! What do you three have planned for this afternoon?"

"We're building a wind funnel," Hugo said.

Mrs. Johnson gave her son a fond, proud look. "Is that so? Well, Marcus is out back with the twins, but you should get him to help you when he comes in. You know how good he is at building things."

"I do not require Marcus's assistance," Hugo said firmly. "I am perfectly capable of constructing a wind funnel on my own."

"On *our* own," Shirin corrected.

"That's what I said," Hugo replied.

Mrs. Johnson sighed, a small, weary sound. "Up to you, Hugo. I put some chili on; it'll be ready in a few hours. I thought it was appropriate with this terrible weather. Still no sign of spring, and it always sounds like a storm is coming too!"

"Apologies," Hugo replied, "but we don't have time to eat."

"Oh my goodness," Shirin said. "I'd like some chili, please."

"Me too," Alma said. "Chili sounds great."

"We'll make sure you get a break," Mrs. Johnson assured them with a wink. "Help yourself to the supplies in the garage. And Hugo—you need to let Alma and Shirin help you. You hear me?"

CHAPTER 51

Two hours later, the reason for Mrs. Johnson's warning to her son was abundantly clear.

Books had been opened—by Hugo.

Sketches had been drawn—by Hugo.

And Hugo sat on the ground, struggling to encase the plastic-piping funnel he had made in yellow material that he had measured and cut himself.

"Are you going to let us do anything?" Shirin complained. "What are we even here for? Ugh. This is boring."

Hugo eyed her warily from behind his visor-glasses. Shirin had already knocked a toolbox to the ground, smashed into the vise on the edge of the workbench, and dropped a bucket of paint while searching for pliers.

So there was a reason for his wariness. Still, Alma had to agree.

Watching Hugo was extremely boring. He didn't seem to need them at all.

"I could hold the material in place," she offered.

"I'd prefer to do it," Hugo said. "Neither of you have the engineering experience I have."

"Oh, is that right?" Shirin said. "I didn't realize you'd had professional training. I thought you were in sixth grade like me."

Hugo ignored her.

"What are you using?" Alma asked, hoping to defuse the tension.

"It's an old hammock," Hugo replied. "It's made of ripstop nylon, the same fabric used in parachutes and tents. No water—and more importantly for our purposes, no air—can get through. It has zero porosity."

"You have zero porosity," Shirin muttered.

The tension in the garage didn't lessen as the evening wore on. With nothing to do, Alma's mind turned back to yesterday's fears—that this was all useless, that she was going to fail the Starling anyway—and the thoughts sounded over and over like an echo that would not die. Even though Hugo protested, she was relieved when Lexi and Isaac came bursting in to tell them it was time for dinner.

"Your mom told me you're making some kind of windmill?" Marcus said to Hugo while scooping out bowls of chili for everyone.

"Wind *funnel*," Hugo muttered, not making eye contact with his stepfather.

"What's a wind funnel?" Isaac cried.

187

"I could take a look at it," Marcus said. "If you want an extra pair of eyes."

"Do you *have* extra eyes, Daddy?" Lexi asked. "Where are they?"

"On your bottom?" Isaac shouted, causing Lexi—and Shirin—to burst into giggles. All three received a stern look from Mrs. Johnson.

"I do not require assistance," Hugo said.

"Hugo won't even let *us* help," Shirin said, accepting her bowl of chili very, very carefully.

Mrs. Johnson turned her stern look on her son. "Hugo!" she said. "What did I tell you?"

"No one wants to be friends with a know-it-all!" Lexi shouted.

It was, Alma was sure, something that had been said in the Johnson house before.

Mrs. Johnson looked embarrassed—for herself or Hugo or both. "No, I said let your friends help," she said. "Because no one knows everything. We need one another."

"We need one another," Alma echoed. It was like the book said, and in that moment, it seemed like the words were for her as much as they were for Hugo. Wasn't that why she was here, even though she felt certain that she was going to fail the Starling? She was here because she needed Hugo and Shirin, wasn't she? She was here because, failure or not, the Starling needed her.

Mrs. Johnson nodded. She didn't seem to think it was odd that Alma was repeating her.

"We do, Alma," she said. "We certainly do."

188

CHAPTER 52

Before Alma and Shirin left, the three of them decided to meet that night at 11:50 at the bus stop near Hugo's house.

Hugo and Shirin had consulted the bus schedule by the library the day before, after Alma had run off. There wasn't a stop on Second Point Peak, but there was one at the bottom of the mountain.

"It wasn't part of the official schedule though," Hugo had told Alma.

"What do you mean?" Alma had asked.

"It was written in pen at the bottom," Shirin had explained. "And the other buses had their last stops at like eight thirty."

Why, Alma had wondered, would there be a bus so late at night in a town as small as Four Points? And why wouldn't it be on the regular schedule?

"I propose we meet and wait for the bus," Hugo had said. "If it does not come, we can abort the mission. If it does come, I will get to conduct my research."

"If Hugo's in, then I'm in," Shirin had replied. "It's going to be amazing—unless we get caught!"

"I'm in too," Alma had said.

When she rode up to the bus stop that night, quintescope in her bicycle basket, Shirin was just riding up too and Hugo was waiting. He was holding the wind funnel, disassembled for ease of carrying, in his gloved hands.

"You still don't look right," Shirin said, frowning at Alma as she climbed off her bike. "You were so, like, bright the other day. Are you feeling okay?"

Alma looked down at herself. She half expected to see a flickering, nearly burned-out flame somewhere around her stomach. Of course there was nothing, only her jacket.

"I'm fine," she said. "Really."

"So you say," Shirin said with another sharp, searching look. "But you know what? I'm still worried. Tell us the truth. What's going on with you?"

Alma opened her mouth, but no words came out.

And then she didn't have to say anything. Because from down the street there came a squeaking, groaning, grating noise. It sounded like a tin roof caving in. It sounded like a blender full of knives. It sounded like—

A bus. It was their bus, coming down the street.

CHAPTER 53

Four Points Transit Authority buses usually looked like this: white with four stripes down the side—red, blue, green, and yellow. Since Four Points wasn't a big town, there weren't a lot of buses, but they were all relatively well kept up.

This bus . . . well, this bus was the opposite of well kept up.

It wasn't white, for one thing. And it wasn't just that this bus sounded and looked like it was *ready* for the junkyard. No, this bus sounded and looked like it had been *made* in the junkyard. It was a hodgepodge of mismatched metals—a rust-red hood, a tarnished silver body, blackened brass window casings, and a door that glimmered gold under a thick layer of grime.

And the driver who leaned toward them after the door creaked open was as strange as her bus.

She had silver hair piled high on her head—impossibly high. Even in the limited light, it was clear that she had on a tremendous amount of makeup. She wore a much-patched, stain-covered electric-blue jumpsuit with a brass name tag that read CELCY, and large, tinted glasses.

"Only three of you?" Celcy the bus driver cried. "Wasn't there another one?"

Alma peeked at Hugo and Shirin and saw that they appeared as startled as she felt.

"No," Shirin said cautiously. "Just us."

"All right, all right, my dear souls!" Celcy replied. "Where are you headed, then?"

Alma exchanged another glance with Hugo and Shirin.

"The mountain base stop," Hugo said slowly, clearly. "That is the route of this bus, correct?"

"Sure, sure, that's the route, my darling dear." The bus driver let out a cackle. "But this late at night, eh? Not much up there."

"We're stargazing," Shirin said, pointing to Alma's quintescope case.

"We're in an Astronomy Club," Alma added.

"And that there, my loves?" Celcy asked, pointing to the pole that Hugo had over his shoulder and the funnel he carried in his other hand.

"It's a wind sock," Hugo said. He had taught Alma and Shirin about those too, material tubes on poles used to measure wind speed and direction. "We're also amateur meteorologists."

"Ah, I see! I see!" The driver cackled again, delightedly this time,

192

and nodded. She nodded so hard that her hair slipped sideways; the prodigious nest of silver was suddenly over one ear.

"Oh my stars!" she croaked, scrambling to right it. "What a mess I am tonight. But time's a-wastin'! Climb aboard, my dear souls. Climb aboard!"

No one moved toward the bus.

"This is—this is a Four Points bus, isn't it?" Alma asked. "I mean . . . you work for the town?"

"I drive the bus," the driver said, nodding again, carefully this time. "I drive to the mountains."

Which wasn't really what Alma had asked, but Celcy didn't say anything else, just stared expectantly. Even through her glasses, her eyes shone a piercing blue beneath long, black lashes and fluorescent green eyeshadow.

Alma waited for Shirin the adventurer to take the lead, but Shirin was hanging back, as if reluctant to board the bus. It was Hugo who stepped forward.

"These hypotheses aren't going to test themselves," he said. "On to Second Point Peak."

And he led the way aboard.

CHAPTER 54

The bus rattled and creaked its way through the deserted streets. Once they left the Second Point neighborhood, there were no longer any streetlights, and inside the bus there were no lights either. Only the half-moon and the stars shining through the windows lit their ride.

Alma had taken the seat behind the driver, the quintescope case next to her. Shirin sat across from her, and Hugo behind, the windfunnel pole stretching across the aisle.

The jangling and clanging of the bus was so loud that Alma would have had to yell to talk to her friends. Since Celcy was a foot away, that ruled out any private conversation. So Alma set up the quintescope and gazed through it at the darkness outside her window. If only she could see the Starling again—or even her light somewhere in the distance—then maybe she could banish the thoughts that had started up after her panic attack. Maybe she would feel connected to the Starling again. Maybe she wouldn't feel like she was going to fail. Maybe she would feel that spark again.

After a few unsuccessful minutes, she sighed and set the scope in her lap. Then she noticed that in the rearview mirror, Celcy was watching her.

"Isn't that a pretty thing!" the bus driver called. "Think you'll find what you're looking for up there on the mountain, my dear soul?"

Alma met the driver's piercing gaze in the mirror, then focused back on the scope's copper casing. "Maybe," she said. "I don't know. I hope so, but I don't know for sure."

"Can't know anything for sure, can you?" the bus driver cried, smacking the steering wheel. "But the only way to find something you're looking for is to keep searching, isn't that right, my darling dear?"

The bus driver turned from the road to wink at Alma—and her eyelashes fell right off that eye.

Alma gaped at her.

"Oh my stars!" Celcy cackled. "Falling apart, I am. Back to your searching, my dear. Don't let old Celcy stop you!"

Alma hesitated, then lifted the quintescope up again. She watched as outside the landscape grew rockier and rockier. The bus went higher and higher. The bus driver sang a wordless tune. Until—

"Here we are, my darlings!" Celcy called as the bus door

squeaked open. "Second Point Peak, the Eastern Wonder of Four Points."

Alma, Shirin, and Hugo filed off into the windswept outdoors.

"All right, all right, my dear souls!" The driver had her hand on the door lever. Her hair was slipping over her forehead. She had no eyelashes left. No eyebrows either. "I'll see you here then."

"Here?" Alma asked. "Isn't this the last bus?"

"There's always another bus," the driver replied. "Wills and ways, wills and ways, dear souls."

"It wasn't on the schedule," Shirin said. "When will you be back?"

"By and by!" the driver cried.

"But when exactly—" Hugo began.

"By and by!" The door slammed shut. The bus squealed away.

CHAPTER 55

It was a disconcerting way to be left. For a few minutes, Alma, Shirin, and Hugo stood and peered up and down the road as if the bus might return immediately.

"Well, at least we got a ride here," Alma said finally.

"And maybe one back," Shirin added.

"The chances of that bus returning—" Hugo began.

"I know, I know," Shirin cut him off. "But we thought we'd have to walk home anyway."

"That will take us a very long time though," Hugo said. "Longer than I realized. We need to hurry."

There was no bus stop stand at the place they had disembarked. There were no signs and no pull-off. There was only an empty road, heading down in both directions, and the mountain rising steeply above them on one side. On the other side, the earth dropped away.

Peering over the edge, Alma could see the lights of Four Points and the shape of the Fifth Point, a black silhouette against the night sky.

"This definitely isn't the bus stop at the base of the mountain," she said. "We're really high up. But where do we go now?"

"Even higher?" Shirin suggested with a grin.

They walked up and down the edge of the road, pointing their flashlights at the foliage, searching for the path that Hugo vaguely remembered hiking with Marcus. Finally, Alma found it—an overgrown, steeply rising trail.

"Eureka!" Hugo cried, and pole and funnel in hand, he hurried intently ahead.

Shirin went next, and Alma followed. The hike was steadily uphill with no flat spaces or breaks, and the rocks were slick with moss and mud in some places. At first, Shirin slipped every few minutes, and Alma had to stay focused enough to steady her friend. But after hiking for an hour or so, Shirin seemed to have found her footing.

As she climbed, now less afraid of being knocked off the mountain, Alma took deep gulps of the bracing wind. She watched the backs of her friends, rising higher and higher. She listened to Celcy's cackled words playing in her mind—*keep searching, keep searching.*

And when she reached the summit, when she stepped out of the shelter of the trees and stood side by side with Shirin and Hugo, with Four Points unfurled beneath them like a star-spangled banner, like a field of glowing flowers, Alma felt the tiniest of sparks reigniting inside her. Maybe she wasn't sure what was going to happen next. But maybe this was still where she was supposed to be.

CHAPTER 56

Hugo had never actually let Alma and Shirin help the afternoon before. He had used the workbench vise to hold the funnel in place while he wrapped it in ripstop inside and out. Then he had built a smaller funnel to cap the large one, then connected that to some tubing that would go into the cloud-swirled container with the little windmill inside.

Now, up on the mountain, Hugo set about assembling the apparatus.

By himself.

"The springwater showed such unusual properties," he said as he unrolled the tubing from its coil, leaving plenty of slack. "I'm very interested to see what my experiment here may yield."

"*Our* experiment," Shirin corrected him.

"It appears that the writer of the book—the True Paracelsus, as he calls himself—did in fact discover an alchemical system," he continued. "A metaphysical overlay of sorts. My results here could continue that work."

Before Shirin could snap at Hugo again, Alma picked up the pole that the funnel would attach to. "Here," she said. "I'll help you."

Hugo snatched the pole from her. "I'd prefer to do it myself," he said.

Alma pulled her hand back and held it, as if it was her hand that had been hurt rather than her feelings. Hugo, she knew, was smarter than she was, smarter than most people. He was focused right now, intense about finding this knowledge he was seeking. She understood that.

But she had gotten the quintescope. Shirin had found the containers. They were on this quest together.

"Hugo, I think you should—" she started.

"You need to let us help!" Shirin interrupted her. Her hands were on her hips and she was glaring at Hugo. The wind whipped her braids around her head, like two snakes coiling and striking, coiling and striking. "You already built this whole thing yourself. Don't you remember what your mother said?"

"We need one another," Alma said quietly.

Hugo busied himself with the assemblage again, avoiding their eyes. "I've got it under control," he said.

"Oh yeah?" Shirin shot back. "Fine! I'd like to see you hold the pole, the container, and the tubing, *and* put the cap on by yourself!"

She threw herself down on a nearby rock. Alma sat next to her.

They watched as Hugo finished attaching the components. Then he tucked the wind container under one arm, put the cap in his mouth, and hoisted up the wind-funnel pole with both hands.

The wind was blowing strong and cold there at the top of the mountain. When Hugo got the pole upright, the yellow nylon fluttered and flapped wildly, this way and that. He turned the pole, slowly and decisively, until the funnel billowed out. The air flowed into the tubing.

Inside the bottle, the windmill began to turn.

"It's working, Hugo!" Alma called to him. Even Shirin was leaning forward in anticipation. "Put the cap on!"

Hugo was trying. He was wriggling his upper body around in an effort to dislodge the tubing with his elbow. Instead, his movements caused the pole to slip. The wind funnel deflated.

"Need help yet?" Shirin cried.

Hugo didn't answer. He bent his knees and squeezed the pole between them for extra stability. He twisted it slowly, searching for the wind again, the container still clutched between his arm and his side.

Then a gust of wind came howling out of the starry sky. The wind funnel inflated with a sudden *SWOOSH*. The windmill spun.

And Hugo, knees bent, hands full, elbows akimbo, went toppling backward with a shout that sent the cap flying from his mouth.

"Help!" he shouted as the bottle fell to the ground with a sharp crash.

CHAPTER 57

Alma and Shirin raced forward in the same instant. The wind screeched around them, an eerie, high-pitched keening.

Shirin grabbed the bottle from the ground.

"I don't know how, but it's not broken!" she yelled, holding it up.

Alma spotted the cap, the silver reflecting back the starlight. "And I've got the top!" she called.

They hurried over to Hugo, who was trying to wrestle the pole upright. Shirin shoved the tubing back into the container. Alma stood by, cap in hand.

Then there was another burst of wind, the strongest one yet, the loudest one yet. The top of the mountain was alive with a bone-chilling cold and an earsplitting shrieking that sent the three of them staggering backward.

Inside the bottle, the windmill began to turn again.

"Alma, check it!" Hugo cried over his shoulder.

Alma grabbed the quintescope from the ground. She aimed it at the wind jar and—

There was the light. Inside the jar it was like there were a thousand tiny fireflies lit up and dancing in unison. The intensity grew and grew, sparks to flames, a swirling, shimmering silver that was bright, bright, breathtakingly bright.

"That's it!" Alma cried, sticking the quintescope under her arm. "That's true wind!" In two quick motions, she pulled the tubing from the bottle and jammed the cap onto the opening.

Inside the jar, the windmill kept turning.

"How can it still be moving?" Hugo asked, dropping the pole and rushing over to her. "And is it really glowing like the water?"

Alma handed him the quintescope.

"Eureka!" Hugo shouted as he peered through the lens. "We did it!"

"Together," Shirin added.

Hugo held the wind jar up to his face. He stared for a long time without saying anything. The light from above caught his glasses, making it look like he had twinkling stars for eyes.

"Apologies," he finally said, pulling away from the jar. "The truth is I'm used to doing everything on my own. I don't—I don't have a lot of experience with friends."

"Me neither," Alma said. And briefly, she considered that this would be a good time to tell them her own truth—the truth she had been hiding for months, the truth that made her fear she would never be able to save the Starling, the truth about why she had left the library yesterday.

But then Shirin said, "Lucky for you, Hugo, Alma and I are very gracious and forgiving."

So instead, Alma smiled and bowed graciously, which made Shirin burst into laughter, infectious and full-bodied. Which made Alma laugh. Which made even Hugo laugh.

They stood under the stars, with wind in a jar, and laughed together. And even though she hadn't told her truth yet, Alma was sure now. Whether she failed or not, whether her episodes stopped or continued, this was where she was supposed to be. She was going to keep trying.

That was when she saw it.

CHAPTER 58

Farther down the mountain, on the trail they had taken up, there was a light. It was a copper light, flitting in and out of sight, moving rapidly toward the road.

"The Starling!" Alma cried. "We have to follow her!"

She shoved the wind jar into her jacket pocket, grabbed the quintescope, and took off. She ran as fast as she could, knowing this was her chance, a chance that might not come again. The descent was steep, and she stumbled a few times, careening into trees and grasping branches and bushes to steady herself, but she managed to stay upright.

She could hear Hugo and especially Shirin crashing along behind her. She didn't stop to check on them though. She kept moving forward, sure that if she could make it to the road, where the trees cleared, she would spot the Starling again.

Before she got there, she saw the light. Not ahead of her, but above.

"Oh my goodness," Shirin shouted from somewhere behind. "There she is!"

"Zonks!" Hugo cried. "She's real."

The Starling had burst over the tops of the trees, her fiery hair streaming behind her, her arms pointing up like an arrow. She wasn't as bright as Alma remembered, but she was just as beautiful.

And she was flying. She was going to go back to the sky!

But as Alma watched in fear, the Starling lost momentum. Her limbs flailed outward. Her body spun and for a brief instant, Alma saw her face again. Those enormous black eyes were filled with the same fear Alma had seen when she'd startled her by the crater.

Then the Starling fell.

Alma let out a cry and started forward. The Starling would be injured, she was sure of it. She threw herself down the rest of the path and burst onto the road. Shoving the lens of the quintescope up to her eye, she located the gold trail that led down the rest of the mountain, ending in—

A tiny pinprick of copper streaking wildly southwest, toward Third Point. Toward Alma's neighborhood.

Alma stood gasping for breath on the side of the road. She wasn't going to be able to catch the Starling now. She had once again failed to help her.

Still, seeing her had made the light in Alma feel brighter. And the Starling was running toward her house. Maybe she was hiding somewhere nearby. Maybe if Alma searched again tomorrow night, she would find her. Maybe—

Her thoughts were interrupted as Hugo and Shirin came racing up next to her, and the clacking, clanking, jangling, squealing of the junkyard bus filled the air.

CHAPTER 59

"Climb aboard, my lovelies!" the bus driver cackled, throwing open the door with a rusty metal squeak. "Climb aboard, my dear souls!"

Alma held the wind jar in her hands the whole way home, watching the blades spin round and round. She wanted to talk to Shirin and Hugo about what they'd seen, but every time she peeked up, she found that Celcy was watching her in the rearview mirror again. Alma wondered if she was paying attention to the road at all.

The bus driver didn't speak on the ride home, however. She seemed pleased about something, humming a high, piercing tune, but she seemed exhausted too. By the time they reached the bus stop by Hugo's house, she was slumped low in her seat.

"Goodbye, my darling dears," she said with a sigh. "Keep searching, and old Celcy will keep on too."

The sky was changing from black to gray, a slow, languid change. Hugo took the wind funnel and set off, awkwardly weighed down, toward his house, while Shirin and Alma leaped on their bicycles and rode as fast as they could.

At home, Alma scrambled onto the flat roof. She realized that she had forgotten to close the window, and when she climbed into her room, she found that it was nearly the same temperature as outside. She shut the window carefully.

Then she heard footsteps on the stairs.

As quickly and silently as possible, Alma removed her shoes and her coat, shoving them under the bed. The door started to open, and she didn't have time to get under the covers.

Instead she was sitting there, fully clothed, guilty-eyed, and red-handed, when her mother came in.

"Alma," her mother said. "I thought I heard something up here. Why are you awake already?"

"Oh. You know I don't sleep very well," Alma said after a much-too-long pause.

Her mother was staring at her. She wasn't smiling. "Why are you dressed?"

There were more footsteps on the stairs, and then Alma's father was there too, looking sleepy and perplexed.

"What's going on?" he asked. "Alma, why are you awake?"

Alma didn't answer.

"You know, I found some clothes hanging in the shower last week," Alma's mother said slowly. "They were soaked. I also found some in your closet yesterday with dirt stains and little briars stuck all over."

Alma still didn't answer. She had washed her dirty sheets herself the other day, but she had forgotten about the clothes. She had forgotten about the clothes twice.

"Also," Alma's father said, a little more alert now, "your window was open the other morning."

Alma's mother peered down at her with a probing, concerned look. "You know we don't object to you exploring, Alma. You've always loved to wander. And we're glad that you're—you're doing things. But you know that you're not allowed to leave the house at night, don't you? Surely we don't have to tell you that."

"We've noticed that you've been acting . . . strange," Alma's father added.

"Different strange," her mother said.

"We're worried," her father said.

Alma had thought about telling her friends the truth, and now she thought about telling her parents. But she rejected that idea almost as soon as it came into her mind for the same reason she'd rejected it before.

Her parents would try to stop her from saving the Starling.

And she couldn't stop now.

She wasn't going to tell them anything.

"There's nothing to be worried about," Alma lied. "Nothing at all."

CHAPTER 60

The ShopKeeper had been a young Star when he fell.

A blue supergiant, he had been fifty thousand times more lumi-nous than the sun, destined to someday collapse into himself and then explode magnificently. That was to be his fate someday, and it was a fate that did not disappoint him. He could not have imagined a more glorious end.

But then that glorious end had happened to someone else, to a star nearby, and he had fallen.

Runaway Stars didn't always fall to Earth—in this never-ending Universe, there is very seldom an always—but many did. The Shop-Keeper, who was the first ever to study such things, speculated that there was something about the Earth's Elements that drew the Stars to it. There was no denying that it was a special place, a place where Quintessence could be created.

Although he hadn't felt that way at first.

Oh, how weak he had been those first days! Oh, how lost and afraid! And how changed, with an Elemental-like body and an uncertain and possibly very brief future ahead of him.

That first night, he had lain on the rocky mountain peak that had broken his fall and wept desperately under Stars that shone down on him like cold, distant strangers. Yet their light, unreachable as it seemed, had revived him.

That Quintessence-filled light had kept him alive as he had figured out how to walk, how to talk. It had kept him alive as he had learned to disguise his true nature and live among the Elementals. It had kept him alive as he had uncovered the secrets of the fifth Element, and befriended other Stars, and begun his life's work—to save the fallen.

He had found that with time his Quintessence could be grown, even in this new home. With every Star he helped, with every Keeper he trained, with every thrown-away item he loved, his Quintessence had increased.

But there is more than one way for a Star to burn out. It wasn't the ShopKeeper's Quintessence that was running low now. No, he was simply, finally getting old. He was running out of fuel.

He sat on the top of the Fifth Point now, feet swinging over the edge of the platform, there between his old home and his new home. Wearily, he wiped his eyes with his patched blue sleeve. The sleeve came away with green and black and tan smears.

He too had seen the Starling that night. She had not been as bright as he would have hoped, but at least she had not lost all her Quintessence. If only he could find her, he could teach her to collect starlight,

212

he could help her grow her Quintessence as he had, while she waited for the Elementals to complete their quest and send her home.

But the Starling did not want to be found; she didn't know that help was here.

As the sun rose, the ShopKeeper rose too. He opened the trapdoor and descended the stairs at the center of the platform, back into the shop.

He had more to do. Starting with another phone call.

"Hello," he said into the receiver. "I'm calling from Four Points Middle School."

PART 7

Earth

....

CHAPTER 61

At lunchtime the next day, Shirin stood indecisively in the aisle between tables. Her tray was tilting, Alma noticed, to one side. The tip of a piece of pizza dangled over the edge. She was about to call out to Shirin, to warn her, when Shirin straightened her tray and headed down the aisle.

Right to Alma and Hugo's table.

"Okay, after last night," she said, sitting down, "I feel like things are sort of different. Like, I thought the Starling was real before, but now I've *seen* her, you know what I mean?"

"Are you going to sit here?" Hugo asked.

"That's what I'm doing, isn't it?" Shirin said. She tugged a braid with one hand and picked up her pizza with the other. "No one will notice anyway. Plus, we've got things to discuss."

"We do," Alma said, smiling at her. "I'm glad you're here. And I'm glad you both saw the Starling."

"I can't believe she's real," Hugo said, shaking his head in amazement.

"I can," Shirin said. "It's not like Alma would lie to us." Alma felt her face turning hot, and she was relieved when Shirin continued, "So we know the Starling is in mortal peril, and we need earth and fire. What's our plan?"

"We don't have one," Hugo replied. "I discussed the remaining elements with Mrs. Brisa this morning—very discreetly, of course. She made several purely hypothetical suggestions—utilizing a lightning rod to create fire or collecting volcanic rocks. But I remain highly skeptical that even these nearly impossible methods would produce *true* fire or earth."

"You were highly skeptical about water and wind too," Alma reminded him. Even though she hadn't been able to get to the Starling last night, and even though she'd almost been caught by her parents, and even though she felt terrible about lying to them and to her friends, after seeing the Starling and getting the wind, Alma felt bright inside again. Even brighter because now Shirin was sitting with them, and they were making plans. Plans that would lead to the next element—*her* element, she was sure.

Hugo frowned at his turkey sandwich, then shrugged. "That," he said, "is true. What do—what do *you* suggest, then?"

"Since we don't have a fire container, we should focus on Earth," Shirin said, taking a bite of her pizza. "What about a quarry? Are there any of those around here?"

Hugo shook his head. "I don't think so."

"Or caves," Alma said. "What about caves?"

"What are you weirdos talking about?"

What could ruin Alma's happiness? What could make the magic and the light vanish in an instant?

Of course it was Dustin. He stood behind them, glaring down. A paper-bag lunch was clutched in one hand, his backpack strap in the other.

"Oh my goodness." Shirin sighed. "Go away. Right now."

Dustin ignored her. "I heard you. You're looking for caves," he said, and Alma was alarmed to find that he was staring right at her.

Alma wanted to dive under the table. She wanted to burrow into the earth herself, dig her way through the linoleum and the concrete foundation and the layers of soil and limestone and bedrock and molten metal until she reached the core. Maybe that was where she'd find the element she was looking for. Far, far away from here.

When Alma didn't answer, Dustin snorted in disgust. "That's what she said, right?" he demanded, directing his words to Hugo now. "Well, what about the Deep Downs?"

"What are the Deep Downs?" Shirin asked. Then she shook her head. "Never mind. I don't want to know. We're not looking for caves. Bye-bye."

"And even if we were," Hugo said, "you're not invited." He spoke slowly and robotically, but loudly, firmly.

Dustin's face started to redden the way it had at the lecture. "You think I want to be invited? You think I want to hang out with you freaks? I don't!"

218

Alma didn't know what would come next. She had a fleeting image of Dustin hitting Hugo or hitting her or hitting Shirin or maybe hitting all three of them, one after another, like that arcade game where you bopped moles with a padded mallet.

Instead, he stomped off.

Kids were staring at them. Shirin's entire table of friends had turned around. Some were even standing up to get a better view, mouths gaping.

Then the whispering started.

Shirin pulled her tray of pizza to herself.

"For such a bully, he certainly is sensitive," she said, deliberately keeping her gaze on the slice she picked up.

"At least he was useful," Alma whispered. She took a long, shaky breath, trying to slow her pounding heart. "The Deep Downs. That sounds like a good place to start."

CHAPTER 62

After Dustin stormed off, Hugo was quiet. He was quiet for most of the lunch period. It wasn't until he had eaten every last carrot stick and finished every last bite of turkey sandwich that he said, "I know where the Deep Downs are."

"What?" Shirin cried. She jolted backward so fast that Alma had to grab her arm to keep her from flying off the bench. "You do?"

"Where, Hugo?" Alma asked after righting her friend.

"Up by Dustin's house," Hugo replied. "Dustin wanted us to go in them when we were much younger, first grade, I think. But I was—I was afraid. Cave systems are extremely dangerous."

"We can go tonight!" Alma cried. "We have to go tonight!"

But Shirin and Hugo didn't seem to share her eagerness.

"I'm not sure I can do that," Hugo said.

"Yeah, me neither," Shirin agreed. "Like Hugo said, caves are dangerous. And my parents are totally going to notice if we sneak out again so soon. Maybe we can just meet up at my house tomorrow after school and, like, make a plan?"

Alma didn't want to plan. She didn't want to wait.

But she knew they were right. Going into a cave system was a serious undertaking. And her parents already *had* noticed, and they hadn't seemed to fully believe the story she'd finally stammered that morning about how she'd been out exploring the backyard.

So she agreed.

It was impossible to think of anything else though. They had water. They had wind. They needed earth and fire and the Starling. Water, wind, earth, fire, Starling. Water, wind, earth, fire, Starling.

"So, Alma," her father began that night after dinner.

Water, wind, earth, fire, Starling, Alma thought. She kept her gaze on her half-eaten taco. She recognized the tone of voice. She knew what was coming. It was time for another Discussion.

But then her father said something he'd never said before.

"Your mother and I have been talking," he said, "and we've decided that it would be a good idea for you to meet with a"—he paused and cleared his throat—"professional."

Alma stopped her elemental recitation. She stopped staring at her taco. She looked up at her father, then her mother.

"You mean like the doctor I saw last time?"

Her father shook his head. "Not a medical doctor. A psychologist. Someone who can listen and give . . . advice, I suppose."

"You give me advice," Alma said. "You give me advice all the time. Constantly."

"Maybe that's true," her father said. His voice was softer than it usually was, gentler. "Our advice hasn't exactly been working, though, has it? You've been doing better . . . we think. But we've also been more worried about you. Well, we've been worried about you for different reasons. We've been considering this course of action for some time, and then we received a call from the school today. They also feel you would benefit from . . . those services."

"We just think, Alma," her mother began, her voice more serious than it usually was, less silly. "That things might have gotten . . ." She rolled her wrists, fingers outstretched, and bobbed her head back and forth, searching for the right words. "Beyond us."

"They haven't," Alma said. "Things haven't gotten beyond you. I joined the Astronomy Club, remember? I'm going places, remember? I'm acclimating!"

"You are," her father replied, "in some ways. But in other ways . . ." He trailed off.

"It isn't a punishment, Alma Llama Ding Dong," Alma's mother said.

"I'm not going to go," Alma said.

"I'm afraid," her father said, still gentle, "that you absolutely must. You have an appointment on Monday, in fact."

"It isn't a punishment," her mother repeated, still serious.

Alma wanted to tell them that they were wrong about her. She wanted to tell them that she was already doing something, something important.

But she didn't.

There were too many lies wrapped around those truths. She didn't know how to untangle them.

And even if she could, even if she told her parents everything, she was sure they still wouldn't understand. They didn't seem to understand her at all anymore.

So she didn't say anything.

CHAPTER 63

That night, the phone rang. Alma was in her room, studying her rock collection through the quintescope eyepiece. It wasn't the first time she'd done this. She kept hoping that one of her own rocks would be "earthy" enough, but none of them ever gave her the feeling that the water from Fourth Point Spring and the wind from Second Point Peak did.

Also, none of them glowed.

Hopefully, what she was looking for would be in the Deep Downs.

Her father knocked on her door, then stuck his head in.

"James is on the phone for you," he said.

"For me?" Alma asked. James called and talked to her parents every now and then. But Alma hadn't spoken to him since winter break.

"For you," her father said, handing her the phone. Then he shut the door, leaving Alma alone.

"Hello?" she said into the phone.

"Hey, Alms," James said. "What's going on?"

Hearing James's voice made Alma want to burst into tears. Which didn't make sense. It wasn't like they had been best friends before he left. James was so much older, more than five years, and they were so different. James was smart and focused, while Alma had always been imaginative and distracted.

But James had always been there. He had known her, and she had known him. And when he was gone, like everything else, Alma had missed him.

"Nothing," she said, but her voice cracked.

"Alms," James said, sadly this time. "Don't cry. Mom told me you've been doing really well, actually. She told me you joined a club."

"Astronomy," Alma said.

"Nerd," James said.

Alma laughed. "I guess I am. Who would have thought."

"But listen." James's voice was suddenly serious. "Mom also said she's worried about you. Dad too. They said you've been acting weird."

"I've always been weird," Alma replied.

"Well, that's definitely true," James said.

"And a lot has happened. You haven't seen me in a long time."

There was a pause. "I saw you for almost a month during winter break, remember?" James finally said, his voice serious again but softer. "You didn't want to go anywhere with me? You stayed

225

in the house the whole time? You were—you were having a hard time."

Alma remembered now. They had only been in Four Points for a few weeks when James had come home for his break. She had already met with the doctor about her panic attacks, and she'd spent James's visit holed up in her room, making excuses for why she didn't want to leave the house, trying to convince everyone that she was doing better. Even though she wasn't. "That seems like forever ago," she told James. "I am different now. But it's a good different, I think."

"You *sound* good," James said. "You sound . . . happier. More like yourself."

"That's exactly how I feel," Alma said, pleased that he could tell that without even seeing her. "And I'm learning a lot too. When do you come home for spring break? I can show you my quintescope. It's a kind of telescope."

"I've never heard of a quintescope," James replied. "I'll be home next weekend; maybe we can set it up on the top of that tower. What's it called?"

"The Fifth Point," Alma replied with a smile. "I'd like that."

After the phone call, once her parents had gone to bed, Alma slipped out onto her roof again. She was tired after a day of ups and downs, but if she was changed, if she was happier, if she was more herself like James had said, it was because of the quest.

Thunder thrummed in the south, a sound that soothed her as she watched the golden spheres burning in the stars above her. She found the place where the supernova had been and saw that the cloud of debris was vaster than ever and just as radiant. Then she moved the scope back down to earth and followed the trails of quintessence through the woods around her house, back to the fields and the old silo.

"I'll find you, Starling," Alma said to the darkness. "I'll save you, just like you're saving me."

CHAPTER 64

Alma had been so distracted by her thoughts about the Starling and then by her parents' announcement about the school psychologist that she'd forgotten to ask permission to go to Shirin's house.

She finally remembered on Friday morning, right before they walked out the door for school.

"It's the same kids I've been meeting at the library," she said, trying to sound calm and cheerful. "The Astronomy Club kids. Hugo and Shirin."

"You've been spending a lot of time with those two," Alma's mother said. "And we've never met them. Or even seen them."

"We've been a little overly permissive," her father added, "because we wanted you to make friends."

"They're really smart," Alma said, because she knew her father would like that. "And nice," she added, because she knew her mother would like that. "And we still have a lot of work to do on the project."

"What if they come to our house?" Alma's mother offered.

Alma knew exactly what would happen if Shirin and Hugo came over. Her parents would hover around. They would make suggestions when her friends left about how she could smile more or be more talkative. They would listen to her conversations, and then later ask her questions. *What did I hear about elements?* they would say. *And where are these caves?*

"The supplies are at Shirin's," Alma said. "Maybe we can do her house tonight and our house next weekend? How about that?"

Her parents glanced at each other, eyebrows raised in what-do-you-think looks.

"Okeydoke, Alma Llama," her mother said, nodding.

"Next weekend," her father agreed. "Or sooner."

CHAPTER 65

Alma hurried down the school hall that afternoon. She had only waited for five minutes instead of ten today so that she wouldn't be too late meeting Shirin and Hugo. There were a few kids milling around, but even so, she felt surprisingly calm.

"We need to make our plan," Shirin was saying when Alma walked up to them outside. She was being, as usual, entirely too loud. "I guess we could go this weekend?"

"Sunday night would be ideal for me," Hugo said. "My mother has a night shift. She is a much lighter sleeper than Marcus, so I prefer not to leave the house when she's there."

"I can go Sun—" Alma started to answer when she felt a prickling on her scalp, like someone was watching her. She turned—

There was Dustin, unlocking his bike a few feet away.

He rode off without saying a word.

"Ugh," Shirin said, wrinkling her nose. "That boy. I am not a fan."

Four Points Middle School was near the center of town. They set off for Shirin's house in Fourth Point, westward toward the afternoon sun.

"What's the deal with you and Dustin anyway?" Shirin demanded as they strolled down the tree-lined streets that Alma had only seen by moonlight.

"What do you mean?" Hugo asked, his voice shifting, flattening.

"Mrs. Brisa said you two were, like, best friends," Shirin said.

"A duo," Alma corrected her. "She said you both liked science."

Hugo shoved his glasses up, then pushed them down, then shoved them up. Then pushed them down. It was the most uncomfortable Alma had ever seen him, even more uncomfortable than when Shirin had asked him about Marcus. "We were friends," he said. "Our mothers work together—they're both nurses at First Point Medical. But Dustin—I don't know, he started acting very unusual over the summer. He started yelling at me every time we hung out. He—he broke my microscope. And when school started he just—he stopped sitting with me at lunch. He stopped talking to me."

"I wonder why," Alma said.

"Not that it's right, but maybe"—Shirin glanced quickly at Hugo, then away—"maybe he didn't want people to know you were friends. Things change in middle school, you know. Sometimes you have to—to act different for people to like you."

"Perhaps," Hugo replied stiffly. "As I told you the other night, friendship is not my area of expertise."

Alma shook her head. "I'm sure there's another reason," she said.

Hugo shrugged and walked on, staring down at the ground through his visor. Shirin tugged on her braids and avoided Alma's eyes. They both looked miserable.

Alma had never had a best friend, but she could imagine how it would feel to have someone who was close to her suddenly become the person who seemed to dislike her the most. She thought about how Shirin must feel too. At the Fourth Point Spring, Shirin had said she didn't want to worry about being popular. She'd said she wanted to be herself. Alma had seen her staring wistfully at her table of old friends, friends who were now talking about her behind her back.

"Well, neither of you have to change for me," she told Hugo and Shirin, the closest friends she'd ever had. "I like both of you just the way you are."

Hugo didn't look at her, but he smiled a tiny smile. Shirin rolled her eyes and said, "Oh my goodness." But she linked her arm through Alma's as the three of them climbed the steps to her front door.

CHAPTER 66

Shirin's room was a predictable explosion of colors and prints, with clothing and books scattered on every surface. Alma liked it. It was like Shirin in room form—messy and fun and full of energy.

Shirin cleared a space on the patchwork rug that covered much of her floor—*cleared a space* meaning she shoved everything into a big pile. Alma sat next to her. Hugo joined them a moment later, after staring around the room in undisguised shock.

"This," he said, "should be declared a disaster zone."

"So my parents say," Shirin replied with a grin. "Now read us the Earth section of *Quintessence*, please."

Hugo got out the book and sat gingerly on a corner of the rug. In his monotone voice, he read:

We come to Earth now.
Earth is the substance beneath our feet,

familiar and foundational on the surface.
Yet, farther in, farther below, down and down,
there are other Earths,
layers and layers, some shining and precious,
some hard and unyielding.
And those Elementals of Earth,
do they not share this disposition?
Are they not quarrelsome and guarded,
yet brave and determined?
Are they not unapproachable
until they have been approached?
Are they not loyal beyond measure
when loyalty has been won?

Hugo finished the passage but kept his gaze on the page. "This may sound ludicrous," he said. "But this description sounds— perhaps—just slightly like Dustin."

"Ugh, how does it sound like him?" Shirin said, covering her ears with her braids. "He's the worst!"

Alma didn't think it sounded like Dustin, and she didn't want it to either. More and more, she had been thinking about how Shirin had led them to the water and how Hugo had been in charge of getting the wind. Those were their elements.

It was her turn now.

Alma wanted to find her element.

She didn't want to say this out loud though. So she picked at the mirrored sequins in one of the rug patches and she said, "Maybe. The 'quarrelsome and guarded' part, I guess."

Hugo shrugged and closed the book.

"Okay, Dustin is like earth," Shirin agreed. "Like a big, mean, dumb rock. But more importantly, this sounds like the Deep Downs to me! What do you two think?"

"It does talk about going underground," Alma said, glad to change the subject.

"A subterranean source makes the most sense," Hugo agreed, his voice loud and rushed like he was eager to talk about something new too. "In fact, it's the easiest explanation. I'd even go so far as to say it's . . . *element*ary." He paused and glanced from Alma to Shirin. "Get it?"

"Oh my goodness, Hugo," Shirin said. Then she collapsed into giggles.

Shirin's laughter always made Alma laugh too. Soon, like the night on Second Point Peak, even Hugo had joined in. Every time they stopped, Shirin would gasp out, "Elementary!" and they would start back up again.

"You know what we should do?" Shirin said, jumping to her feet. "We should actually do some stargazing! We are an Astronomy Club, aren't we?"

Alma, her face hurting from smiling so hard, said, "That would be a great idea, Shirin. Except that it's daytime."

The three of them burst into laughter again. Alma couldn't be-lieve how good it felt to smile and mean it, to laugh and feel it, like sunshine bubbling out of her.

"Fascinating fact: there are things in the sky you can see in the daylight," Hugo told them. "Not a lot, but some. I could show them to you." He paused for a moment, then continued, "If you want me to, that is."

"I'll go find my telescope!" Shirin cried. "I bet my sister—ugh!—has it!"

She ran from the room. Hugo shrugged at Alma, and they fol-lowed in their friend's wake.

CHAPTER 67

"Farah! Farah!" Shirin had thrown open the door of the room next to hers.

Hugo stayed on the other side of the hallway, as far from Farah's room as he could get, but Alma peeked around Shirin. She was curious about the big sister who said high school was better than middle school and who was—ugh!—too cool to hang out with Shirin now.

Farah was like an older version of Shirin, but with makeup, and hair that fell in loose, flowing waves. She looked incredibly sophisticated and pretty, stretched out on her bed with a textbook open in front of her. She didn't look like someone who would have trouble fitting in anywhere. Alma backed away from the door, feeling suddenly as awkward as Hugo.

"Where's my telescope, Farah?" Shirin demanded.

"Get out, Shir!" her sister yelled, throwing a pillow.

Shirin blocked it with the door. "Is it in there? Let me come look!"

"No way!" Farah said. "Last time you were in here you shattered my lamp and pulled my shelves off the wall, remember?"

"I only pulled down the shelves because I was falling!" Shirin protested.

"Yeah, exactly," Farah said. "You were falling. You always fall." Shirin opened her mouth to shriek something back, but Farah cut her off. "It's not in here, Shir! I promise. Why don't you check the tower?"

Shirin wrinkled her nose, then stomped off down the hall. Alma was eager to climb to the top of the window-wrapped tower she'd seen from the outside of the house, but before she followed, she peered through the door one last time. Farah was smiling after her little sister, and when she saw Alma, she smiled at her too.

Alma gave a little wave and then hurried after Shirin. She felt, strangely enough, the way she had after talking to James last night—as if someone who had seemed far away was actually quite close.

Shirin took them to a set of winding stairs that led to the tower. At the top there was a round room so tiny that Alma could almost touch both sides if she stretched her arms out. Curved windows took up much of the wall space. It was stuffy and crowded, and it was the most wonderful place Alma had ever seen.

"I've always wanted a tower," she said. "Was it built for star-gazing?"

"Probably not," Shirin replied. "But that's why my mom liked it. It made her think of her mother, my grandmother, who actually studied astronomy in Iran—that's where she was born. She was like super brilliant. And Persians used to be really into astronomy. Still are, actually."

"Fascinating fact," Hugo said, "some of the earliest and most well-known astronomical texts were written by ancient Persians."

Shirin's telescope was nowhere to be found, and the moon had already set, which was something Hugo had to explain; Alma hadn't realized that the moon didn't rise at sunset and set at sunrise. He *was* able to show them Venus in the just-fading sunlight. Venus, he told them, was known as both the evening and the morning star, despite actually being a planet.

"Betelgeuse—that's a star—will probably be the next supernova visible to the naked eye," Hugo told them. "We'd be able to see the explosion, even in the daylight."

"Will it happen soon?" Alma asked, pressing her nose to a windowpane. "Can we watch it?"

"Maybe tonight," Hugo said. Alma and Shirin gasped until he continued, "But maybe not for a million years."

"Very helpful, Hugo," Shirin said, rolling her eyes.

"Why," Alma wondered, "can't we see the supernova I saw, then? The one that knocked into the Starling and made her a runaway star?"

"If I may propose a very unscientific hypothesis," Hugo said. "When we look at the stars, we are looking into the past. Space is inconceivably immense, and light can only move, well, at the speed of light. Even light from our sun takes eight minutes and twenty seconds to reach us. So by the time light from a very distant super-nova reaches us, the actual supernova event is far in the past. The quintescope, however, appears to show us what is happening right now."

"We see things in real time through the quintescope," Alma said slowly, trying to understand. "No matter how far away. But how?"

"How did the Starling fall to Earth so rapidly? How is there a Starling at all? Why do some elements on Earth seem to light up like fireworks? I don't know." He gave a jerky shrug. "But that is why I like astronomy so much. Because there's so much we don't know. And because everything comes from the stars."

Shirin was spinning slowly in a circle, her gaze taking in the pan-orama of sky. "As amazing as that is, if everything is from the stars," she said, "then everything is the same. Nothing is extraordinary or magical or mysterious or anything like that."

"Logically," Hugo said, "you are correct, Shirin. If everything is extraordinary, then nothing really is."

Alma thought about what she had seen through her quintescope on that first night. She thought of the brilliant light bursting forward, propelling stardust into a universe that was so intricate, so vast, so unfathomable. Somehow, being a part of that made her feel both insignificant and wondrous. It made her feel connected and the same but also separate, also marvelously different.

"Or," Alma said, "everything really is. Everything really and truly is extraordinary."

Alma, made of elements, watched Venus shining up there, a

planet made of elements. She was connected to the stars. She was connected to the earth. And to water and air and fire. And to her friends and to her family and to everything that surrounded her, in Old Haven, her old home, and here in Four Points, a place that was finally beginning to feel like home too.

She was connected, and she was also herself, with Alma-ness inside her and many somethings that could be done, somethings that only she could do.

There was magic in that, magic and a deep mystery.

CHAPTER 68

On Sunday night when Alma went to get her bicycle from the shed, she found that it was locked to her parents' bikes. It took quite a while, but finally she found the key, tucked under a potted plant outside the shed door.

She rode as fast as she could to compensate for the time she'd wasted. Her friends were waiting for her in the middle of town, across the street from the Fifth Point.

"We already knocked," Shirin told her as she pulled up. "No answer, obviously."

They rode north together, the three of them, and by now, Alma no longer felt it was strange. It felt like they had done this for years, leaving their homes in the middle of the night, finding one another on darkened streets and riding off to magic and adventures. This was part of her life now.

Except that tonight, everyone was unusually quiet. Alma didn't know what Hugo and Shirin were thinking, but she knew that the closer they got to the caves, the more afraid she felt. Fear bloomed inside her, foreboding-laced blossoms of something poisonous, like the oleander she had once unknowingly brought home to dry between the pages of her books before James had stopped her and told her what it was. The fear grew and grew, another petal unfolding with each rotation of the pedals.

It was Shirin who finally broke the silence.

"Listen, you two," she said as they rode past First Point Medical. "I didn't want to say anything before, but I have to sit this one out."

"What do you mean?" Alma asked, surprised.

"I can't go in the Deep Downs," Shirin replied. "I'm—I have claustrophobia."

"What?"

"It means," Hugo explained, "that she experiences intense fear and anxiety when confined."

"I know what claustrophobia means," Alma said. "I just didn't know that Shirin had it."

"I can't do it," Shirin said. Her voice was tight and she was gripping her bike's handlebars with one hand and tugging on one braid with the other hand so hard it made Alma wince. "I don't, like, freak out or anything but I almost do. That bus made me so nervous the other night. I don't like to fly in airplanes or ride in elevators or even put my head under the covers! I can't go in the caves. I'm sorry, I really can't."

Alma had never considered that Shirin would be afraid. Shirin had led them into the woods that first night. She had tromped up the mountain to get the wind. She was always so excited about each journey, about each element, about everything.

She wondered if Shirin would consider her episodes "freaking out."

"I meant to say this Friday, Alma," Hugo said, "but then we were having, well, fun, so I didn't. But I'm not sure we should be doing this either. Streams and mountains are potentially dangerous, of course, but it is absolutely foolhardy to wander into a cave system. Animals may live there. We could get lost. There are bodies of water underground, sudden drop-offs, possible cave-ins. We have very little knowledge of what we'll be facing."

Alma knew these things, of course. It was why she felt afraid herself. "What else can we do though?" she asked. "We have to get the earth."

"I think now that we've seen the error of our ways," Hugo replied, "we should abort this mission and return during the day."

"We won't be able to see the true earth during the day!" Alma protested. "The sunlight is too strong."

"But Alma," Shirin said, "there isn't any sunlight in a cave."

Alma hadn't thought of this before. They were right, of course. They were right about all of it. This was foolhardy. They would have to go home.

"I'm just worried," she said sadly. "Worried about the Star—"

And then Alma fell silent.

Because somewhere in the woods, something bright flashed.

244

CHAPTER 69

Alma came to a sudden halt.

Hugo and Shirin, not realizing she had stopped, pedaled onward.

"What should I do?" Alma whispered to herself.

And then—

The light came again, deeper in the woods now.

The light was copper, but it was nothing like it had been the first time Alma had seen it. That light had washed out the whole world, had forced her eyes closed, had burned with a radiance that could not be contained or hidden from.

This light sparked, flickered, sputtered. This light was struggling. This light, Alma thought, was almost out.

It moved farther and farther away. Then it was gone.

"Alma!" Shirin was riding back toward her, with Hugo following behind. "Are you turning around? Are we going home?"

"I thought I saw the Starling," Alma said, her voice hushed.

"What? Where?" Shirin cried.

"Don't run," Hugo cautioned. "Let's just see if we can approach her calmly."

They hopped off their bikes and headed into the woods, tiptoeing over dirt and winter debris. Hugo had taken the quintescope and was leading them along a path of gold. Alma hardly dared to breathe as they moved farther and farther within.

Hugo stopped.

"The trail ends here," he said softly. "Maybe she jumped into the air again? I'm not sure. Perhaps when we return tomorrow to see the caves we can also search this portion of the woods."

Inside herself, Alma felt her own light burning.

And somewhere inside these woods, somewhere far away now, the Starling was growing dimmer and dimmer. What would happen, Alma wondered, if the light went out?

She couldn't let the Starling go out while she shone. She couldn't give up on her.

"No," she said. "No, I'm not going home. I have to go to the caves. Tonight."

CHAPTER 70

Shirin and Hugo were still not completely convinced, but at her insistence, they agreed to go *to* the caves but not *in* them. They could scout things out, figure out their next steps.

As they biked on, the houses began to thin and spread. The pieces of land they occupied were bigger, with trees and ponds and so much space that the homeowners couldn't possibly know everything that was happening in their own backyards.

"That's where Dustin lives," Hugo said quietly as they rode past a small brick house tucked back from the road and surrounded by needly pines and bare-branched oaks. One of the oaks had a rickety tree house in it that Alma would have loved, although she couldn't imagine Dustin playing there.

"Ugh!" Shirin cried. "Don't even mention his name."

Finally, they came to the fork in the road that Hugo

remembered. They turned down the packed dirt path, and the woods rose up around them, blocking the light of the stars. Alma worried that they might miss the caves in the moonless darkness, but her worries were unnecessary.

The path dead-ended right into the gaping black hole of the cave's entrance.

The opening was surrounded by rock that looked like a purple-blue bruise in the shadows. There was no sign, but scratched into the walls of stone were the words: *Deep Downs*.

"I guess this is it," Alma said. Fear made her voice shake. "I'm going to go in."

"You can't go in alone," Shirin said, but she stayed on her bike, a good forty feet away from the entrance.

"No one should go in," Hugo said. He wasn't as far back as Shirin, but he wasn't close either. "We're just supposed to be looking around, remember?"

"I won't go far," Alma said. "A few feet. That's all. To see what it's like. Then we can decide what to do."

Before Hugo could protest further—and before she could lose her nerve—Alma grabbed her flashlight and the quintescope and darted in.

The smell of the cave was not inviting. The smell of the cave was heavy with dampness and dirt and rotting things. It was the scent of a place that a human should not go.

Here under the earth, it was dark. True dark, an almost tangible dark. If darkness was an element, the Deep Downs would be the place to gather it.

Alma kept glancing back at the entrance to the cave, the window of inky sky and starlight and silhouettes of trees. That window grew smaller and smaller and smaller the farther in she went.

Even though she'd said she was only going to go a few feet in, that wasn't her plan. Her plan was to go until she found true earth. Shirin had gotten water; she had even seemed to shine when she bottled it. Hugo—well, there was no denying that Hugo's element was the wind. He had said that Dustin sounded like earth, but Dustin wasn't part of this, even if he had been Hugo's friend.

Earth, Alma knew, was *her* element. It had to be. It was her turn.

And more than that, she couldn't help but feel that she was somehow the most responsible for the Starling. She was the one who had seen her fall. She was the one who knew about being lost, about being lonely. Who knew what it was like to fear that her light would go out completely, forever.

She was the one who had to go, even if the others were afraid.

She tried to focus in front of her, tried not to look at the walls surrounding her. Every time she did, she imagined that she could see things she did not want to see. The things that lurked in the dark. The things that crawled underneath her feet, deep in the core of the earth. Pale things, slimy things, eyeless and heartless.

On and on she crept, down that dark subterranean hallway lined in dirt and stone and sometimes glimmering veins of something precious—heavy elements, she now knew. She wondered which stars they had been born in.

The air grew heavier, thicker, wetter, and Alma's breath came faster as she tried to get as much oxygen in as she could. She was far, far below the surface now. All that earth, piled on top of her, crushing her down, weighing her down.

And then it was too hard to breathe and Alma was seized with a deeper fear than she had ever known.

She turned and ran.

Her footsteps echoed up the tunnel of stone. Her thoughts were a tangle of terror. She ran until she burst out of the cave entrance, into the starlight, where she knelt and gasped and gasped, drawing in the cold-sharp, quick-moving air.

"Alma!" Shirin was there, wrapping an arm around her. "Alma, are you okay?"

"I can't get it!" Alma cried, her voice catching. "I thought I could. I thought maybe this was my element, like yours was water and Hugo's was wind. But I can't do it. I can't get it."

"You weren't even supposed to, Alma," Shirin said, rubbing her shoulders.

"Yes, we can come back tomorrow," Hugo said. "We'll do more research."

"But the Starling—" Alma paused, then took another shuddering breath. "She's running out of time. She needs to get home, and I have to do something. I'm not doing enough."

The thoughts that had been written in her books of fears after the panic attack at the library returned. The Starling had fallen into the wrong backyard. The quintescope had come to the wrong person. She didn't have an element.

There's nothing you can do, her mind said. *There's nothing you can do.*

Then it came again, that terrible crescendo of emotion. She felt it rising up in her, choking her, squeezing her and squeezing her. She felt herself turning brittle and sharp, fragile, breakable.

As if through a fog, she heard that voice.

"What are you weirdos doing out here?"

And Alma shattered.

CHAPTER 71

She was running. She was running blindly into the caves.

She couldn't hear anything except the gasping, tearing sounds of her own breath. She couldn't feel anything except the wild hammering of her heartbeat. Every one of her senses seemed simultaneously sharpened and dulled, and she felt the strange sensation of not being herself, of not being anyone at all, just a body in a tunnel in the center of the earth.

The passage widened and widened, and then Alma found herself in a cavern.

It was immense, far larger than her flashlight could let her see, with stalactites reaching bony fingers down and stalagmites curling crookedly upward. Rocks were piled high here too, nearly to the ceiling. There was the dripping sound of water on stone, but otherwise, the cavern was silent.

Alma ran on. But she was tired. She was so tired of running,

running from classes and from libraries and from friends. And most of all she was tired of running from her own thoughts, from her own self.

She wanted to stop running, but she didn't know how. She didn't know how to stop.

Before she could figure it out, she fell.

CHAPTER 72

Alma lay at the bottom of a pit in a cave. Her eyes were closed. She gripped the quintescope. She couldn't breathe.

Suddenly, someone was next to her. "Are you okay?" a voice said, a voice she didn't recognize. "Just breathe. Breathe with me. Ready? In—one, two, three, four. Hold your breath. Now breathe out slowly—one, two, three, four, five, six, seven, eight. Ready to breathe in?"

At first, Alma didn't think she was breathing. Then, she realized that someone was. Someone was lying on the cold stone ground, filling and emptying her lungs.

And slowly, slowly, she started to realize that someone was her. She started to feel like she was herself again.

Her heartbeat slowed and slowed. Her hands stopped shaking. The whir of thoughts that had been so fast and terrible that they weren't even real words but only the never-ending clamor of dread and fear quieted.

She breathed. She breathed along with the voice. Over and over.

And finally, after what seemed like a long time, she felt not entirely better, but okay enough to open her eyes.

Sitting on the ground next to her was Dustin.

CHAPTER 73

Alma couldn't have been any more surprised if it was the Starling herself sitting next to her.

Actually, she had hoped it *was* the Starling. She had imagined, as she lay there, that instead of her finding the Starling, the Starling had come to find her. She had imagined that the Starling had gathered her up and held her tight and that their quintessences had connected and that the flawed, all-wrong emptiness that kept opening up inside her had been fixed in that instant, fixed for good and forever.

But it was Dustin. The last person in the world—in the universe—that she wanted to see.

"Why are you here?" she asked, sitting up. "Did you follow us?"

Dustin scowled at her. "Maybe you haven't noticed, but we're stuck in a hole in a cave. Maybe we can talk about that later."

Alma looked around her then. The quintescope was on the

ground, and so was her flashlight, illuminating a small circle of stone. Dustin was holding a flashlight too, and in its light, she could see the pit she had fallen into. The pit Dustin had, presumably, leaped into to help her.

The pit they were stuck in.

She nodded. "Okay, we'll talk later. How do we get out of here?"

They stood next to each other, surveying their predicament. Dustin was tall, but even when he jumped, his fingers didn't quite touch the lip of the pit. The sides of the hole were so smooth that there was nowhere to wedge a hand or a foot. They both tried to scramble up with no success.

"I would boost you," Dustin said hesitantly. "But you'd never be able to pull me out of here."

Alma eyed Dustin. He was a lot bigger than her, taller and heavier, but if she pulled and he braced himself against the rocks, she thought they could probably do it.

"I can get you out," she said.

Dustin considered her, doubt etched into every feature of his face. "I guess we can try." He paused for a minute. "What will you do if I'm too heavy?"

There was something in his voice that made Alma look closer at him. His eyes were narrowed and his arms were crossed, but Alma saw suddenly that he was afraid.

"Do you think I'll leave you in here?" she asked, surprised.

Dustin's glare deepened. He looked like he was going to deny it, like he was going to yell at her. Then his stony expression seemed to crack and beneath it his eyes were wide with fear. "Yeah," he said. "I do. Why wouldn't you?"

Dustin had been nothing but mean to Alma since she'd moved to Four Points, that was true. He had been nothing but mean to her friends. Still, it would never have occurred to her to leave him trapped in a hole, even if he hadn't climbed into that hole to help her. Even if he hadn't spoken to her so kindly, so gently that she hadn't recognized his voice.

"I won't leave you," Alma said. "We'll both get out."

Dustin studied her in the flashlight beam for a long, searching moment more. Then he nodded and crouched, making a platform with his hands.

With a boost, Alma was able to scramble over the edge of the pit. When she looked back in, Dustin was scowling again, scowling up at her.

"You *are* going to leave me in here, aren't you?"

Alma shook her head. "I already said I wouldn't do that."

He handed up the flashlights and the quintescope. Then she leaned down as far as she could without feeling like she was going to fall back in herself. She held out her hand.

Dustin reached up and grasped it.

It took a few tries, including a particularly terrifying one where Alma almost tumbled headfirst back into the pit, but finally, when they were both drenched in sweat and coated in dust and out of breath in the thick Deep Downs air, finally, Dustin was out. They lay on the ground, side by side, catching their breath.

Alma got up first.

She wanted to get out of the cave right away, but she had come for earth.

She reached her hand down to Dustin again.

"Let's get out of here," she said. "I can look as I walk."

This time he didn't glare at her. He half smiled, and he took her hand.

"Look for what?" he asked as Alma pulled him to his feet.

Before she answered, Alma pressed the quintescope to her eye. And right there, right underneath where Dustin had been lying, she saw it.

There was a stone there the size of a fist. It was shining with a dark russet gleam, like iron ore. Beams of light shot out from its surface, dappling a pattern on the cave ceiling.

And Dustin: he was shining too.

"Dustin!" Alma cried. "You found it!"

"What are you talking about?" he asked, following her gaze. "This?" He picked up the stone. Without the quintescope it was dusty and dirty and not one bit special.

He didn't know, Alma realized, about any of it. He didn't know about the elements or the Starling. He didn't know why they were here in the middle of the night. She felt a surge of panic as she thought about him laughing at her, calling her a weirdo. Then she held the quintescope out to him.

Hugo had been right. This was Dustin's element, not hers. He would see.

"Look at it through this," she said.

"Whoa," he breathed a moment later. "What's making it shine like that?"

"I'll tell you about it," Alma replied, "under the stars."

Together, they hurried out of the cavern, down the tunnels, and then out into the open air, where Shirin threw herself at Alma.

"Oh my goodness! Are you all right?" Shirin cried. "What happened? I was about to go get help!"

"I'm fine," Alma said. "Dustin helped me. And look—" She took the stone from Dustin's hands and held it up.

It was a plain rock, but Hugo and Shirin knew—even without looking through the quintescope they knew.

It was true earth.

CHAPTER 74

Dustin had been in his tree house when he heard them coming down the road.

"My mom lets me sleep there sometimes," he said. "I knew you were going to go to the Deep Downs tonight—I heard you say that—but I didn't really think you'd be stupid enough to go in the *middle* of the night."

They were sitting a little away from the cave entrance. They had told Dustin about the book and the jars. No one had mentioned the Starling, but then Dustin said, "What about that thing that fell out of the sky the other week? Does this have anything to do with that?"

"How do you know about that?" Alma asked with a gasp.

"I was in the tree house that night. I—I saw it. And then I heard you three talking about it at Astronomy Club. That's why I've been, you know, interested in hanging out."

"Interested in *following* us," Shirin corrected him. "Like you did tonight."

Dustin glowered at her. "Yeah," he muttered. "So you wouldn't *die*. You don't know anything about these caves. It's a good thing I did too, since Alma had a panic attack and fell in a pit . . . although some of that might have been my fault."

Alma flinched. It was so easy for him to call her episode what it was—*a panic attack*—as if it was nothing. As if this secret that she kept so carefully hidden was no big deal.

"A panic attack?" Shirin turned to Alma, mouth open. "Wait! Are you claustrophobic too?"

"No," Alma said. She shook her head, wishing she didn't have to answer. "I'm—I don't know what I am. I just get anxious. Really anxious. Especially in new situations or when there's lots of people or—"

"Or around me," Dustin said. "Right?"

Alma wanted to deny it, but then she thought of her first panic attack. She could still feel the way her shoulder had jerked forward when he had run into her, how her hands had slammed into the lockers to keep herself upright. She could still hear his voice yelling, "Watch out, weirdo!" And then, the part she really tried not to think about, after she had crumpled to the ground: "Hey! Look at this! Look at this girl!"

"You—you were there," she said quietly. "The day I had my first panic attack. You pushed me. You—you yelled at me. You told everyone to look at me. You were making fun of me."

Dustin stared at her, aghast. "That's not what happened!" he cried. "I wasn't making fun of you. I was trying to get someone to come help you!" When Alma didn't answer, he continued, "My mom gets panic attacks, okay? She used to only get them sometimes, but after my dad—after he left last summer, she got them a lot. Like every day. So I know about them. I know how to help her with them. But that day—I didn't know you, you know? I thought someone else should help."

Alma tried to make this new information fit into the image of Dustin she had formed three months ago. It was hard to reimagine her first panic attack. It was hard to think of him as someone trying to help, not hurt her. Although not as hard, now that he had helped her again.

"Yeah, but you're mean to us," Shirin said, getting to the point. "Like constantly. And you and Hugo were best friends! Why are you so awful to him? Do you think you're too cool for him now or something?"

Dustin's face contorted in confusion. "What? No!" he said. "I don't care about that. Why would I care about that? I just wanted—I wanted to be by myself."

"Okay, but why were you so mean?" Shirin persisted.

"Because of all the stuff I told you!" Dustin yelled. "About my dad leaving and my mom's panic attacks and everything I just said!"

Alma shook her head slowly. "That sounds really hard," she said. "But it's still not—you know that doesn't make it okay, right?"

263

Dustin was silent. He glared at her. He glared at Shirin. He glared up at the stars. He glared down at the ground. Then he mumbled, "I know."

Hugo had been sitting as still as a deactivated robot this entire time. Now he pushed his glasses up very slowly and said, "I didn't know about your father leaving."

In an instant, Dustin's glare returned. "Yeah, because you never asked, weirdo!"

Hugo went back to being tense and stiff. Dustin went back to being angry. To Alma, it seemed as if both boys had stepped out of their own caves, just for a moment, and were now retreating back inside.

When Hugo spoke again, it was to Alma only, and his voice was flat and emotionless.

"I observed that you were breathing very rapidly immediately prior to the panic attack," he said. "The ratio of oxygen to carbon dioxide that you were creating in your bloodstream was unconducive for a calm outlook."

"You closed your eyes too," Shirin added. "And you got very tense and shaky."

"It may be helpful to know that a panic attack is a self-limited phenomenon," Hugo continued. "The human body cannot produce adrenaline indefinitely."

"So it can't last forever," Alma said. "Is that what you're saying?"

"From what I have read, symptoms usually peak within ten minutes, then gradually subside," Hugo agreed.

Shirin, at least, seemed encouraged by this news. "Ten minutes isn't that long!" she said. "You can do anything for ten minutes."

Alma laughed, although it wasn't funny. It was, to use a Hugo-ism, ludicrous. "That's what you think," she said. "I just wish— I wish I didn't have them. I wish I could just be happy."

There was silence in the woods as the four stood by the entrance to the Deep Downs. Alma kept her gaze fixed on the stone gray and pine-needle-and-dirt-brown ground beneath her feet. How could so many precious, glittering things be buried there, in mud and rock?

"No one can be happy all the time," Shirin said finally.

Alma glanced at Shirin out of the corner of her eye. Next to her mother, Shirin was the happiest person she knew. "Not even you?" she asked.

Shirin shook her head, hands on her braids. "Not even me."

"Definitely not me," Dustin muttered.

"Not me either," Hugo said quietly.

What did this mean? Alma wasn't sure yet. But her friends had learned the truth about her, and they were still here. No one thought she was crazy or flawed or destined to fail. And she knew one thing.

"I'm happy right now," she said. "That's worth something."

CHAPTER 75

They had stayed at the caves longer than they intended, and the ride home was longer than Alma remembered. The sun was rising as she pedaled up to her house, and it had risen by the time she climbed in her window.

And her parents were there, sitting side by side on her bed.

"Alma!" Her mother leaped to her feet. Her eyes were red-rimmed, and she was gripping her phone with both hands. "What's happening? Where were you? Why are you covered in mud?"

"I'm not," Alma said. She put her hands, dirt-streaked, behind her back. As if that would help. As if her entire self wasn't coated in earth.

"Is this what you've been doing?" Her father shut her window, hard. "Sneaking out in the middle of the night?"

"I just went into the backyard," Alma said. "Like last time."

"And rolled around on the ground?" her father asked.

"Yes," Alma said. "No. I don't know."

Alma had known this would happen eventually. She had snuck out of her window five times now, and three of those times she had stayed out for hours. She had gone all over Four Points—to the source of a stream, to the top of a mountain, under the ground. She was actually surprised she hadn't been caught—really and truly caught—before now.

She was also surprised when she felt her heartbeat speed up. She felt her muscles tighten. She felt her face tense, not into a smile but into a hard, unapologetic expression. She had been having panic attacks for months, and her parents hadn't been able to help her. They had told her what to do and told her she was doing it wrong and told her to keep trying. They had made it worse.

Her parents were the ones who had started all these problems.

"I was about to call the police, did you know that?" her father said. "This is completely unacceptable!"

"And scary," Alma's mother said. "Do you know how scary it was for us to come in here and find you missing?"

"Okay, I wasn't in the backyard. I was in the Preserve," Alma said, the lie slipping off her tongue easily, defiantly. "I woke up early, and I wanted to be outside. You know I like to be outside. That's all I was doing."

Her parents studied her, her mother's look full of open concern, her father's fear coated in a layer of anger.

"Today is your appointment with the psychologist," he finally

267

said. "We're going to call and let him know about this. We need—we need a plan. We need to figure out what to do here."

Then, before Alma could stop him, he picked up the quintescope case from the floor.

"I'm taking this," he said, heading toward the door. "I don't know what you think you were doing with it, but that's over now."

CHAPTER 76

The Fifth Point was changing. The tarnished signs had been polished, their words now gleaming gold and splendid. The ladders had been wiped clean, rung by rung, their messages now shining bright. For the first time in a long, long time, passersby could see inside the Fifth Point. The four display windows of the square shop shone, clear and clean, inside and outside.

And what would a curious Four Pointer see if they looked through?

Not dust, not dirt, not rubbish, not trash.

No, no. They would see wooden floors that reflected back the sunlight and the barely there blue light. They would see shelves lined with once-thrown-away nothings that had been lovingly mended into somethings.

Re-covered books. Kites with new tails. Tea sets a queen would be proud of.

They would see a home, a home for the lost and homeless made *by one who was once lost and homeless, a home that a Star had made for himself after the Universe had taken his away.*

They might even spot the ShopKeeper himself. He was there now, at his workbench.

Tick tock tickity tock, *went the many now-functioning clocks.* Scritch scratch scritchity scratch, *went the ShopKeeper's quill pen.*

The ShopKeeper had spent the day writing letters to his Keeper friends. They were fallen Stars like him—Stars that had chosen to remain here on Earth instead of returning home. They, like the Shop-Keeper, had created new homes for themselves and a new purpose: to save the fallen. He had visited each one before this quest began, but he wanted to tell them what they had meant to him one last time.

Then the clocks began to chime and ring and cuckoo. The Shop-Keeper set down his quill. He donned his much-patched top hat and pulled on a pair of gloves.

It was time for his meeting.

CHAPTER 77

There was no time for Alma to go back to sleep. But in spite of having been awake all night, she was not tired. She was too angry to be tired.

Her movements were quick and sharp as she showered and got ready for school. She jerked open drawers and shoved her closet door shut. She threw on clothes and stomped downstairs. Her mind was full of thundercloud thoughts during the silent car ride to school.

At lunch, she picked at her grilled cheese while Hugo and Shirin talked about the cave and the stone and what to do next. She didn't want to tell them about getting caught. She didn't want to tell them about the appointment.

She was still angry. But as the day wore on, another feeling was making itself known.

Fear.

Because what was this psychologist going to say? What was he going to tell her about herself? And did she want to know?

The psychologist had given her parents directions to his office, even though it was in the school. Alma was glad she had those directions as she went down halls she hadn't even known existed until that afternoon. She passed a classroom filled with stacked chairs and broken desks, an OUT OF ORDER bathroom, and a side door to the gym before she found what she was looking for.

The door was smaller than a normal classroom door. There were stains around the handle, and dirty drip marks around the bottom, as if muddy water had been sloshed there. It didn't look like the door to an office. It looked like the door to a supply closet.

Except for the sign.

Taped to the door was a piece of paper. The paper was black and the words across it were gold: DR. PARRY: ILLUMINIST, they read, followed by a single blue star.

It was not the kind of sign Alma would have expected the school psychologist to have.

She didn't want to knock. What she wanted to do was run.

So she stood at the door and did not knock.

Until the door flew open, revealing Dr. Parry, Illuminist.

The illuminist was short, very short, even though the patched brown top hat he wore gave him an extra six inches at least. He wore brass-rimmed spectacles with extremely thick glass, but even shrunk by the lenses, his eyes were startlingly large and startlingly blue. He wore a tweed tailcoat, a plaid waistcoat, and a white shirt with a discolored ruffled collar. On his hands were mismatched gloves, one white cotton, the other pink knit. On his feet were purple cowboy boots. Socks with neon-yellow smiley faces peeked over the tops.

If his height and his hair and his apparel choices were not unusual enough, Dr. Parry also seemed to be wearing makeup. Not eyeliner or lipstick. Just layers and layers of foundation on his face and neck, as if he had painted on his skin.

He reminded Alma of someone—of several someones, in fact—but before she could say a word, the illuminist let out a high, wild laugh.

"Alma!" he cried, his voice echoing up and down the empty hallways. "Come in, come in, there's not a moment to waste!"

He ushered Alma inside what was definitely a supply closet. Spray bottles and rolls of paper towels lined the shelves. Brooms and dustpans hung on the walls. The cause of the door drips, a yellow mop bucket, sat in a small puddle in one corner.

Crammed in the middle were two metal chairs. Alma took one, Dr. Parry the other. A bare lightbulb hung above them.

"So," Dr. Parry said, regarding her with a bespectacled blue-eyed stare so bright and so intense that Alma looked away almost immediately. "You're here."

"I have to be," Alma said, eyeing the bottles of Super Duper Clean. "Don't I?"

"Yes!" he said. "You absolutely do. Yes, you do. And I'm delighted."

Alma glanced over at him. He did look delighted. His gloved hands were clasped together, and he was grinning like a small child who had been given a box full of lollipops and kittens. "Why are you delighted?"

"Because I get to meet you!" Dr. Parry said. "I get to talk to you. I get to learn more about Alma Lucas."

"I think," Alma replied, "that you're going to be disappointed."

She returned her gaze to the cleaning supplies, but she could see the illuminist out of the corner of her eye, studying her. Then he gave a long, weighed-down sigh.

"It has been a hard year for you, hasn't it?" he asked, and his voice was very soft now, like a song on a radio with the volume turned down low.

The reasons for not talking to Dr. Parry were there—present and accounted for. Alma was angry. Alma was afraid. Yet inside, deep inside where there were still knots and hurt and darkness, that little light flickered.

Hesitantly, she gave a small nod.

"I know about leaving home," Dr. Parry said. "I left home. I suppose everyone does at some point. And this world can be a cold place. This world can be a lonely place."

Alma nodded again. She felt tears filling her eyes, even though it was silly, even though she shouldn't be crying, and her light flickered again, brighter now.

"Why don't you tell me, my dear soul," the illuminist said, "what brings you here?"

That light had never steered Alma wrong so far. Whenever she had followed it, good things had happened. She didn't want to follow it. But she thought maybe, maybe she should.

As if in reply, the light sparked.

So Alma took a deep breath. Angry or not, afraid or not, she was going to do something. Something only she could do.

She was going to tell the truth.

CHAPTER 78

"I've been having panic attacks," Alma said. "I told my parents that they stopped, but they haven't."

"Ah," Dr. Parry said. "I see, I see. Do you know why you told your parents that?"

Alma shook her head. Then she nodded. "It's because I don't know," she said, "how to fix myself. And my parents want me to be better. Not in a bad way, not like they'll punish me or anything. But if they knew I was still having the panic attacks, they'd be . . . disappointed, maybe. And worried."

Dr. Parry was bobbing his head along with her words. Then he stopped and frowned. He started digging in the pockets of his tailcoat, then in the pocket of his waistcoat. Then he held up one gloved finger, grinned, and dug his hand into his boot. Out came a small, foil-wrapped candy.

"Butterscotch," he said. "Helps me think. One for you?"

"No, thank you," Alma said. Boot-sweets did not sound particularly appetizing.

Dr. Parry opened his candy, popped it into his mouth, and sucked thoughtfully for a moment.

"People," he said, "can be so marvelous. And so difficult. Especially the ones that care about us." His candy bulged in one painted cheek, then the other, back and forth. "Did you know I spoke to your parents? Yes, indeed I did. They want very much to help you. Do you want to know something else? They have no idea what to do."

Alma opened her mouth to tell Dr. Parry that this was simply not true. But then she stopped. Her parents always seemed to know what to do. They seemed to know *exactly* what to do. But they had been trying and trying and trying to make her better, and it hadn't worked.

So maybe—maybe they didn't.

"Alma, other than these panic attacks," Dr. Parry said, "how have you been feeling?"

Alma gripped the metal sides of her chair as she tried to uncover the answer to this question. It took some time to find it, buried as it was beneath the more easily recognized layers of fear.

"Well, actually," she said, "lately I've been feeling different. Four Points has started to seem more like—more like home. I joined a club, and I made some friends, and we've been trying to— to help someone. Sometimes, I feel wonderful. I feel bright. But then other times—other times, I feel like that wonderful brightness gets swallowed up. I feel dark, if that makes sense."

"Ah," said the illuminist. "Ah. But you can't feel wonderful *all* the time, can you?" He leaned forward. "How can you have the light without the darkness?"

Alma shook her head. "Some people are happy," she explained. "And peaceful. Peace-filled. But not me. Ever since the move, sometimes I feel like I'm not even myself. I think there's something wrong with me." The tears spilled out as she spoke this, her deepest fear, like a splinter that had lodged into her heart long ago and was suddenly being forced to the surface.

"Oh, Alma," Dr. Parry said. His voice was melodic and gentle. The smell of butterscotch—sweet and golden as sunshine—filled the air. "No one is happy all the time. No one is at peace all the time. No one, no one, no one. And these things you are doing—it sounds to me, my dear one, like you are doing a remarkable job of finding out what makes you *you*."

"I'm not," Alma said, wiping her cheeks with the heels of her palms. "I have these new friends, and they're filled with all sorts of great things. They're fun and smart and brave." She paused to breathe in a deep, shuddery breath. "But me—sometimes it feels like I have nothing inside. Nothing good."

Dr. Parry was silent for a moment. Alma, who had been staring at the teardrop puddle in the impression between her thumb and pointer finger, glanced up to find him studying her through the butterscotch wrapper. "These are things," he said, "that everyone has to figure out, panic attacks or not." He lowered the wrapper. "I can tell that you are not empty inside, even if it feels that way. Quintessence, you see, is not so easily extinguished."

At this, Alma inhaled sharply and sat up tall. "How do you know about quintessence?" she asked.

The illuminist raised and wiggled his eyebrows at her. "Oh, I know about quintessence because I am an illuminist, my dear one," he said, "among my many other occupations and pastimes. It is my job to know these things. Did you know that that light inside you—that's quintessence?"

"I thought so," Alma whispered, remembering the book, remembering the human figures with spheres at the centers. "I thought it was my Alma-ness."

"Ominous?" Dr. Parry pulled back in his chair, an offended look on his painted face. "My dear girl, what's so ominous about quintessence?"

"Alma-ness," Alma said, enunciating. "That's what I call my—*my* quintessence, I guess."

Dr. Parry clapped and let out a ringing laugh. "A perfect description!" he cried. "Absolutely perfect! It has been called many things over the years—*the core, the heart, the spark, the light, the soul.* Me, I have always preferred *quintessence.*" Dr. Parry clutched at his hat and leaned toward her. "Quintessence is your you-ness distilled down to the truest parts. It is yours to discover, yours to grow, yours to share. Yet somehow—and this is where things get marvelously complex and wondrous—it is also the thing that connects you to everything else that is true. To the earth and the oceans, to the wind and the fire, to friends and family and strangers and enemies, to the very stars and beyond, beyond, beyond! And that connection, oh, that is where the magic and the glory are, dear soul!"

The illuminist was quite excited now. He had stood up on his folding chair. His gloved hands were waving through the air, conducting the melody of his voice. But Alma wasn't alarmed by this fervor. She was too swept away by what he was saying.

"The panic attacks," she said, looking up at him. "It feels like they put the light out."

Dr. Parry's whole body twisted his answer: *no, no, no.* "No one can be everything, Alma!" he cried. "Every single elemental has challenges and obstacles and pain and illness and general badness! And yet they grow their light anyway—in spite of, because of, alongside of."

"But," Alma pressed, "what about elements? Do I have one?"

"You have all of them, Alma," Dr. Parry replied. "Everyone does. But one of them—one of them is more Alma-y than the rest. Think, think, think—what makes you feel alive? What makes you feel like you?"

The first thing that came to Alma was a memory of the wake-up wind that had pushed her along the day she had found the flyer. "Being outside," she said. "Exploring. Imagining. Being alone. But also being with my new friends. And the—the someone we're helping. Helping her makes me feel like me too. Do those things have something to do with my element?"

"They have everything to do with it," the illuminist said. "And you must keep doing those things! You must keep searching!" He leaped from the chair so that he stood directly in front of her. "And tell the truth, Alma." He pressed a gloved hand to his chin. "That's important too."

Home and *truth*, *quintessence* and *elements*—these words, all these words, were like kindling inside Alma. Her lofty thoughts were interrupted, however, by the sight of Dr. Parry's glove as he removed it from his face. It was covered in tan smears. "You're wearing a lot of makeup," she blurted out. "And you remind me— do you have any sisters? Or brothers?"

Dr. Parry, Illuminist, grinned at her. His teeth were so white they seemed to sparkle. His eyes were so blue they seemed to shine. Even his skin, covered in paint as it was, seemed luminous. It was as if he was filled with light, like a jack-o'-lantern.

"Oh yes," he said. "Many. But they are all very, very far away." He held his hand out to Alma. "Alas, our time is up!"

Alma took his hand reluctantly. There was more that she wanted to ask, more that she felt Dr. Parry could tell her. But he was leading her toward the door, his fingers warm on her arm even through his gloves and her sweatshirt.

"Good day, Alma of the Growing Light!" he sang out, flinging open the door. "Keep searching, and I will see you by and by! I'll see you on the top at the end!"

281

"Why are you calling me that?" she asked, stepping backward through the door. "And on the top of what? Do you know the Shop-Keeper?"

"On the top at the end!" Dr. Parry cried.

Then he shut the door firmly in her face.

"Alma of the Growing Light," Alma whispered to herself.

And on the other side, Dr. Parry said it too. "Alma of the Growing Light."

PART 8

Fire

....

CHAPTER 79

On Tuesday, Dustin started sitting with them at lunch, plunking down on the bench next to Alma without comment. It occurred to her that she had never seen him in the cafeteria before. She wondered where he used to sit. Alone somewhere, she guessed.

When he threw himself onto the bench on Friday, he asked, "What are we doing about fire?" He had asked this on Tuesday, Wednesday, and Thursday too. "Let's do something!"

Shirin eyeballed him over her pizza. Hugo arranged carrot sticks on his napkin.

Dustin may have rescued Alma in the cave, but it didn't mean that he was welcome or entirely forgiven. Dustin and Hugo still hadn't talked about their falling-out last summer, and lunches had been tense, with Shirin snapping, "Ugh! Why are you even here?" on more than one occasion and with Hugo reverting to his stiff, robotic behaviors. Alma found that she was no longer afraid of

Dustin, not even a little bit, which was good, since most of the time it fell to her to deal with him.

"Without the quintescope, we don't know what to do," she said.

"I told you to just steal it back from your dad," Dustin grumbled.

"I know," Alma replied. "But my parents are watching me so closely. They're really worried about me."

After the meeting with Dr. Parry, she had felt ready to keep searching, but her parents had become more vigilant than ever. Her father had affixed bolts to her windowsill so that she could only open her window about six inches. She had not been allowed to leave her parents' office after school. She heard them at night sometimes, opening her bedroom door and peeking in to make sure she was there.

So now, days later, they had made no progress in finding the Starling or true fire.

"If only we had the fire container," Hugo said. "It might give us some indication of the type of fire we need to collect, whether it's from a wood fire or some sort of chemical fire or—or a volcano?" He shook his head in frustration. "I keep thinking of Mrs. Brisa's idea to use a lightning rod to ignite a spark, but lightning is incredibly powerful and dangerous. It's not a real possibility."

"Let's read the fire section again," Alma said, struggling to think of something, anything that she actually could do.

Hugo got out the book and handed it to Alma. She opened to the page with the triangle illustration and read:

Finally, at last, we turn to Fire.
Of all the Elements, it is Fire that is
the most enigmatic and most difficult to obtain.
Fire can destroy and burn down to ash.
Fire can blaze wild and raze field and forest and home.
Yet Fire gives way to new life.
Fire purifies and refines.
And Fire Elementals, they contain their own flames—
of passion and compassion.
Flames that can destroy, flames that can blaze wild.
Yet when these Elementals are their truest
and when they connect—
How their ideas can create worlds!
How their spark can change the Universe!

"You know what? I think that sounds like you, Alma," Shirin said
when she was done. "You're not very loud about it, but you're definitely, like, intense. And that's why we're on this whole quest in the
first place. Because you had so much compassion for the Starling,
right?"

Alma shook her head. She had read the fire description over
and over, trying to find herself in it. It was the last element, her
last chance, and it was easy to identify with the parts about being
destroyed, about burning away.

But creating worlds? Changing the universe? That didn't sound
like her one bit.

"Agreed," Hugo said, to Alma's surprise. "The quest would have ended many times without Alma's belief in the Starling. Of course, there are some things I could never have believed in, no matter what. Our pamphlet, as you know, is written by someone who calls himself the *True Paracelsus*, and I have been reading some of the books the librarian gave us about the other Paracelsus. Fascinating fact: the other Paracelsus thought elementals were gnomes, sprites, mermaids, and magical salamanders!"

Alma and Shirin started to laugh, but Dustin snorted. "More like *un*fascinating fact."

Shirin whipped around to snap at him, and her braids knocked her entire tray into her lap. Pizza went everywhere. Hugo and Alma were so used to this that they jumped up to help without even commenting.

Dustin, however, snickered. "Seriously? What's wrong with you?" he said.

The glare Shirin gave him was as fierce as fire shooting from her eyeballs. Alma imagined Dustin turning into a smoldering pile of ash.

Maybe it was because Dustin's presence inhibited their conversation or maybe it was because fire really was the most difficult element, but when the bell sounded for the end of lunch, they still didn't have any real ideas.

"Why don't we meet tonight?" Dustin demanded as they packed up. "Why do we have to have some perfect plan? I have stuff we can use. We can try different things—see what works."

Hugo looked like he wanted to say no. Shirin actually did.

"Nope," she said. "We're not ready. We've been doing this for a while, and the other elements were in really specific places. We didn't just *happen* to find them."

Dustin rolled his eyes and turned to Alma.

"Come on, Alma," he said. "Remember what it says about the Starling being in mortal peril? Don't you want to get the last element? We need to finish this!"

When Hugo talked about finding the elements, it was like a puzzle that needed to be researched and solved. When Shirin talked about it, it was like a thrilling adventure. With Dustin, finding the elements was like a mission, something they had to complete.

Alma loved figuring out the puzzle and sharing the adventure. But Dustin was demanding answers so intensely, and Alma found that she agreed with him. It had been over two weeks since the Starling had fallen, and from what she'd seen at the caves, she was running out of time. Even if she didn't believe that fire was her element, even if she got caught, she had to try.

"I think Dustin's right," Alma told Shirin and Hugo. "The Starling's been here for too long. Somehow we need to get fire. Tonight."

CHAPTER 80

Dustin's house, out in the woods, would have been the perfect spot for the fire. Unfortunately, his mother was working at the hospital that night, which meant his insomniac aunt was staying with him and his three younger brothers.

"She thinks we don't have enough supervision," Dustin had complained. "She spends the night, like, patrolling the halls. No way we can be in the backyard. It'll be hard enough to sneak out."

The second-best option was Hugo's house, since he had a fire pit in his backyard and his mother was also working that night.

"We have to be silent though," Hugo had told them. "*Silent*. If my stepfather wakes up, I'll be in so much trouble."

Dustin had snorted. "Whatever," he had said. "Marcus is so nice. I don't get why you don't like him."

"I like him fine," Hugo had said flatly, stiffly. "However, this is none of his business."

That night, right before midnight, Alma put on her coat and shoes in her room. She put her flashlight in her pocket. Then she tip-tip-tiptoed down the stairs, breath held, movements in slow motion. At the back door, she turned the handle by infinitesimal degrees, and opened and shut the door as if it were made of crystal.

Once outside, she ran to the shed, where she retrieved the bike-lock key from under the potted plant again. She unlocked her bike and then rode, reckless and pell-mell, toward Second Point. She thought, as she flew down the streets, that she would almost certainly be caught—her parents were watching her too closely.

This was her last chance.

Hugo and Shirin were already in the backyard when Alma arrived, and they had a tiny blaze going in the fire pit.

"Do you see anything?" Shirin whispered to her as she walked up. "In the flames, I mean? I don't know how to tell if it's true fire without the quintescope."

"Apologies, but I'm not sure how long we can keep this burning," Hugo said. "If Marcus finds us, we will be in extremely serious trouble."

Alma searched the dancing copper and gold flames. Shirin was right; every single one looked pure and extraordinary, burning and gleaming so brilliantly. And of course Hugo was concerned. They had lit a fire in his backyard in the middle of the night.

"You call that a fire?" Dustin's voice came booming through the yard.

"Oh my goodness! Be quiet," Shirin hissed. Hugo moved to the other side of the fire as Dustin came up.

"Fine," Dustin said. "But that thing's too small. Don't you think, Alma? There isn't going to be any true fire in there."

"It is little," Alma admitted. "We don't want anyone to see it though."

"No, we don't," Hugo said, kneeling to add more kindling to the flames.

Dustin snorted. "So we're not even going to try? Look what I brought, Alma." He held out a small plastic container to her. "Add this, and we'll see what happens. It will only be big for a minute, and then I've got—I've got something for the flames."

Alma took the container. "What is it?" she asked, squinting at the label in the flickering light.

"It's lighter fluid and some other stuff I mixed together," Dustin said. "My dad used to do it all the time when we made bonfires and had cookouts and stuff."

"I don't think that's wise," Hugo said, jerking to a stand. "Mixing accelerants is very risky. There is the possibility that—"

"Why can't you just listen to me for once?" Dustin cried. "You always think I'm wrong. I'm not stupid, Hugo!"

Hugo took a step back. "I never said you were stupid."

"We don't want to do anything dangerous, Dustin," Shirin said, pointing her braids at him. "Anyway, you're not in charge."

"Like you're so careful," Dustin shot back. "I'm surprised you don't break your neck when you bend down to tie your shoes. And I never said I was in charge! But I'm part of the quest, whether you two want me to be here or not."

Alma turned the bottle over in her hands. She didn't know a lot about lighting fires, but she knew that people sometimes used lighter fluid. It couldn't be that dangerous. She wondered if Shirin and Hugo would be objecting if she were the one suggesting it instead of Dustin.

"Just do it, Alma!" Dustin cried. "Why are you waiting forever? Don't you want to finish?" He took a step toward Alma, and his green eyes were burning in the light of the flames. "We can do it, Alma. You don't want the Starling to die, do you?"

She didn't. With her whole heart, desperately, desperately, Alma wanted the Starling to get home. This didn't feel exactly like the right way to do it—it wasn't the way she would have chosen. But maybe Dustin was right. Maybe this would lead to pure and true fire, huge and flaming and brilliant. Maybe this would finally give them the last element.

And maybe it really would be her element.

Alma squeezed the bottle. An arc of golden liquid shot out.

But when it reached the flames, that liquid turned to fire.

A rope of fire.

A rope that blazed right back to Alma.

CHAPTER 81

They were at the hospital.

The fire had momentarily set the sleeves of Alma's jacket aflame. Instead of putting it out herself, Alma had frozen. It had been Dustin who had smothered the fire with his gloved hands, but in spite of this quick action, pain—searing, dizzying pain—had overwhelmed her seconds later.

She hadn't cried. She had felt beyond crying. She had just held her shaking, bright red hands out in front of her.

Shirin had half dragged her to the house. Hugo had raced inside ahead of them, yelling for Marcus, who had come running down the stairs, bleary-eyed and confused. He had taken one look at Alma, ashen and red-handed, then scooped her up and carried her to the kitchen sink. For a long time, he had let the cool water run over her hands, saying quietly and calmly, "This will help. The water will help." Shirin had rubbed her back and cried.

Hugo had hovered in the background, pushing his glasses up and down, up and down.

When Marcus turned off the water, Alma was in less pain, but only slightly less. Marcus had taken her arm and led her outside to the car. Dustin had been waiting there, his face a panic-stricken shade of white.

"Hugo, stay with the twins," Marcus had instructed his stepson. "And call your mother. Tell her we're on our way to the hospital."

He had helped Alma into the front seat, while Shirin had climbed into the back. Dustin had started to follow, but Hugo had reached past him and slammed the door shut.

"You go home, you—you weirdo!" he had yelled.

While the car pulled away, Alma had watched through the window as Dustin held his hands up, as if in surrender, and then ran off down the street. Hugo had still been staring after him when the car rounded the corner and they both disappeared from view.

On the way to the hospital, Alma had felt her pain and her fear shifting, morphing into that familiar panic. It had swelled up inside her, cutting off her breath and making her shake, making her sob. And when they reached the hospital, she had felt so out of control, so not herself, that she couldn't even get out of the car, and Marcus had ended up running inside to get a nurse and a wheelchair.

In the hospital, Shirin was pulled aside and Alma was wheeled to a cool, empty room where a nurse with a gray-and-blond-streaked ponytail helped her onto an examining table. The nurse gave her water and medication and then spoke to her in a soft, soothing voice as she cleaned and bandaged her hands.

Then Mrs. Johnson came in. She didn't look angry, but she looked very stern and ready for answers. Alma wondered what Shirin had told her, what Marcus had said.

But before Mrs. Johnson could say a word, the doors swung open again and Alma's parents came racing in—wide-eyed, breathless, and terrified.

CHAPTER 82

The next morning, lying on the red-plaid couch in her living room, Alma was awakened by the sound of the front door opening. She had spent the night there, because her parents had refused to let her be alone in her room. Her hands were resting on her stomach, both loosely wrapped in clean, white gauze. She had been given medication for the pain, but she could still feel the ache.

"Hey, Alms," said a voice. "What's all this I hear about you setting fires around town?"

James was there in the doorway. Alma could tell he was trying to be lighthearted, but his voice was unnaturally cheerful and his forehead furrows reminded her of their father's.

Alma sat up. She tried to smile, but she didn't know what to make of his sudden presence.

"What are you doing here?" she asked.

"Spring break starts today," James said. "Although I came a little earlier than I would have. Mom and Dad called me in the middle of the night. They think we should talk. The four of us. Together."

Alma knew then. This was what she had been waiting for, what she had been dreading. Her parents had not asked many questions last night because the nurse with the gray-streaked hair had quickly taken them aside and told them about her panic attack and her burns. By the time they had arrived at home, in the early hours of the morning, everyone had been too exhausted to talk.

But now the moment had come. This would be, Alma felt sure, the Discussion to End All Discussions.

After their long night, her parents had been asleep too, but now they came out to the living room. Alma and her mother sat side by side on the couch. Her father and James sat in the matching leaf-print armchairs across from them.

"There are several things we need to discuss," her father began. His fingers laced. His brow furrowed. "Alma, it is imperative that you tell us the truth."

"The truth," Alma repeated. The truth. *Tell the truth, Alma*, Dr. Parry had said.

"The panic attack last night," her mother said gently. "Was that the first one you've had since December?"

Across from Alma, her father unlaced his hands and leaned forward. The creases in his brow deepened. James's movements mimicked their father's. Alma's mother put her arm around Alma.

Every time this had happened before, every time they'd had the Discussion, Alma had felt like she was being shrunk down and taken apart and placed beneath a microscope. She had wanted to hide from view. But today, suddenly, Alma realized that Dr. Parry had been right. Her family was trying to help her.

And they didn't know how.

They needed to know the truth.

Here was something that she could do.

"I'm still getting the panic attacks," she said. "Not just last night either. It hasn't happened as much over the last three weeks, but before that, I was having a lot. Sometimes every day. Sometimes even more."

"Oh, Alma," her mother breathed. She scooched closer to her daughter, pulling her in.

Alma's father's eyebrows lifted, taking his forehead furrows with them. "But why didn't you tell us?" he asked. "All this time—we had no idea."

Alma shook her head. "I couldn't—I didn't want to tell you," she said, "because I didn't know how to fix it, and I kept disappointing you. And I was—I was angry, even though I didn't realize it at first. You made me move here to Four Points, and I didn't want to."

"You really loved Old Haven, didn't you?" Alma's mother said. She touched the dried yellow wildflower that was woven into Alma's hair. That flower had grown by the front steps of their old home.

"I did," Alma replied, her voice breaking, her eyes on her bandaged hands.

"Plus, middle school is tough," James said. "It was tough for me too."

Alma's father was slower to respond. "We bought the law practice," he said finally, "because we had a lot of debt from law school. This seemed like our chance to have a better life. I knew you wouldn't be happy about leaving Old Haven, but I thought you would acclimate. And when you *didn't*, I suppose I thought that you—that you weren't trying."

He paused, and Alma kept her gaze down, her insides heavy and her eyes filling with tears. She wondered if it had been a mistake to tell them about the panic attacks after all. Maybe she had been right to keep it a secret. Maybe her father was going to tell her to try harder, to *do something*.

But he didn't say anything.

And when Alma finally looked up, she found that he was looking right at her, and he was crying.

"You were trying though, weren't you?" he said softly.

Alma's own tears spilled over. "I was," she said. "I was trying, but I couldn't—I couldn't stop the panic attacks. I can't stop them. I can't make myself better. But I was trying. I am trying."

Alma's father came to sit on the other side of her. He put his arm around her shoulders, and she felt a teardrop land in her hair. "I know you were," he said. "We weren't listening. *I* wasn't listening. And you weren't being honest. So we have to figure out—together—how to help you. What *you*, Alma, need."

"We're sorry that you felt you *couldn't* tell us the truth," her

299

mother said. "And that you thought we were"—she paused, and when she continued her voice was choked by tears—"disappointed in you. We're not. We always want to know the truth, Alma, whatever it is, because we love you."

James had scooched forward in his chair, toward the three of them on the couch. "And I'm not so far," he said, bumping Alma's knees with his. "I can come home sometimes. I miss you, you know."

"You do?" Alma asked.

"Of course I do," James said.

These were the things that Alma had wanted to hear for the last three months: that her panic attacks were not her fault, that she was not a disappointment, that she was loved. To hear them now, after she had told the truth she had kept so carefully hidden, gave her the same feeling she'd had when the ShopKeeper and Dr. Parry had called her Alma of the Growing Light.

It was the feeling that her family was seeing her brightness, her Alma-ness, at last.

Her father laced his hands together again, but his brow stayed unfurrowed as he shifted to look her in the eyes. "Now, why don't you tell us," he said, his voice gentle but very definitely firm, "why you've been sneaking out of the house?"

CHAPTER 83

Alma and her parents and James talked all throughout that day. Alma told them about her new friends. She told them about Dr. Parry. She told them about the book and the elements. She even took them into the backyard once the sun set and showed them the spheres of quintessence inside the stars through the quintescope, after her father had retrieved it from its hiding place.

"I've never seen anything like that," James admitted, gazing through the eyepiece.

"That was your astronomy project, Alma Llama Ding Dong?" her mother asked.

Alma nodded. "It was," she said.

The only thing she didn't tell them about was the Starling. It was too painful for her to even think about how she had failed the star-child. She had tried to create fire and instead, she had set herself on fire.

While spending time with her family, their love made her feel temporarily bright. But by late evening, slumped back on the couch in the shadow-filled living room, her hands felt like they were aflame again and the rest of her was heavy with the ache of defeat. She had failed to create quintessence, and her own quintessence, her Alma-ness, had never felt so dark.

Then there was a knock on the door.

Her father came into the living room, and behind him were Shirin and Hugo.

"Alma!" Shirin cried. She ran across the room, then tried to slow down when she saw Alma's bandaged hands and careened backward. Luckily, one of the armchairs broke her fall.

"You can talk in this room for five minutes," her father said. "I will set a timer." Alma's mother, rising from her seat next to Alma, raised her eyebrows at him. "Okay, I won't set a timer, but I will come and get you."

"Okeydoke, Alma Llama Ding Dong?" Alma's mother asked.

"Okeydoke," Alma agreed, surprised that she was allowed to talk to her friends for any minutes.

Her parents left the room, and Shirin and Hugo came to sit on either side of her, Shirin moving at an almost comically slow pace.

"My parents have been totally freaking out," Shirin began. "I'm grounded for life. Even Farah was lecturing me!"

"Then how are you here?" Alma asked. "You didn't—you didn't sneak out, did you?"

"Oh my goodness, no!" Shirin cried. "I don't have a death wish. My parents are actually waiting out front. They drove us because I told them I wanted to check on you and apologize for making everyone go to the creek that first night. They're very into, like, admitting wrongs and all that." Shirin rolled her eyes, then grinned. "Plus, they were kind of impressed when I told them about the supernova and the elements and quintessence and everything I've learned. And Farah wants to go stargazing with us! Everyone said they've never seen me so focused on, well, anything."

"I'm here because Shirin called me," Hugo said. "On the phone. I don't think my mother would have let me go, but no one's ever called me on the phone before." He gave a little shrug. "Also things with Marcus have gotten—well, they're a little better than they were."

Alma smiled back at her friends. It seemed like she wasn't the only one who'd had a Discussion today. Then her smile faded away as she thought of the fourth member of their group.

"Have either of you talked to Dustin?" she asked.

Hugo shook his head, his curls following along. "Did you know I yelled at him?" he said. "I've never done that."

"I was really mad at him too," Shirin admitted. "But he didn't mean for Alma to get hurt."

"I know," Hugo replied, pushing his glasses up and down. "That's not the only reason I yelled, I suppose. I've been angry at him for quite some time." He shrugged. "Although I know I haven't always been the best friend to him either."

"Yeah, you two definitely need to talk," Shirin agreed. "And probably me and Dustin do too. That wasn't why I didn't want to do the bonfire, though. Dustin's way just never seemed right. Fire is your element, Alma, not his."

Sitting with her friends had been having the same effect as sitting with her family had. But now last night was all she could think about again.

"I *thought* it was," she said. She stared down at her bandaged hands, the white wrappings crisscrossing like an endless maze, like a bleached-out bird's nest. "But I was wrong. I don't have an element. And I ruined everything."

Her words were met by silence. When Alma finally looked up, she found Hugo was squinting at her through his visor-glasses, and Shirin had a braid pulled out to each side, her nose scrunched.

"You should stop telling yourself things like that," Hugo said. "Because they aren't true."

"No, they're not!" Shirin cried. "I *know* fire is your element. You believed in the Starling, and you made us believe in her too. You're the one who's kept us going!"

Alma held up her hands. "Then why wasn't I able to get the fire?" she said. "That was our last chance, and now there's nothing we can do!"

"Maybe," Shirin said. "But maybe not. I'm not ready to give up."

"Me neither," Hugo said. "I don't think you are either, Alma. You wouldn't give up on the Starling now. Not you."

Alma was still holding out her hands, still struggling to form words, when her father came back into the room. "Time's up," he said.

CHAPTER 84

After her friends left, Alma headed up to bed. Her parents had agreed to let her sleep in her room that night.

"We'll be checking on you though, Alma," her father had said. "You're going to have to earn our trust back."

In her room, Alma turned out her light. Her curtains were open, and starlight was filtering in, glinting off the element containers on her bookshelf. Without the quintescope, the earth was a dusty rock. The water was muddy and stagnant. And the wind jar looked completely empty, with the windmill barely fluttering within.

Her friends wanted to keep trying. But Alma didn't think she could.

"I'm sorry, Starling," she whispered to the closed window. "I don't know what else to do."

Then there was a knock—the second knock of the night—and Dustin's scowling face appeared.

Alma scrambled over to the window, trying to move quickly so that Dustin wouldn't knock again but not so quickly that her parents or James would hear her. The window was still blocked by the bolts her parents had installed, but she lifted it the six inches she could.

"Hey, were you talking to yourself?" Dustin asked, peering through the opening at her.

"Shh," Alma whispered. "Yes, I was."

"You do that a lot," Dustin said.

"I know," Alma replied. "What are you doing here?"

She noticed suddenly that he looked terrible. There were dark circles around his eyes, and he was chewing on his lip, and his hands kept balling into fists, then opening, over and over.

"I climbed up," he said. "I just—I wanted to tell you that I was sorry. I'm sorry about everything. About pushing you and yelling at you that one day and about—about the fire." He shook his head, eyes down. "I'm so sorry about the fire. My mom told me how bad your hands were."

"Your mom?"

"Yeah, my mom. She said she and Mrs. Johnson were your nurses last night."

Alma pictured the woman with the blond-gray ponytail who had helped her so expertly last night, who had spoken so soothingly. "I thought your mom had panic attacks like me," she said.

Dustin shrugged. "Yeah, but not like twenty-four hours a day. She's still a normal person with a normal job. Anyway, I'm sorry. I don't know why I'm—why I'm not nice. I've always been that way."

"Always? I don't think you can be born not nice," Alma said, tucking what Dustin had said about his mother away to consider later.

"I don't know about that," Dustin replied, gripping the window ledge. "I just know I've never—you know how Shirin is always smiling? And you know how Hugo is—he's always right? He always knows everything."

"I'm not like that though," Alma said. "I'm not always happy. I'm not always right."

"But you have other stuff," Dustin said. "You have ideas and you—you believe in things. Not everyone has that."

It was the same thing that Shirin and Hugo had said, and Alma still didn't know what to make of this, so she said, "Well, you saved me in the Deep Downs."

"Only because it was my fault," Dustin muttered. "And then you saved me."

"You were brave," Alma said. "You *are* brave. And—and determined. You wanted to help us."

"You didn't want me there though. I followed you."

Alma couldn't deny that this was true. "We didn't want you there," she agreed. "And you know why. But maybe now we understand you better, and maybe now you understand us better. I'm glad you were part of our quest. We needed someone determined and brave."

Dustin was quiet for a minute. "I'd rather be happy all the time," he said. "Or know everything."

"No one's happy all the time," Alma said, smiling a little as she said the words that had been said to her over and over again now. "No one can know anything for sure. And no one can be everything. That's why we need each other."

Dustin seemed to consider this for a moment. Then he put his head down and started rooting through something he'd brought with him to the roof. A moment later, he came back up with a gleaming object clutched in his hands.

It was a jar. A bronze-tinted jar with a copper triangle on its rounded side and a bronze cap that he unscrewed and removed. Inside, there was a small copper spike, and Alma watched as Dustin pulled on it, extending it like a radio antenna. The spike, now several feet high, was connected to dozens of strands of copper wiring that filled the bottom of the jar.

The fire jar.

"I found it a while ago," Dustin said. "In the Fifth Point. I think you light the top, like a candle, and then the fire travels down to those little wires. When we were at Hugo's, I thought—I thought that if you lit the fire, I could get the flames in there. I wanted to be the one to do it. I wanted to be—I don't know, part of the Astronomy Club, I guess. But I think I'm supposed to give it to you."

"Why do you think that?" Alma asked.

Dustin placed the jar on the windowsill. "I've been out here for a while," he said. "I came because I thought—I thought I saw a light outside my window."

Alma gasped. "Was it sort of red gold?" she asked, hardly daring to hope.

"No," Dustin said. He shook his head. "It was blue. Anyway, I followed it, and it led me here, to your house. I thought maybe I'd apologize, but then I got nervous. So I went around back, and I saw that crater you told me about. Your quintescope was out there—did you know you left it out there? Here." He grabbed the scope from the roof and shoved it through the gap in the window. "Anyway, I was looking through that, and then I thought I saw that light again, only this time it *was* kind of reddish and gold. But it was inside your house, this light. And it wasn't a star. It was you, Alma. I could see you through your window. And you were shining."

CHAPTER 85

The ShopKeeper did not know if he could go on.

He had been out once already, leading the first Elemental to the third's home. As soon as he had arrived back at the Fifth Point, he had collapsed on the bottom step of the spiral staircase, surrounded by his dolls and clocks and books and vases and quilts and kites. Finally, he had managed to clean and polish and shine each one. Finally, he had put his home in order.

Now he was the only thing in this place that was falling apart. He was the only thing that could not be mended, could not be made new with paint and thread and patience.

But there was still so much to do. Everything had to happen tonight. Tonight or never.

Somehow the Fire had to be gathered. Somehow the Starling had to be found. Somehow Quintessence had to be created.

He had known all along, of course, that this was it. This Starling was the last he would ever be able to help.

Yet to end this way, to fail at the last quest he had set for himself—to let the Starling burn out alone and afraid—it was more than he could stand.

And indeed, he would not stand for it.

All that talk of Quintessence, all that talk of growing Light. Well, wasn't that his truth too?

"Am I not filled with Quintessence as well?" he murmured to the ticking clocks, the polished doll eyes, and the ribbon-tailed kites, to the mended vases and the patched quilts, to the air so bitter and sweet, to the remaining dust motes that may have come from some distant Star he once knew.

The ShopKeeper struggled to his feet. His skin was like a bruise, mottled and indigo. His body felt run-down and weak. His visible light was so dim, he doubted he could illuminate the inside of a thimble.

But he was not ready to give up. No, he would try one last time. He would try for the Starling. He would try for the Elementals. He would try for all of them.

CHAPTER 86

In Alma's room, there was a lovely white wooden bed that she had spent too many nights lying awake in, and recently quite a few nights not lying in at all. In Alma's room, there was a lovely white wooden desk with a collection of Old Haven feathers hanging above. In Alma's room, there was a lovely white wooden bookshelf filled with books with Old Haven flowers pressed inside and a collection of Old Haven rocks and three jars.

A jar of springwater.

A jar with a windmill.

A jar with a dirt-coated rock.

Alma sat on that lovely white wooden bed after Dustin had left. She held the fourth jar as she watched the other three, and she listened to the fearful thoughts that filled her mind.

Now that they know the truth about you, Alma's mind said, *your parents will never trust you again.*

Now that the quest is over, her mind said, *you won't have friends anymore.*

And worst of all, her mind said, *you failed. You didn't get the fire. You didn't save the Starling. Your quintessence is gone, gone, gone.*

And there's nothing to be done.

Alma sat and watched and listened and listened and listened.

But then she lifted the quintescope to her eye.

The springwater glistened. The rock gleamed. The glimmering wind began to blow hard and strong, spinning the windmill faster and faster and faster.

For months, Alma had felt like a failure, like a disappointment. For months, she had felt like a stranger to herself, unknown and unknowable, empty and lost. For months, she had felt like she was far from home.

Then she had done something. She had taken the flyer. She had joined the club. She had asked for Hugo's help. She had followed Shirin into the woods. She had faced an enemy who was becoming a friend. She had connected to a Starling who seemed so much like herself, afraid and alone and hidden.

Time and time again, Alma had taken risks. She had left her safe places and gone out into the world.

And her light had grown and grown and grown.

Her parents still loved her, and they wanted to help her. Shirin and Hugo believed in her. And Dustin, Dustin had said that she was shining.

She didn't feel like it. She didn't feel like she was shining at all.

But that didn't mean she wasn't.

She had been so sure she had failed, but how did she know? What if she could still get the fire? What if the Starling was still out there? What if she could still be saved?

She can't be saved, her mind said. *You can't be saved. There's nothing to be done.*

"For the last time," Alma said out loud. "Be quiet."

She turned the quintescope to the window.

The quintessence that had zigzagged and spiraled through the entire Preserve was gone now. The only gold path that Alma could see was the one that led from the crater into the woods. And the gold still ended in that same place, in the middle of the untended farmland near the silo.

Alma fixed her gaze on the point where the trail left off. If the light was bright there, then the Starling must have come that way recently. She must have returned there again and again. But why? Where was she going?

Alma moved the quintescope, scanning the field, searching for some sign, some light—

Until she saw it.

Something new that hadn't been there before. A slight glimmer next to an opening at the top of the silo. A fresh streak of quintessence.

Alma remembered how the Starling had seemed to disappear

the night she had chased her, vanishing into thin air. And she remembered how the Starling had flown that night on the mountain, leaping into the sky, high, high up.

A clap of thunder startled her from her thoughts. The sound was nearby, not too far from the fields she was watching.

And suddenly, Alma knew what she had to do.

She got out of bed.

She loaded the fire jar and the jar of water and the jar of earth and the jar of wind into her backpack.

She put on her coat.

She took her flashlight and the quintescope.

She was going to gather the last element, her element.

And she was going to save the Starling.

CHAPTER 87

Everyone was asleep as Alma slipped out her bedroom door and padded toward the stairs, shoes in hand. She held her breath as she passed James's room, but there were no sounds from behind his door. Downstairs, her parents had left their bedroom door open, and Alma crept through the shadows of the living room until she was clear of it.

Her greatest hurdle, however, was her own guilt, heavy as a stone in her stomach. She had told her parents the truth about herself only hours before, and now she was back to lying.

She left a note, scribbled hastily, on the table by the red-plaid couch:

There is someone I need to help. I will explain everything when I get home. Don't worry.

Once she made it outside, Alma headed toward the back of the yard, then past the crater, until she came to the first singed tree.

Here was the trail that the Starling had taken that first night. If she was reading the quintessence right, it was a path the Starling had traversed many times since then.

The Starling had followed Alma up the mountain. She had followed her to the Deep Downs. She had stayed near Alma's home, coming to her backyard over and over.

Maybe the Starling knew all along what Alma had doubted so many times: that Alma could help her get home.

Alma hurried from one blackened patch of bark to the next, guided by her flashlight and the still-lingering smell of burned wood. The misting rain that wanted to be snow had returned again. It filtered through the still-leafless branches, settling on her coat in tiny, rounded domes that collapsed into wet circles. The moon was not in the sky that night, but looking up, Alma could see the evening star that was the morning star that was the planet Venus, and she could see real stars, although, she realized, she didn't know what any of them were called except Betelgeuse, the red supergiant that was destined to explode sometime in the next million years.

Then Alma was out of the woods, and the farmland was spread out before her, barely visible in the light of those unknown stars.

Even in the limited light though, Alma could tell that the fields of Third Point Farm were blackened. It was a good thing that no one had tried to grow anything there for many years, because any crops would have been reduced to ash. The air was thick with the smell of old, wet kindling, and Alma wondered if the Starling had done it or if the fire had been the one she was supposed to gather, and now she was too late. She swept her flashlight across the field until it came to rest on the silo, towering high above the ravaged farmland.

"There," she said.

There was where the Starling was hiding.

This was what Alma had realized as she gazed through the quintescope from her bedroom window. She could picture how it had happened—the Starling soaring into the air and diving into the opening in the silo the night that she fled from Alma. She must have returned here, to this safe place, time after time.

Alma hoped she was there now.

Charred stubble crunched beneath her feet, and the wind blew ash into her face as she trekked across the field. The silo was the color of rust, except at the top where it was soot black. When Alma grew closer, she saw that there was a ladder up its side.

The silo was rusty, but the ladder looked like it was made *entirely* of rust. When Alma pushed against the lowest rung, it didn't creak or shift though. It seemed sturdy enough. So she began to climb, her bandaged hands clumsy and sore.

The opening was near the top of the ladder. And when Alma was high enough, she leaned toward the hole, flashlight in hand, breath in her throat, hope in her heart, and she peered in.

The silo was empty.

CHAPTER 88

Alma was still high up and whole, but her heart and her hope felt broken and low as she swept the flashlight beam around the metal interior of the silo again. And again and again.

Nothing.

She had been so certain the Starling would be there. Her hands ached from gripping the ladder and the flashlight. The books of fear began to open.

Then a bolt of lightning ripped across the sky, a line of light like a door cracked in a darkened room, and thunder sounded, closer this time.

Alma shoved the flashlight back into her pocket and reached up for the next ladder rung.

The Starling was not there, but that was not the only reason she had come to this silo.

Alma was almost to the top when the storm that had been threat-ening to break loose for weeks finally swept in.

Wind whipped through the burned fields. Lightning struck, illu-minating the farmland and the woods beyond. Thunder rumbled a second later, and the silo thrummed, its metal sides vibrating with the sound.

Alma climbed the last few rungs.

The top of the silo was rounded, with a flat circle at its center. The smell of smoke was stronger, and it was clear that lightning had struck there before. There were sagging, blackened patches and tiny holes in the dome, places where fire had eaten away at the metal surface.

Alma scrambled her way up the curving slope and to the center. She knelt there and opened her bag as lightning flashed again, fol-lowed immediately by thunder. Fumbling with her gauze-covered hands, she drew out the fire jar with the copper spike.

It wasn't a candle, she had realized in her room as she watched the storm approaching.

It was a lightning rod.

Transforming the energy of lightning into true fire was an idea that Hugo had mentioned many times—in the General Store while they were gathering supplies, during his lecture with the image of the flaming forest under a forked-lightning sky, and as a possible solution suggested by Mrs. Brisa. It had seemed impossible because lightning was so powerful, but Alma understood now how it would work with the fire jar. She removed the lid and pulled the spike out to its full length.

The lightning would spark the fire just like the flyer and the quintescope and the Starling had sparked her Alma-ness weeks ago.

So Alma stood atop the silo in the middle of the burned fields with the wind howling and the rain falling and the stars shining.

"I am Alma of the Growing Light!" she called to the wind and the earth and the water and the stars, to everything, everything around her. "And I am here for fire!"

She lifted the jar into the air. The metal rod extended upward, pointing up to the heavens, up to those billions and trillions of stars whose names she did not yet know, those stars shining with the light that shone inside her.

Alma felt like that light was flowing into her, flowing in through her eyes, into her body, meeting her Alma-ness, until she felt like another star herself.

She felt as bright as the Starling had been that first night.

Then the thunder crashed, and the lightning flashed. The sky was split wide open, split by a jagged line.

A jagged line that dead-ended at the copper rod on the fire jar that Alma was lifting up high.

Suddenly, the world was alight. The world was on fire. And Alma was flying. She heard the wind screaming through the silo's burned-out holes. She felt the rain, sharp and stinging on her face. And the earth, the earth was reaching up to meet her.

Alma fell from the silo. She fell and fell.

Until something caught her.

Something warm and strong.

Something that sang like a thousand bells.

Something that carried her, gently, gently, down to the ground, where the world went dark.

CHAPTER 89

Alma woke up.

At first, her vision was checkered with black. Her mouth felt dry, and her body was stiff. She was lying on the ground, flat on her back.

The jar, clutched in her hand, was full of fire. Every copper tip flickered with red-gold flames.

And next to her was the Starling.

Right away, it was clear to Alma that the Starling did not have long left. She wasn't glowing, not one bit. Her skin was dull and flat, like tarnished metal. Her eyes were closed. Her hair was limp and tangled. The sound coming from her was low-pitched and dragging, like the tolling of a funeral bell.

"Can you hear me?" Alma whispered.

The Starling stirred. Two great black eyes blinked open. Alma held her breath as the Starling's gaze focused on her for a moment. There was light inside the Starling, at least. Alma could see it. But it was so dim, it was so weak.

The Starling's eyes closed again.

"Hold on," Alma said. "I'm going to get you home."

Alma placed the fire jar and the quintescope into her backpack, and pulled the straps on. She put her flashlight into her pocket. Bending down, she lifted the Starling with her now-dingy-gray-bandaged hands and cradled her like an infant, her long limbs hanging limply down.

And then Alma, with her light burning and growing inside her, set out.

To the south was the silo, smoking and smoldering. To the east, Second Point Peak towered above like some watchful stone giant. To the west, there were trees, their roots drinking from the source of the Fourth Point Creek. And who knew how far the Deep Downs extended? Maybe its tunnels were beneath her feet even here.

Alma wasn't going to any of those places though. She was heading to the center of town, to the very center.

The ShopKeeper had told her to come to the top at the end.

This, she was certain, was the end.

Alma set out for the Fifth Point.

PART 9

Quintessence

CHAPTER 90

Engraved in the ladder rungs on the south side of the Fifth Point were letters that were no longer blackened by time and pollution and oxygen. They were gold now, and the words were illuminated by the stars:

> *Come right up, dear souls.*
> *See the lights above.*
> *Grow the Light inside.*

Alma stood at the base of the ladder after a long walk through the stormy, middle-of-the-night empty streets. She wanted to come right up. She wanted to see the lights. She wanted to grow the light.

But she was carrying a pack full of elements on her back, and she was carrying a Starling in her aching, burned hands, and she had been struck by lightning and thrown off a silo and she had not slept enough in almost three weeks.

She wished that her friends were there to help her.

She shifted the Starling so that she was upright, her forehead pressing against Alma's shoulder. When Alma had first picked her up, the star-child had felt so fragile and light, and now she was practically weightless, as if her insides were almost empty, as if she was little more than a shell of herself.

"Can you hold on?" she whispered, and the Starling's small hands wrapped around her neck and held on.

It was the best Alma could do. She started to climb her second ladder of the night.

Every step was a struggle. Every rung bit into her hands. She wanted to stop. She wanted to cry. Instead, she climbed onward, upward, until she reached the top.

At the center of the platform, there was a small metal door with a handle. Alma gently laid the Starling next to it. The wind whipped around them, up so high, and the clouds appeared, then vanished, appeared, then vanished, as lightning flashed within them. Alma had been sure the ShopKeeper would be waiting here, but he wasn't. She didn't know what to do next.

The Starling let out a small, whimpering chime.

"Don't worry, Starling," Alma said, pulling off her backpack. "I'll figure it out."

She unloaded the element jars and the quintescope. The book

had said that connecting the true elements would produce quintessence, but it hadn't given any other instructions. It was up to her to decide what to do.

"I'm going to mix them together," she told the Starling after a long moment of hesitation. "That should do it."

First, she opened the fire jar. The flames inside flickered steady and strong. To this jar, Alma added the earth. When they joined together, the two elements burned all the brighter, all the more brilliantly, sending out sparks and flares.

"It's working," Alma whispered. "Almost there."

What could she add next though? The water might put the fire out. Perhaps the wind had to come next.

Alma opened the wind jar—

And the air came whooshing out. Alma jumped to her feet and pressed the quintescope to her eye, thinking she could somehow scoop the wind back into its container. She saw the shining, dancing silver light, but it was flying up into the sky, scattering like dandelion seeds. Then it blew to the west, back to where it had come from, back to Second Point Peak.

Alma fell to her knees. In desperation, she grabbed the jar of water, uncorked it, and dumped it into the fire container.

The fire went out. Black smoke rose up from the jar, smoke tinged with the acrid scent of burned metal. Alma stared down in horror at what she had done. The elements were all either gone or ruined now.

And next to her, the Starling was silent, not moving, not shining at all.

"Starling," Alma whispered. She touched the small copper hand carefully. It was cold, cold, cold.

"Starling!" she cried, shaking the Starling's arm now. "Starling, hold on. You can't burn out yet!"

The Starling didn't open her eyes.

After everything, Alma had failed. She had failed. She felt her throat tighten. She felt her heart pounding faster and faster and faster. The books in her mind began to open.

But then Alma took a deep breath. She took another one. And another one and another one.

"Quintessence and elements," she whispered to herself.

Then she banged on the trapdoor with all her might.

"ShopKeeper!" she shouted. "ShopKeeper, we're here! This is the end, and we're here, and we need help!"

CHAPTER 91

There was a noise inside the Fifth Point. Something was moving, slowly, slowly. Something was climbing stairs, *thud*, *thud*, *thudding* with heavy, labored steps.

The trapdoor opened.

And out of it climbed a creature with mottled, violet-blue skin. The creature was thin, with long limbs, and there was little hair on his oversize head. He carried a quintescope in his hands, and inside his enormous indigo eyes, there was only the faintest flicker of light.

He was a star, Alma could see that, but he was a worn, bruised, exhausted star.

A worn, bruised, exhausted star that she recognized.

"I know you, don't I?" Alma whispered, pushing her words past the tightness of her throat, over the pounding of her heartbeat.

The ShopKeeper smiled at her as he sank down next to the Starling. "In a way," he said. "In several ways, actually, Alma of the Growing Light."

"Dr. Parry," Alma breathed in recognition. "You're Dr. Parry!" She turned her head from one side to the other. "And you're also—you kind of look like Susie, the librarian. And the—the bus driver—Celcy." She gasped, hands pressed to her cheeks. "Parry. Celcy. Susie. Paracelsus! You're Paracelsus!"

"The *true* Paracelsus," the ShopKeeper corrected.

"You wrote the book! And you're the ShopKeeper! But how?" Alma asked, too overwhelmed to sort through her revelations.

The ShopKeeper wanted to be sensitive. He wanted to explain things slowly and patiently. He wanted to tell his story. It was, he had to admit, a spellbinding story full of identity changes and fact-finding missions and, above all else, the light of the stars.

But, looking at the Starling next to him, touching her much-too-cold cheek, he knew there wasn't time for that.

"Oh, I've been many things," the ShopKeeper said, his melodic voice now barely more than a rasp. "With the right disguise, even the brightest of stars can live among you elementals. I've been a doctor, an alchemist, a preacher, an illuminist, a dancer—briefly though, not enough starlight-coverage in those leotards. My life's work, however, has been helping the fallen to rise. I find fallen stars, and I find the elementals who can send those stars home—elementals like you. For centuries I have done this, and I have taught

333

many other stars around the world to do the same. And tonight, I would very much like to send this young Starling home, but I will need your assistance. Can you help me, Alma of the Growing Light?"

Alma listened to this with wide, amazed eyes. The ShopKeeper watched her, hoping that he had not been wrong after all, hoping that this girl was truly of fire.

When she started to nod, he closed his eyes in relief. But when he opened them again, she was shaking her head.

"I can't," Alma said, tears spilling down her cheeks. "I had the elements, just like the book said. But now—now look. I ruined everything."

The ShopKeeper followed Alma's pointing finger and saw the jar for the first time, filled with dirty water and a burned stone. "Oh, I see, I see," he said. "Yes, indeed, those true elements are ruined. Luckily for us, there are other true elements, even greater ones, that are still very much intact."

"Where?" Alma asked the ShopKeeper, who, through her tears, was a blue smudge against the black sky.

"Tell me," the ShopKeeper said, "did you find these elements alone?"

Alma shook her head. "No. I had help. My friend Shirin led us to the water. Hugo got the wind. And Dustin, he found the earth."

"And you?" the ShopKeeper prompted. "What was your element, my dear soul?"

"Fire," Alma said. "I found fire."

The ShopKeeper clapped his hands together. "I knew it," he said. "And I see you have your quintescope. Marvelous! Let's find the other three, shall we?"

The ShopKeeper rose laboriously to his feet, his quintescope in his hands. Alma followed him to the west point of the platform, where he positioned the scope on the railings and pressed an eye to the glass.

"One!" he cried, growing more animated by the second. "Do you want to see?"

Alma pointed her quintescope in the same direction. For a moment, she saw only the dark outlines of houses and trees, but then—

There was Shirin, running toward the Fifth Point.

A rainbow light streamed from behind her, like a cape, like a banner. And in her center, there was a sphere of golden light.

The ShopKeeper was moving across the platform, crossing to the east side. Looking through his scope, he sang out, "Two!"

Alma hurried over, held up her quintescope and—

There was Hugo, a silver spotlight streaking toward the middle of town, with that same golden sphere inside.

"Three!"

The ShopKeeper was on the north point now, and when Alma reached him and peered down, she saw him—

Dustin. He was barreling toward the Fifth Point, lit with a rusty light, and at his center, there was gold, gold, gold.

The ShopKeeper did a little dance, brandishing the scope above his head. "Here they come, here they come! And oh, aren't they shining so brightly with their own quintessences? We just may do it! Now you."

He lifted the quintescope and pointed it right at Alma. She was reminded of how he had studied her that first day in the Fifth Point. *Only a spark*, he had said. *But it's growing!* She held her breath, wondering what he would see now.

"Glorious!" the ShopKeeper cried. "Wondrous! Extraordinary! Alma of the Growing Light, you are filled with quintessence! A quintessence with a heavy dose of fire—true fire. Can you feel it?"

Alma knelt down next to the Starling. She stroked the little figure's knotted, dulled hair and thought of the many adventures of that night, the many adventures of the past three weeks. Now, finally, finally, they were going to send the Starling home.

That made her feel brighter than she had ever felt.

"I can," she said.

"That is good," the ShopKeeper replied. "Because it's time."

CHAPTER 92

Someone was on the ladder. No, not someone. Someones. Three elementals were climbing, one up the north side, one up the east, and one up the west. Climbing to the top of the Fifth Point, where a Starling and a star and the final elemental were waiting.

"Alma, oh my goodness! Are you up there?" It was Shirin's voice calling over the sound of the thunder and wind.

"We're coming! Hang on." That was Dustin.

And Hugo was there too. "We are extremely high!" he was shouting.

Up on the platform, the ShopKeeper was doubled over, hands on knees, his skin a blotchy midnight blue.

"You should know, Alma of the Growing Light," he said with a gasp, "that I am going to go out soon. This very night, I believe."

Alma, still next to the Starling, looked up with alarm. "Go out?"

she said. "You're a star though. We can—can't we send you back too? Can't we send you home?"

"Oh, my dear soul," the ShopKeeper whispered, "I am home. This is my home now. You, I think, understand that." He closed his eyes for a moment, inhaled a shaky breath, then continued. "I was the first to learn how to create quintessence and send stars back to the sky. Once I had learned such a powerful secret, I couldn't leave. The stars needed me. This world needed me. So I created a new life for myself here. And it has been glorious. My only regret is that I will not end as a supernova. I always thought that would be a marvelous thing—to return to the universe and beyond!" He straightened up, and he seemed to suddenly brighten. "To become part of what I have loved so deeply as I move on to whatever comes next!" His voice rang out from the tower, down to Four Points below. Then he gave a shrug and dimmed again. "But I have made my peace with that."

Alma did not feel at peace with that. She did not want any stars to go out, not after she had spent so much time saving the Starling. She wanted to say more, but the footsteps on the ladder had come to an end.

Dustin reached the top first, bursting onto the platform like he was ready to charge into battle. Shirin came next, stumbling off her ladder with her mouth agape and her eyes shining. Finally, Hugo arrived, gripping the railing with both hands but still moving forward.

There they were, three friends, each on a corner of the platform, coming to meet the Starling and the ShopKeeper and Alma.

"Ah!" the ShopKeeper cried, spreading his tiny, slender arms wide. "Here you all are at long last! Shall we begin?"

CHAPTER 93

The ShopKeeper was certainly a strange sight to take in, and for a long moment, no one spoke.

Finally, Hugo asked, "What exactly is happening here?"

"I saw a light outside my window," Shirin said, words tumbling out of her mouth. "A blue light. I thought—I thought it might be the Starling. So I followed it."

"Me too!" Dustin shouted.

"Me three," Hugo said.

The ShopKeeper clapped his hands and gave a little leap. "Oh, that was me!" he cried. "I needed to bring you here, you see. Because the time is now, now is the time. We have a Starling to send home."

Shirin's eyes widened, as she looked past the ShopKeeper for the first time. "The Starling!" she shrieked. "Alma, you found her."

"I did," Alma said from the platform floor. She didn't want to leave the Starling's side. "Well, actually, she found me."

"I require further information," Hugo said, his voice robotic and stiff. "Where are the elements? What is the protocol? How do we create the quintessence?"

"Not to worry, Hugo of the Growing Light," the ShopKeeper said. "The quintessence is already created. It is inside you! Isn't that extraordinary? That was the secret I learned many, many years ago. That is why I had you gather water, wind, earth, and fire. As you collected those elements, one connected to each of you, you grew the elements inside you. And when your element grows—when it grows true and strong—your quintessence brightens as well."

Alma's hand was on the Starling's heart as she listened, and the star-child was colder than ever, duller and more tarnished than ever. "What do we do, ShopKeeper?" Alma asked.

The ShopKeeper beamed at each of them in turn. "This," he sang, "is my favorite part! My dear souls, each of you is filled with that wondrous light, but alone you could never send a star home. You are only elementals, after all. That is why four are needed: One elemental of water"—he pointed to Shirin at the west point of the platform—"one of wind"—to Hugo on the east point—"one of earth"—to Dustin on the north point—"and one of fire." Instead of pointing, he reached his hand down to Alma. "To the south of the platform, Alma of the Growing Light."

Alma pressed her hand to the Starling's heart one last time. Then she picked up her quintescope and took her place. She stood with her friends, each on a point of the platform, with the Starling and the ShopKeeper in the center.

"Do we have to do something?" Dustin cried. "Like say a magic spell or—or hold hands or something?"

"You are already doing it," the ShopKeeper said. He was swaying in the wind, as if he might topple over at any moment. But he stayed upright. He kept on. "You created this quintessence for the Starling, to save her. You created it together. That quintessence will go where it is meant to go."

As he finished speaking, in the center of the platform, the Starling began to glow.

CHAPTER 94

Brighter and brighter and brighter the Starling grew, brighter and brighter until she seemed to be made of nothing but light, until Alma could hardly look at her. Beneath them, the town of Four Points was illuminated by the pulsing, shimmering copper glow, and all sound—the howling wind, the rolling thunder, the creak of the tower, Alma's own heartbeat and breath—was drowned out by the rising star song. It was a song of bells, ringing and ringing, not a funeral toll now but wild and wondrous.

And it wasn't only the Starling who was changing. The Shop-Keeper was suddenly shining too.

"How glorious!" he cried, holding his hands up in amazement. "This has never happened to me before. But stars are always brightest before the end!"

The bell sound rang on. The light grew. The ShopKeeper laughed a high, delighted laugh and began to sing his own star song.

Then the Starling stood up.

She was, once again, luminous and other-worldly, the most beautiful thing Alma had ever seen. Her hair was aloft, blown by her own stellar winds. Her body was in perpetual motion, stretching her slender arms out, twisting from side to side with her face tilted toward the sky. Then she turned to the south point of the platform.

With her eyes burning like two embers, the Starling—strange but familiar, distant but near, the same but extraordinary—smiled and held up one hand to Alma.

And Alma was sure that the song she was singing was for her. She was sure that she had done the something that she was meant to do and that a universe of somethings was now open to her.

"Goodbye," Alma whispered, holding up her own hand. "Goodbye, Starling."

Then the light intensified and the bell sound shifted into a high-pitched sustained note that seemed to be on the precipice of breaking and—

The Starling and the ShopKeeper—the two stars—began to rise.

"Until we meet again." The ShopKeeper's voice rang out across the town. "By and by, my dear souls! By and by!"

Two lights shot up through the blackness of the sky, one small and copper, one blazingly blue. Up and up they went, up toward the stars that seemed to be waiting for them, back to the place in the universe that they had once called home.

But before he had gone too far, the brilliant blue star—the ShopKeeper—broke free.

For a moment, Alma thought he was going to fall. She let out a cry and pressed the quintescope to her eye.

He had changed, the ShopKeeper. He was no longer human-shaped but a round, fiery ball. He was not quite a star, small as he was, but he was certainly not a creature of Earth.

And he was filled, brimming, overflowing with quintessence.

Then the sky was awash in blue and gold brilliance as the Shop-Keeper got his wish, his last wish.

"Glorious," Alma whispered, as she watched the supernova expand and brighten, as the gold light flowed up into space and down to the earth, from home to home, and who could say for certain where else.

And far, far above, a copper star glowed and twinkled, smaller and smaller, as she went up and up, closer and closer to her place in the Universe.

"Oh my goodness." Shirin was running across the star-shaped platform, braids streaming, eyes enormous. She flung herself at Alma, who caught her. "This is amazing!"

"Zounds!" Hugo cried, crossing carefully to the south point. "Zonks."

Dustin came to stand by them but didn't say a word.

They passed the quintescope around, watching the Shop-Keeper's supernova, watching until the Starling seemed to be stationary. Up in the sky, there was a star where there had been a blank space before. Her red-gold light twinkled, as if she was sending a message to the Earth below.

345

"Look how bright she's shining!" Shirin cried, pointing with both braids and smiling her widest smile.

Alma knew that she was shining too.

She was made of elements. She was made of fire, and made of water and wind and earth.

She was filled with quintessence.

They all were.

PART 10

The Fifth Point

·················

✦

CHAPTER 95

Alma could have stood at the top of the Fifth Point for the rest of the night. She could have stood there for a lifetime of nights, staring up at the Starling shining down on them, basking in the quintessence that filled the air.

However, around the iron spire, lights were turning on. Apparently, having a star—even a very, very small one—go supernova directly above them was enough to wake up the town of Four Points.

The four friends hurried down their ladders, and there was no time to meet up at the bottom, no time to talk. Alma raced toward Third Point, the jars of ruined elements in her backpack, her quintescope in hand.

She flew down the streets, as fast as she could go, until she saw a car coming her way.

The car jerked to a stop. The doors opened. Her parents and James came running toward her.

And Alma ran toward them.

CHAPTER 96

Of course, Alma was grounded. Big-time grounded. Maybe for-life grounded.

The next day, she slept, soundly and deeply, for the first time in a long time. When she finally woke up, she talked to her family, giving answers that seemed impossible but that were true nonetheless. They didn't believe her, of course, not about everything, but Alma knew that she couldn't lie anymore.

On Monday, Alma went to a doctor's appointment where her burns were cleaned and redressed, but she didn't go to school. Her parents were too worried to let her out of their sight. Alma didn't blame them, but that evening, at dinner, she decided it was time for another Discussion.

"The old school psychologist is . . . gone now," she said, "but I think I'd like to see someone else. I mean, I think it might help."

Alma met with her new therapist, Vera, the very next day. Vera didn't give Alma a butterscotch candy from her boot and she didn't talk about quintessence or elements. But she listened, and she explained panic attacks again, and she talked with Alma's parents and then with Alma about what she had already done and what she could continue to do.

It was, Alma thought, her second-best therapy appointment ever.

CHAPTER 97

Almost three weeks later, the doorbell rang at the Lucas house.

Alma was still grounded. She'd had two panic attacks since the night at the top of the Fifth Point, but Vera had not been worried by this and Alma wasn't either.

"Panic attacks are very treatable," Vera had told her, "but nothing happens overnight."

"Will they be gone forever though?" Alma had asked. "How can we be sure?"

"You can never be sure of anything," Vera had said. "All you can do is tell your truth, ask for help, give help, and do the things that make you feel like yourself."

So that was what Alma had been doing. She ate lunch with her friends every day. She did her homework, most of the time. She left her classes when the bell rang, moving through the halls with the rest of the students.

In spite of being grounded, she had seen more of Four Points than ever before—by day, at least. She had hiked up Second Point Peak with her mother one Saturday morning, and they had lain at the top and watched the clouds go by. On Monday afternoons, she and her father started going to Bean There Donut That for coffee and hot chocolate and conversation that didn't include brow-furrowing or finger-lacing. She had explored the backyard, picking and drying the wildflowers that were beginning to blossom as April progressed and the warmth that had eluded the town for so long finally settled in.

And now she was opening the door.

"Oh my goodness!" cried Shirin, throwing herself at Alma. "It's been forever!"

"I saw you at lunch today." Alma laughed.

"Yeah, but I used to see you like every single night," Shirin said without releasing Alma. "Thirty minutes while I shove pizza in my face is not nearly enough."

Shirin stopped hugging Alma then because her sister gave one of her braids a little tug. "Are you going to formally introduce me to the famous Alma or what, Shir?" Farah asked. "And then you have to show me this quintescope you've been talking nonstop about."

Shirin's whole family had come over. Hugo, his mother, Marcus, and the twins were right behind them, and a little later Dustin, his mother, and his three younger brothers arrived. It was the get-together that Alma had once tried to put off and had now been looking forward to all week.

They had a cookout in the backyard, where the crater was now covered in a layer of new, green grass. Hugo, Farah, and a somewhat awkward-looking James were involved in a very intense science-y conversation that Alma had been unable to decipher. Marcus, Alma's mother, Shirin's mother, and Shirin were laughing uproariously about something, about everything, at the picnic table. Alma's father was cleaning up and explaining real estate law to a serious-faced Dustin, who was following him and nodding along, while Shirin's father, Hugo's mother, and Dustin's mother talked quietly and watched the younger kids climb trees and pick flowers and run in and out of the crater.

Alma moved from group to group, mostly listening, mostly just feeling content and at home, until the sun set.

"It's getting dark out," Alma's mother said, coming up and putting her arm around her. "Are you ready to go?"

"Ready," Alma replied. "Let's go to the Fifth Point."

CHAPTER 98

Alma's father had not wanted her to go to the Fifth Point, but he had agreed, at Vera's urging, on a number of conditions.

"You and I can go up together for two minutes," he had said at first. "I'll set a timer."

The next day, he had amended this. "We can go up for exactly ten minutes. We might as well see a few things while we're up there."

Finally, only yesterday, he had agreed that Alma and her friends could climb the tower alone while the families waited in Bean There Donut That. "We will join you," he had said, "after half an hour."

"Perfect," Alma had replied, smiling and meaning it. "That sounds perfect."

When Alma, Hugo, Shirin, and Dustin reached the Fifth Point, they tried the four doors, but they were all locked. They peered through the windows—not as clean after nearly three weeks of neglect, but certainly nowhere near their previous dismal state—and saw the changes the ShopKeeper had made on the first floor.

The dolls were lined up next to one another. The kites and model planes hung from the ceiling. Clock pendulums swung back and forth, back and forth. The entire shop seemed to be waiting, waiting for what would come next.

"What do you think will happen?" Shirin asked, her voice quiet and solemn. "Like, who gets the shop?"

"Yeah, I doubt the star had any kids," Dustin said.

Alma remembered what the ShopKeeper had said to her on the tower. "There are others," she told them. "Other fallen stars living among us. Maybe one of them will come here."

"Ooh, what if?" Shirin cried.

"I would like to meet another star," Hugo said. "I have many questions."

Alma nodded. "Me too," she said. "Although I also have a lot more answers now than I ever thought I would."

They each climbed up their ladder. On the platform, Hugo, Shirin, and Dustin set up their telescopes, and Alma set up her quintescope, easily and without hesitation now.

Dustin showed them the hazy band of the Milky Way, and Hugo found galaxies within the Leo constellation and the Owl Nebula in Ursa Major. Shirin pointed out the stars her mother had been teaching her and told them some of the Arabic names. Alma showed them the spheres of quintessence and watched the Starling twinkling, which she did nearly every night.

And then a light came streaking across the sky.

"It's the April Lyrids," Hugo told them. "A meteor shower. It happens every year around this time. Fascinating fact: it was first recorded in Zuo's *Commentary*, where it says 'stars fell like rain' in 687 BCE."

It seemed like only a few minutes had passed before their families emerged from the coffee shop. From her perch above, Alma pointed her quintescope at them.

In each one of them there was a light, some big and burning, some small and growing. Alma could see the light inside all these people who had become her home, who were heading up the streets that had become her home, toward her, at home in herself.

They came up the ladders, every one of them, even though Alma's father expressed concern about the construction and durability of the platform several times. They stood together and watched the night sky from the top of the Fifth Point, from the top of the world, it seemed.

And down below them, the words that the ShopKeeper had polished shone and glistened, waiting, beckoning, welcoming:

Come right up, dear souls.
See the lights above.
Grow the Light inside.

Acknowledgments

"A book, too, can be a star . . . a living fire to lighten the darkness, leading out into the expanding universe."
—Madeleine L'Engle

All my thanks to everyone who contributed so many elements to the creation of this *Quintessence* star, including:

- My brilliant editor, Janine O'Malley, who is almost definitely a fallen star on a quest to bring light and love to the world through words.
- My stellar agent, Sara Crowe, who is probably made entirely of quintessence. Yes, she's that awesome.
- Melissa Warten, who I thank my lucky stars for every day. Seriously. Thank you.
- Hayley Jozwiak and Chandra Wohleber, guiding stars who have kept me from crashing into so many asteroids.
- Elizabeth Clark, whose gorgeous book design has me over the moon once again.

- Matt Rockefeller, for dazzling me with another glorious cover illustration.
- JP Coovert, for making a map to the stars!
- The entire team at FSG and Macmillan Children's, including Jen Besser, Madison Furr, Katie Quinn, Katie Halata, and many more. There would be no *Quintessence* without your wisdom, passion, energy, and support.
- Holly McGhee and everyone at Pippin Properties—what brightness you bring to our little planet!
- My early readers and advisers, whose feedback and encouragement sparked me again and again: Sarah Baughman, Luisa Brown, Sheena Wilber, Meghan Mayo, Sarah and Mani Amini, Meagan Bandy Bell, and Brigid Misselhorn.
- A Novel Bunch, for their stellar support and enthusiasm. My book club is the best of all book clubs.
- The kidlit community—teachers, librarians, fellow authors, story lovers. If books are stars, then we are the intergalactic travelers, and I'm so grateful I get to cross this universe with all of you.
- Every reader of this story, especially those of you who feel lonely or lost or out of place. I hope this story makes you feel lighter, brighter. I hope this story helps you feel found.
- My parents, for always listening to my truth and for always believing that I could do anything, even when I didn't believe it myself.

- Russ, who complements and inspires and sparks me. Together, we can do all the somethings.
- And finally, to Coral Mae and Everett Reef, who bring immeasurable light to my life and the world. I love you both to the farthest reaches of this ever-expanding universe and beyond.

Onward! Ever onward!

Keep reading for an excerpt.

CHAPTER 1

A Letter for Milton P. Greene

On June 3 of the Most Totally, Terribly, Horribly, Heinously Rotten Year of All Time, a letter was delivered to Milton P. Greene's house. The envelope had probably been white once, but now it was a sort of phlegmy green, and it was covered in about a hundred stamps. That letter had traveled a long, long way.

Only moments after the letter's arrival, a bus pulled up at the corner.

And even before the doors could fully open, Milton P. Greene squeezed himself out onto the sidewalk and took off running.

From behind him, he could hear someone calling, "See you tomorrow, Elaina!"

"Bye, Nico!" someone else shouted.

"So long!" Milton hollered over his shoulder. "Until we meet again!"

No one yelled *So long, Milton!* back, but he hadn't really expected anyone to. Milton had been practically so-longless for the entire Most Totally, Terribly, Horribly, Heinously Rotten Year of All Time and completely so-longless since the Bird Brain Incident.

As expected as it was, the silence still felt like some great, invisible hand reaching out from the bus and shoving him forward, shoving him away. Milton stumbled, then raced on, a small, pale bespectacled blur with an oversize backpack beelining toward home.

Where the letter was waiting.

But when Milton reached his house, he didn't take so much as a peek inside the mailbox that hung beneath the doorbell. He didn't see the bills or the credit card offers or the dental-cleaning reminder (*We miss seeing your smile!*)—or the phlegmy-green envelope.

He flung open his front door and threw himself inside.

The house that Milton ran through was empty. His mother had been working more and more lately, but she'd told him she would be home at 5:50, and she was a very punctual lady.

His father, however, would not be coming home at 5:50 or 6:15 or midnight or ever. He had moved out three months ago, and now Milton only saw him on Tuesday afternoons and every other weekend.

Milton's former best friend, Dev, who used to go on backyard expeditions and play video games with him after school, wouldn't be coming over either. Dev had hardly spoken to Milton since November.

Yes, it had been a rough year. It had been the Most Totally, Terribly, Horribly, Heinously Rotten Year of All Time.

Except for one thing.

The thing that Milton was running to.

Isle of Wild.

In his room, Milton collapsed onto his bed and pulled his HandHeld out from under his pillow. He had finally convinced his parents to buy him the HandHeld last summer, when things had already begun to get a little rotten around the edges. He used to sneak it to school every day, but after the Bird Brain Incident, his mother started checking his backpack before he left to catch the bus. She didn't always remember, but she had remembered this morning, much to his dismay.

Breathless, Milton jabbed at the *Power* button. Then he pressed the green-eyed-bobcat icon.

It seemed to take too long, it seemed to take forever, but then—

Isle of Wild's opening story began.

Sea Hawk Ferox, Naturalist and Explorer Extraordinaire, came bursting onto the screen. Dashing, brawny, and brilliant, Sea Hawk had been en route to the Flora & Fauna Federation headquarters when his ship had capsized in a raging tempest. He had washed ashore on an uninhabited island where he found a most unusual mixture of flora and fauna, including umbrellabirds, corpse flowers, aardvarks, and a miniature green-eyed bobcat that he named Dear Lady DeeDee.

Instead of trying to escape from the island, Sea Hawk (somehow still sporting his signature straw hat with a peacock feather tucked in the band) had opened his (somehow not waterlogged) field journal and set off into the underbrush with his new feline friend.

On the HandHeld's screen now, Sea Hawk was leaping out of a towering redwood, DeeDee perched on his shoulder, binoculars around his neck.

"The adventure is now!" he cried, his voice deep and booming and chock-full of awesomeness.

"The adventure is now," Milton agreed. "And boy, am I ready."

With a lung-emptying sigh of relief, Milton shed his skinny, bespectacled, Bird-Brained, un-so-longed, soon-to-be-divorced-parented skin and became Sea Hawk—dashing, brawny, and brilliant.

It was the best feeling he'd had all day.

He didn't know that twenty feet away, a message from another island was waiting.

The Lone Island.

He didn't know that an adventure was just around the corner.

Not an adventure for Sea Hawk.

An adventure for Milton P. Greene.

CHAPTER 2

Mortal Peril

On June 4 of the Most Totally, Terribly, Horribly, Heinously Rotten Year of All Time, at exactly 5:52, Milton P. Greene's mother handed him the letter from the Lone Island.

Well, she tried to, anyway. Milton was in his room again, lying on his bed playing *Isle of Wild*. And *Isle of Wild* required two hands.

"Milton, turn that off for a minute," said Milton's father.

Since Milton's father had not set foot inside the house in three months, his inexplicable presence was enough to make Milton jerk his head up in surprise. As soon as he did, however, there was a howl of pain from the HandHeld.

"I definitely will," Milton said, returning his gaze to the screen, "as soon as Sea Hawk is out of mortal peril."

Sea Hawk was currently being pursued by the huge-eyed, many-appendaged cephalopod he had been observing. While Sea Hawk carried a machete in his utility belt, he didn't use it on the island's fauna. He was a naturalist, after all. He explored and studied and researched. He did not de-appendage.

So instead, Milton was frantically button-pressing and joystick-jiggling to make Sea Hawk duck, twist, and emit his signature bird-of-prey call in an attempt to intimidate the creature. Milton knew from a vast wealth of *Isle of Wild* experience that if he so much as blinked, Sea Hawk would be a goner for sure.

"Mighty moles and voles!" yelled the feather-hatted naturalist as a bright red tentacle snaked around his throat. Milton increased his rate of button-pressing and joystick-jiggling.

Milton's mother, seemingly oblivious to Sea Hawk's plight, reached over and plucked the HandHeld from Milton's grasp.

"Mighty moles and voles!" Milton cried, making a desperate grab for the device. "At least pause it. You've almost certainly killed me!"

"We have some wonderful news," Milton's mother replied firmly. She held out the letter again. "You'll want to read this."

There had been zero wonderful news this year, and Milton was 99.99 percent sure that whatever was inside the envelope was not going to change that.

But even though he was leaning as far from the letter as he could and even though he was staring unblinkingly at the little screen in his mother's hand and *only* at that screen, his parents were not getting the hint.

"Take the letter," his father urged. "It's for you. Uncle Evan sent it all the way from the Lone Island."

Milton gasped and pressed his hands to his heart. The Lone Island, he knew, was an itty-bitty, teeny-tiny, super-duper-remote island in the middle of the Atlantic, much like the Isle of Wild. Milton's uncle was a naturalist who ran research studies there, much like Sea Hawk (except not nearly as brawny or dashing . . . also, not shipwrecked). Milton had only met Uncle Evan one time, back when he was five years old, and he had *never* been to the Lone Island, but once upon a time, it had been his favorite place in the whole entire world.

"In that case," he said, "perhaps I'll have a look."

CHAPTER 3

The Lone Island Letter

Inside that phlegmy-green, stamp-covered envelope, there was a slightly cleaner piece of notebook paper with a few pen-scrawled lines. Milton adjusted his glasses and read:

> Dear Milton,
>
> I'm looking forward to your visit. It's pretty tricky to get here, so I arranged your flights. I'm enclosing the itinerary.
>
> I'll be waiting for you at the airstrip. See you on June 8.
>
> Uncle Evan
>
> P.S. Tell your dad the Incredible Symphonic Cicadas should be emerging soon, and this might be his last chance to hear them.

Behind the letter was a paper filled with flight numbers and times and finally, at the very bottom, these words: *ARRIVAL: The Lone Island.*

"Can this possibly mean what I think it means?" Milton asked. His parents both wore huge, frozen smiles—the kind of smile you smile when you're trying to convince someone that a letter contains wonderful news.

"It means you're going to the Lone Island for the summer!" Milton's father cried, sounding peppier than he had all year. "You get to stay with Uncle Evan."

"It'll be like visiting a real *Isle of Wild*," Milton's mother added.

Milton glanced back and forth between them, openmouthed and bug-eyed. "Well, that's—that's very—egad. Really?"

"You've been wanting to go there ever since Uncle Evan's visit," his father replied. "Remember?"

Of course Milton remembered. During that visit seven years ago, Uncle Evan had taken Milton and his parents birdwatching and hiking and even camping. Over roasted marshmallows, he had told them about his life on the nearly deserted Lone Island and about the island's famous explorer, Dr. Ada Paradis. Dr. Paradis claimed the island's jungle was filled with never-before-seen creatures like a pachyderm that burrowed underground, a tree that shot poison arrows, a bird with stars in its tail feathers, and thousands more just waiting to be found. And Uncle Evan had been sure, absolutely sure, that he would find them all.

That visit had been the start of Milton's Nature Phase. His parents had gotten him a pair of neon-green binoculars with seagull decals on the sides, and he had spent many an after-school hour in their row house's minuscule backyard cataloging types of grass and peering up at pigeons and crows. On Sundays, Milton and his parents (and sometimes Dev) would head to a local park. These expeditions had been the highlight of Milton's week, and he had been pretty sure they were the highlight of his parents' week too.

Yes, if he'd gotten this letter a year ago, back in fifth grade, Milton would have wept tears of joy. But things had changed. His parents hadn't offered to take him on an expedition in months, and he hadn't asked. His Nature Phase was over.

"I *used* to want to go there," Milton said. "I'm not entirely certain that I still do."

"This is a once-in-a-lifetime opportunity." His mother hadn't stopped smiling, but Milton could hear the impatience that had become nearly constant this year creeping into her voice. "And your father and I, we need—we need some time to sort things out."

"You mean . . . getting-back-together things?" Milton asked, even though he knew the answer.

Milton's father shook his head. Milton's mother stopped smiling.

"No, Milton," she said softly. "The opposite is what I mean."

Now Milton understood.

The opposite. Like his father cleaning out the last of his stuff.

Like finalizing the custody plan. Like divorcing, completely, at last, for good. The End.

And they didn't want him here while that happened.

The kids at school, they didn't want him here. Not even Dev, who mostly pretended he didn't exist.

No one wanted him here.

So long, Milton.

"Well, that is a very tempting offer," he said. He folded up the itinerary and the letter and replaced them in the envelope. "And I truly do hate to disappoint Uncle Evan, but unfortunately, I must decline."

From the corner of his eye, Milton could see his parents exchanging glances—say-something, no-you-say-something glances—but neither of them spoke, and when Milton reached for his HandHeld, his mother gave it to him.

He had been right though. When the screen lit back up, Sea Hawk was dead. Milton would have to start over.

"I have plans with Sea Hawk this summer," he said. He pressed *Restart*, and the shipwrecked naturalist sprang back to life. "I'm not going anywhere."

"Onward! Ever onward!" Sea Hawk bellowed.

"Indeed," Milton agreed.

But as he maneuvered Sea Hawk toward the bay where the territorial cephalopod was once again hiding in the shallows, Milton had this (very disturbing) thought: This was the first time in months that his parents had been together in the same room without biting each other's heads off.

If they'd been willing to do this, if they'd been willing to work together and smile and be as patient and peppy as possible—well, then they really might mean business.

Milton might be going to the Lone Island.

CHAPTER 4

Business

As it turned out, they did mean business.

The next day, which was the last day of school, Milton's father was waiting for him at the bus stop. In spite of Milton's very emphatic initial protests, his father drove them to the outdoor store, where they spent the afternoon picking out hiking boots and a utility belt and a brand-new field journal and even a straw hat with a peacock feather tucked in its band. It was, Milton had to admit, a truly magnificent piece of headwear, and he hadn't seen his father smile so much in a long time.

"You're going to have the best trip, Milt," his father said when they pulled up to the house afterward. "I can't wait to hear about it."

The next day, which was the day before he was supposed to fly out, Milton's mother didn't work from her home office or on her phone like she usually did on Saturdays. Instead she helped Milton pack his belongings into a canvas backpack.

Well, actually, mostly *she* packed his belongings, while Milton (wearing his magnificent headwear) tried to talk her out of packing his belongings.

"This summer is going to be just what you need," she said before she left his room for the night. Her voice wasn't one bit impatient, and her hands were on his shoulders, her eyes searching for his under the brim of his lowered hat. "What we all need. I promise."

After she left, Milton couldn't sleep. That wasn't unusual though. At night, in the darkness and silence, with his HandHeld turned off, Milton's thoughts turned on.

Thoughts about how his father was living downtown in an apartment now.

Thoughts about how his parents had snapped and spat out words (and sometimes even yelled them) before his father had moved into that downtown apartment.

Thoughts about the Bird Brain Incident and his former best friend, Dev.

Totally, terribly, horribly, heinously rotten thoughts.

Most nights, Milton tried to distract himself from all that rottenness with *Isle of Wild* scenarios. He would imagine that he was Sea Hawk scaling to the spidery-frond tops of palm trees to pluck coconuts or being brought offerings of decapitated lizards by Dear

Lady DeeDee, who would then meow-snarl words in a language only he could understand. Pretending to be Sea Hawk didn't always help him fall asleep, but it was better than being Milton P. Greene.

But tonight, try as he might, he could not distract himself. Tonight, he couldn't stop thinking about how he did not want to be sent halfway around the world.

And he couldn't stop thinking about how he sort of *did* want to be sent halfway around the world.

His thoughts were loud and jumbly and terrified and eager and achy, and when he finally fell asleep, he still had not come anywhere close to sorting them out.